PATRICIA WENTWORTH
THE BLACK CABINET

PATRICIA WENTWORTH was born Dora Amy Elles in India in 1877 (not 1878 as has sometimes been stated). She was first educated privately in India, and later at Blackheath School for Girls. Her first husband was George Dillon, with whom she had her only child, a daughter. She also had two stepsons from her first marriage, one of whom died in the Somme during World War I.

Her first novel was published in 1910, but it wasn't until the 1920's that she embarked on her long career as a writer of mysteries. Her most famous creation was Miss Maud Silver, who appeared in 32 novels, though there were a further 33 full-length mysteries not featuring Miss Silver—the entire run of these is now reissued by Dean Street Press.

Patricia Wentworth died in 1961. She is recognized today as one of the pre-eminent exponents of the classic British golden age mystery novel.

By Patricia Wentworth

PATRICIA WENTWORTH

THE BLACK CABINET

With an introduction by
Curtis Evans

DEAN STREET PRESS

Introduction

BRITISH AUTHOR Patricia Wentworth published her first novel, a gripping tale of desperate love during the French Revolution entitled *A Marriage under the Terror*, a little over a century ago, in 1910. The book won first prize in the Melrose Novel Competition and was a popular success in both the United States and the United Kingdom. Over the next five years Wentworth published five additional novels, the majority of them historical fiction, the best-known of which today is *The Devil's Wind* (1912), another sweeping period romance, this one set during the Sepoy Mutiny (1857-58) in India, a region with which the author, as we shall see, had extensive familiarity. Like *A Marriage under the Terror*, *The Devil's Wind* received much praise from reviewers for its sheer storytelling élan. One notice, for example, pronounced the novel "an achievement of some magnitude" on account of "the extraordinary vividness...the reality of the atmosphere...the scenes that shift and move with the swiftness of a moving picture...." (*The Bookman*, August 1912) With her knack for spinning a yarn, it perhaps should come as no surprise that Patricia Wentworth during the early years of the Golden Age of mystery fiction (roughly from 1920 into the 1940s) launched upon her own mystery-writing career, a course charted most successfully for nearly four decades by the prolific author, right up to the year of her death in 1961.

Considering that Patricia Wentworth belongs to the select company of Golden Age mystery writers with books which have remained in print in every decade for nearly a century now (the centenary of Agatha Christie's first mystery, *The Mysterious Affair at Styles*, is in 2020; the centenary of Wentworth's first mystery, *The Astonishing Adventure of Jane Smith*, follows merely three years later, in 2023), relatively little is known about the author herself. It appears, for example, that even the widely given year of Wentworth's birth, 1878, is incorrect. Yet it is sufficiently clear that Wentworth lived a varied and intriguing life that provided her ample inspiration for a writing career devoted to imaginative fiction.

It is usually stated that Patricia Wentworth was born Dora Amy Elles on 10 November 1878 in Mussoorie, India, during the heyday of the British Raj; however, her Indian birth and baptismal record states that she in fact was born on 15 October 1877 and was baptized on 26 November of that same year in Gwalior. Whatever doubts surround her actual birth year, however, unquestionably the future author came from a prominent Anglo-Indian military family. Her father, Edmond Roche Elles, a son of Malcolm Jamieson Elles, a Porto, Portugal wine merchant originally from Ardrossan, Scotland, entered the British Royal Artillery in 1867, a decade before Wentworth's birth, and first saw service in India during the Lushai Expedition of 1871-72. The next year Elles in India wed Clara Gertrude Rothney, daughter of Brigadier-General Octavius Edward Rothney, commander of the Gwalior District, and Maria (Dempster) Rothney, daughter of a surgeon in the Bengal Medical Service. Four children were born of the union of Edmond and Clara Elles, Wentworth being the only daughter.

Before his retirement from the army in 1908, Edmond Elles rose to the rank of lieutenant-general and was awarded the KCB (Knight Commander of the Order of Bath), as was the case with his elder brother, Wentworth's uncle, Lieutenant-General Sir William Kidston Elles, of the Bengal Command. Edmond Elles also served as Military Member to the Council of the Governor-General of India from 1901 to 1905. Two of Wentworth's brothers, Malcolm Rothney Elles and Edmond Claude Elles, served in the Indian Army as well, though both of them died young (Malcolm in 1906 drowned in the Ganges Canal while attempting to rescue his orderly, who had fallen into the water), while her youngest brother, Hugh Jamieson Elles, achieved great distinction in the British Army. During the First World War he catapulted, at the relatively youthful age of 37, to the rank of brigadier-general and the command of the British Tank Corps, at the Battle of Cambrai personally leading the advance of more than 350 tanks against the German line. Years later Hugh Elles also played a major role in British civil defense during the Second World War. In the event of a German invasion of Great Britain, something which seemed all too possible in 1940, he was tasked with leading the defense of southwestern England. Like Sir Edmond and Sir William,

Hugh Elles attained the rank of lieutenant-general and was awarded the KCB.

Although she was born in India, Patricia Wentworth spent much of her childhood in England. In 1881 she with her mother and two younger brothers was at Tunbridge Wells, Kent, on what appears to have been a rather extended visit in her ancestral country; while a decade later the same family group resided at Blackheath, London at Lennox House, domicile of Wentworth's widowed maternal grandmother, Maria Rothney. (Her eldest brother, Malcolm, was in Bristol attending Clifton College.) During her years at Lennox House, Wentworth attended Blackheath High School for Girls, then only recently founded as "one of the first schools in the country to give girls a proper education" (*The London Encyclopaedia*, 3rd ed., p. 74). Lennox House was an ample Victorian villa with a great glassed-in conservatory running all along the back and a substantial garden--most happily, one presumes, for Wentworth, who resided there not only with her grandmother, mother and two brothers, but also five aunts (Maria Rothney's unmarried daughters, aged 26 to 42), one adult first cousin once removed and nine first cousins, adolescents like Wentworth herself, from no less than three different families (one Barrow, three Masons and five Dempsters); their parents, like Wentworth's father, presumably were living many miles away in various far-flung British dominions. Three servants--a cook, parlourmaid and housemaid--were tasked with serving this full score of individuals.

Sometime after graduating from Blackheath High School in the mid-1890s, Wentworth returned to India, where in a local British newspaper she is said to have published her first fiction. In 1901 the 23-year-old Wentworth married widower George Fredrick Horace Dillon, a 41-year-old lieutenant-colonel in the Indian Army with three sons from his prior marriage. Two years later Wentworth gave birth to her only child, a daughter named Clare Roche Dillon. (In some sources it is erroneously stated that Clare was the offspring of Wentworth's second marriage.) However in 1906, after just five years of marriage, George Dillon died suddenly on a sea voyage, leaving Wentworth with sole responsibly for her three teenaged stepsons and baby daughter. A very short span of years, 1904 to 1907, saw the deaths of Wentworth's husband, mother, grandmother and brothers Malcolm and Edmond, removing much of her support network. In 1908, however, her father, who was now sixty years old, retired from the army and returned to England, settling at Guildford, Surrey with an older unmarried sister named Dora (for whom his daughter presumably had been named). Wentworth joined this household as well, along with her daughter and her youngest stepson. Here in Surrey Wentworth, presumably with the goal of making herself financially independent for the first time in her life (she was now in her early thirties), wrote the novel that changed the course of her life, *A Marriage under the Terror*, for the first time we know of utilizing her famous *nom de plume*.

The burst of creative energy that resulted in Wentworth's publication of six novels in six years suddenly halted after the appearance of *Queen Anne Is Dead* in 1915. It seems not unlikely that the Great War impinged in various ways on her writing. One tragic episode was the death on the western front of one of her stepsons, George Charles Tracey Dillon. Mining in Colorado when war was declared, young Dillon worked his passage from Galveston, Texas to Bristol, England as a shipboard muleteer (mule-tender) and joined the Gloucestershire Regiment. In 1916 he died at the Somme at the age of 29 (about the age of Wentworth's two brothers when they had passed away in India).

A couple of years after the conflict's cessation in 1918, a happy event occurred in Wentworth's life when at Frimley, Surrey she wed George Oliver Turnbull, up to this time a lifelong bachelor who like the author's first husband was a lieutenant-colonel in the Indian Army. Like his bride now forty-two years old, George Turnbull as a younger man had distinguished himself for his athletic prowess, playing forward for eight years for the Scottish rugby team and while a student at the Royal Military Academy winning the medal awarded the best athlete of his term. It seems not unlikely that Turnbull played a role in his wife's turn toward writing mystery fiction, for he is said to have strongly supported Wentworth's career, even assisting her in preparing manuscripts for publication. In 1936 the couple in Camberley, Surrey built Heatherglade House, a large two-story structure on substantial grounds, where they resided until Wentworth's death a quarter of a century later. (George Turnbull survived his wife by nearly a decade, passing away in 1970 at the age of 92.) This highly successful middle-aged companionate marriage contrasts sharply with the more youthful yet rocky union of Agatha and Archie Christie, which was three years away from sundering when Wentworth published *The Astonishing Adventure of Jane Smith* (1923), the first of her sixty-five mystery novels.

Although Patricia Wentworth became best-known for her cozy tales of the criminal investigations of consulting detective Miss Maud Silver, one of the mystery genre's most prominent spinster sleuths, in truth the Miss Silver tales account for just under half of Wentworth's 65 mystery novels. Miss Silver did not make her debut until 1928 and she did not come to predominate in Wentworth's fictional criminous output until the 1940s. Between 1923 and 1945 Wentworth published 33 mystery novels without Miss Silver, a handsome and substantial legacy in and of itself to vintage crime fiction fans. Many of these books are standalone tales of mystery, but nine of them have series characters. Debuting in the novel *Fool Errant* in 1929, a year after Miss Silver first appeared in print, was the enigmatic, nautically-named *eminence grise* Benbow Collingwood Horatio Smith, owner of a most expressively opinionated parrot named Ananias (and quite a colorful character in his own right). Benbow Smith went on to appear in three additional Wentworth mysteries: *Danger Calling* (1931), *Walk with Care* (1933) and *Down Under* (1937). Working in tandem with Smith in the investigation of sinister affairs threatening the security of Great Britain in *Danger Calling* and *Walk with Care* is Frank Garrett, Head of Intelligence for the Foreign Office, who also appears solo in *Dead or Alive* (1936) and *Rolling Stone* (1940) and collaborates with additional series characters, Scotland Yard's Inspector Ernest Lamb and Sergeant Frank Abbott, in *Pursuit of a Parcel* (1942). Inspector Lamb and Sergeant Abbott headlined a further pair of mysteries, *The Blind Side* (1939) and *Who Pays the Piper?* (1940), before they became absorbed, beginning with *Miss Silver Deals with Death* (1943), into the burgeoning Miss Silver canon. Lamb would make his farewell appearance in 1955 in *The Listening Eye*, while

Abbott would take his final bow in mystery fiction with Wentworth's last published novel, *The Girl in the Cellar* (1961), which went into print the year of the author's death at the age of 83.

The remaining two dozen Wentworth mysteries, from the fantastical *The Astonishing Adventure of Jane Smith* in 1923 to the intense legal drama *Silence in Court* in 1945, are, like the author's series novels, highly imaginative and entertaining tales of mystery and adventure, told by a writer gifted with a consummate flair for storytelling. As one confirmed Patricia Wentworth mystery fiction addict, American Golden Age mystery writer Todd Downing, admiringly declared in the 1930s, "There's something about Miss Wentworth's yarns that is contagious." This attractive new series of Patricia Wentworth reissues by Dean Street Press provides modern fans of vintage mystery a splendid opportunity to catch the Wentworth fever.

Curtis Evans

Chapter One

MISS ALLARDYCE always felt that her house had what she called "a nice appearance." It stood at the top of Maxton High Street, a little withdrawn from the busy pavement. It had bright green railings. A flagged path fully five feet long led to the green front door. Every time that Miss Allardyce came up from the High Street she thought how nice and cheerful her green railings looked, and she nearly always said to herself, "The house really has a very nice appearance—it really has—yes, very nice indeed."

There was a brass plate on either side of the front door. The one on the side nearest the High Street bore the words:

"MISS ALLARDYCE,
Dressmaking and Renovations."

The one on the other side was inscribed:

"ALLARDYCE,
Robes et Modes."

With the former Miss Allardyce appealed to what she herself termed "business circles"; with the latter she designed to attract "The County."

The workroom was on the second floor, and looked over what Miss Allardyce called "the garden"; it was really a dingy yard which happened to contain a battered remnant of lilac and the pollarded remains of an elm tree.

Chloe Dane, looking out of the window on an October afternoon, could see chimney-pots and out-houses, other people's back yards, and other people's washing, all rather drab and depressing. Not that Chloe was depressed; it took a good deal more than a view from a back window to depress Chloe. She turned back to the room with a laugh.

"This frightful abomination that I'm making is the own twin of old Mrs. Duffy's flannelette nightgowns. There's one hanging on her line now, all pink and bulging. I'm sure that's where Ally got the inspiration from. I say, Rose, it's pretty bad, isn't it?"

Rose Smith looked up from the black moiré which was to grace the Mayoress of Maxton. Chloe was holding out a very large pink satin garment which certainly bore some resemblance to a nightgown. It was adorned with pink ostrich-feather trimmings and incrustations of pink and green beads. Rose shrugged her shoulders.

"It wasn't Ally's fault this time. Miss Jones had it planned to the last bead—and oh, Chloe, won't she look awful in it!"

"There ought to be a law to stop red-haired women wearing pink," said Chloe. "I say, Rose, I've got a ripping idea. Let's start a society for the prevention of criminal clothes. I'd love to. You know, I could make Miss Jones look—well, quite *decent*; but she'll never give me a chance."

"What would you do with her?"

"Put her into black velvet, and give her hair and skin a chance. Dead plain, you know,—not a flower, not a feather, not a bead." Chloe stabbed the pink ostrich feathers fiercely as she spoke, and then broke into sudden, bubbling laughter. "Poor Miss Jones, she'd be bored stiff, wouldn't she? She does love her bead and feather abominations. And I'd put that poor little, shrivelled Mayoress into grey. She'll look like nothing on earth in that hard black moiré; but I could turn her into a sort of French fairy godmother if she'd let me—only she won't. But, oh, Rose, wouldn't it be heavenly to have a free hand and make the right things for the right people?"

Rose Smith smiled, dimpled, blushed. She was a pretty, soft thing, all curves, and colour, and big brown eyes. She was going to be married in a month, and leave Maxton and dressmaking behind her for ever.

"It'll be much more heavenly not to have to make other people's things at all. Chloe, I wish you were going to be married too."

Chloe tossed her head. Her black curls danced, and so did her black eyes.

"My angel Rose, I don't want to be married."

"You'll hate it without me, Chloe. Ally's going to get in the Shingleton girl, and she's not your sort a bit. You'll simply hate it. I wish you'd get married."

"Nobody axed me, sir, she said,"—Chloe's cheeks wore a geranium flush—"well, nobody that I'd have anyhow."

"Bernard Austin would be awfully good to you."

Chloe stamped.

"Rose, I won't have it! I'm not the deserving poor. Who wants a husband to be good to them?"

"I do," said Rose with her eyes soft.

Chloe jumped up and kissed her.

"Shall have," she murmured caressingly; and then, "I shall go adventuring." She gathered the pink satin on to her lap again and began to sew. "I'm full of ideas. I've got a feeling in the tips of my eyelashes that Ally and I are going to be torn asunder. Our ways will lie far, far apart. It's sad, but it's just got to be."

"What will you do?"

"Don't know. What do you think of an advertisement in *The Times*, or the *Daily Herald*, or the *Maxton Post*?—'Chloe Dane, young, lovely, talented, wants something amusing to do. Dancing, dressmaking, driving, dining out—in fact, anything, so long as it's respectable. N.B. She is quite respectable and has been *most* strictly brought up. Apply care of Miss Allardyce, High Street, Maxton.' Just think of Ally's face!"

Rose laughed; but when she spoke, it was to say rather seriously:

"Aren't you sometimes sorry that you didn't stay on at Miss Tankerville's and teach?"

Chloe shook her head so vehemently that a curl whisked into her eye. She tucked it behind her ear, and said:

"Never—never once—never for half a second—in fact, my angel, *never*."

"I can't think why."

"Teaching's all right if you've got things to teach. I haven't. I should just have frumped and grown blue mould all over me. Look at poor old Tanks herself—there's an awful warning for you."

"You couldn't get like Miss Tankerville if you tried," said Rose. "And—and you wouldn't have been so cut off from all your old friends."

"Haven't got any."

"Your grandfather must have had some."

Chloe snipped a length of pink feather trimming.

"Well, I was only nine when he died, and he hadn't really been keeping up Danesborough for years before that. I can look back and see how neglected everything must have been. I can only remember about four servants indoors—and a place like that must have wanted at least a dozen to run it decently. Then I think my grandfather wasn't very much liked. He had the sort of row with the local hunt that thoroughly endears you to everyone within fifteen miles or so. He was queer, and crotchety, and bad-tempered, and people just dropped away, I think. Anyhow, no one worried about me. There was enough money to keep me at Miss Tankerville's till I was eighteen, and that was all."

"The place went to your uncle, didn't it?"

"Yes, Uncle Robert in Australia. He didn't come over or take any interest; he didn't even answer letters, I believe. He just let it all slide and go to rack and ruin. And two years ago, when he died, his son sold Danesborough to a man called Mitchell Dane who's simply rolling. I believe he's some sort of distant cousin. It's comic, isn't it? None of the Danes have had a penny since they ruined themselves for the Stuarts in the Civil Wars; and now there's this sort of cousin from nobody knows where with such a lot of money that he doesn't know what to do with it. I think it's *frightfully* funny."

Rose Smith dropped her thimble, picked it up, and inquired ingenuously:

"Chloe, is he married?"

"Widower," said Chloe—"old as the hills. I haven't seen him myself, but Monica Gresson told me. They went and stayed with some people near Danesborough for the hunting last winter, and met him. He's done Danesborough up absolutely regardless—new ball-room floor, electric light and telephones everywhere, central heating, and ten bath-rooms. Monica was much struck with the bath-rooms. He took them over the house, and she said they were full of the most thrilling contraptions."

"Chloe, perhaps he'll ask you to stay."

"Perhaps he won't. I shouldn't go anyhow."

"Why not?"

"For the same reason that I won't go to stay with the Gressons." Chloe set her red lips very firmly.

"I think you're silly," said Rose.

"I know you do."

"It's silly to be proud."

Chloe stuck her chin in the air. Her black eyes sparkled.

"I won't go and stay with people when I can't afford the things that are just a matter of course to them. It's—it's undignified. At the present moment, for instance, I have got a pair of evening shoes, but not an evening dress, or a coat that I could go to a dance in, or bedroom slippers, or a proper dressing-gown. Of course, if I were the lovely, impecunious heroine of the sort of novel that the Tank adores, I should go and stay with the Gressons and discover that they were giving a ball that very night to the whole County. I should retire to my room and drape myself gracefully in a chair-cover, or an eiderdown, or a muslin window curtain. My hair, of course, would be done in a simple knot. I should then arrive in the ball-room and instantly make a conquest of every eligible young man in the room. The alternative to the eiderdown, chair-cover, window curtain scheme is that you wear the black bombazine bequeathed to you by your Great-Aunt Matilda. The result is exactly the same: the young men simply tumble over one another to propose to you, and you become the blushing bride of a wealthy and virtuous young duke, if there is such a thing—there would be, of course, in a novel."

Rose giggled softly. Chloe always told her that she laughed like a fat baby.

"Chloe, if you could *choose*, what sort of dress would you have? I mean, suppose you were going to the County Ball."

"Well, I wouldn't have black moiré, or pink satin, or ostrich feathers—that's a cert. I think silver tissue; there's a sort—frightfully expensive, of course—that's exactly like a dull silver bath-towel; and I'd have it just as plain as plain; and perhaps dark fur, but I'm not sure about the fur. What would you have?"

"Gold," said Rose. "I do look nice in gold. I should love to have a gold wedding dress, but of course I can't."

"Edward thinks you perfectly lovely anyhow, so it doesn't really matter," said Chloe. "My old nurse used to say a rhyme about gold and silver, but I believe I've forgotten it—no, I haven't." She put her head on one side, and sang:

'Silver and gold, silver and gold,
    And just as much joy as your heart'll hold.'

"You've got the last line all right, so I wouldn't worry about the wedding dress."

"I don't," said Rose. She got up, stretched herself, and shook out the black moiré. "There, that's done. And thank goodness, it's Saturday. How's yours?"

"Acres of ostrich feathers still. But it can wait till Monday. The minute the hooter goes I stop. Edward coming by the two-twenty?"

Rose nodded.

"Chloe, do change your mind and go to the Gressons."

Chloe made a face.

"Monica bores me rather. She's all over me one day; and then, next time I see her, she's trying hard to remember that she's Miss Gresson of Ranbourne and I'm just Chloe Dane that she used to be at school with, and: 'One tries to keep up with her and be just as nice as ever, only of course—well, you know how *difficult* it is—'" Chloe made her pretty voice sound dry and thin. She broke off laughing. "No, that's Lady Gresson, not Monica. Monica's bun-faced and a bit of a snob, but she's not as bad as that. I expect I shall go out there this afternoon. There, not one stitch more till Monday." She sprang up, gave the pink satin garment a swing round at arm's length, and launched it at Rose's head.

Rose screamed faintly. Chloe fell into a chair, laughing, and the door opened.

"Young ladies, young ladies!" said Miss Allardyce.

Chapter Two

ROSE AND CHLOE shared a bed-sitting room. They had lived together for two years—ever since Chloe left school. And next month Rose was going to Assam with Edward Anderson. Chloe tried not to think too much about next month. She was very fond of Rose, and Maxton wouldn't be a bit the same without her.

She saw Rose off to the station, and then bicycled up the High Street, past Miss Allardyce's house, and out upon the Ranbourne road.

It was a grey afternoon, but windless. The Ranbourne road ran straight and level for a couple of miles before it began to dip and turn. On a very fine, clear day you could imagine that the dazzle of blue far away at the edge of the sky was the sea; quite certainly when the wind was from the south-west you could smell sea-weed and feel a hint of salt upon your lips. The country fell away to the marshes, and then rose again where Luttrell met the sea. Ranbourne lay away on the other side. Chloe would have liked going to Ranbourne better if it had lain seawards. She had not really seen the sea since she was eight years old.

Chloe began to think what she should do when Rose was gone.

"If I'd only been to a proper school instead of a genteel survival like the poor old Tank's, there'd be more chance. As it is, I can sew and I can do housework; that's about all. Well, something'll turn up, I suppose. You never know what's waiting for you round the next corner, so why worry?"

She came to a corner then and there, a corner well sign-posted, with an arm that read "To Ranbourne." As she swung round it she heard voices—or, to be strictly accurate, a voice—and saw, a dozen yards down the slope, a stranded car with an old lady in it. The voice was the old lady's voice. As Chloe drew nearer she observed that there was a chauffeur with his head buried in the bonnet of the car. The old lady was very angry with him. She wore an immense fur coat, and clasped a very small Pekinese dog. Whenever she paused to take breath the Pekinese gave a short, angry bark which subsided to a snarl as soon as his mistress resumed.

Chloe had slackened pace a little. She was just passing the car, when the old lady addressed her:

"You—yes, you on the bicycle—come here!"

The Pekinese yapped. Chloe got off her bicycle, and said, "Why?"

"Come here!" repeated the old lady.

The Pekinese yapped again. Chloe came up to the car, hoping that she would never develop a red face, a peacock voice, or a passion for Pekinese dogs.

"What's the matter?" she asked.

It was the chauffeur who answered her question. He lifted his head, cast a restrained glance in her direction, and said briefly:

"Ignition."

"Disgraceful carelessness!" said the old lady—"disgraceful! It's all part and parcel of this modern way of scamping everything. No thoroughness. No attention to detail. A smattering of this and a smattering of that. That's your modern education—just putting ideas into the heads of the lower classes instead of teaching them to order themselves lowly and reverently to all their betters like the Catechism says. Bolsheviks, the whole lot of them! Bolsheviks, and Communists, and upstarts, instead of decent, respectable working folk that learnt a trade and learnt it well, and weren't too fine to touch their caps when they met you, or to drop a curtsey if it was a woman. No one's *got* any manners nowadays!"

"No, they don't seem to have," said Chloe sweetly. She wasn't looking at the chauffeur, but she was aware of a hurried movement on his part. It occurred to her afterwards that he had turned his head aside to hide a grin.

"No manners at all!" said the old lady severely. "Mannerless and incompetent—that's the present generation. Where we shall all be in fifty years' time, goodness knows."

"I know," said Chloe. "But what about now?"

The old lady fixed her with a pair of small, pale blue eyes.

"Do you know Ranbourne?" she inquired.

"I'm going there—don't do that!" The last words were addressed to the Pekinese who had just made a vicious snap at her hand.

"Darling angel Toto mustn't bite," said the old lady in quite a different voice. One might almost have said that she cooed the words. "Darling angel Toto shall have his tea if he's a real angel boy, he shall." She resumed normal speech, and once more addressed Chloe:

"Owing to the chauffeur's incompetence I have already been stranded here for at least a quarter of an hour." She consulted a jewelled watch. "It is three o'clock, and if Toto doesn't get his tea and biscuit at three, he screams—doesn't ums, a darling angel? He knows the time as well, and once three o'clock has struck, he knows it's time for his tea, and he screams till he gets it—a precious. And we ought to have been at Ranbourne at least ten minutes ago."

At this moment Toto's snarl ran rapidly up the scale and merged into an undoubted scream. The old lady gazed at him with fond pride. Chloe had a fleeting impression of the chauffeur as a large, fair, young man who looked as if he would like to murder Toto. She hoped it was only Toto.

"There!" said the old lady as scream succeeded scream. "He does want his tea—a precious, a clever, darling angel boy."

Chloe caught the chauffeur's eye. She looked away again instantly. The eye was an angry one, but behind the anger there had certainly been a twinkle.

"Well, I don't see what we can do about it," she said. "I can take a message if you like—I'm going to Ranbourne."

"Not a message," said the old lady. "Let Mother speak, a darling angel"—this to Toto. "Not a message, but Toto himself. Take him with you, and ask them to let him have his tea at once—China tea, half milk; and a Marie biscuit; and just one teeny lump of sugar in the tea."

Chloe began to shake with inward laughter. She bit the corners of her lips to keep them steady.

"Do you mean bicycle with him?"

"Oh, no! Certainly not! How could you think of such a thing? My precious Toto! No, no, you must walk your bicycle of course, and have Toto in the basket in front with his own eiderdown—my precious, darling angel, do hush, just for a minute."

Chloe felt that, if she stood there any longer, she would say or do something outrageous. She therefore murmured, "All right," and submitted to endless instructions as to the proper preparation of Toto's tea, whilst the chauffeur lined her bicycle basket with a purple satin eiderdown. Toto, snarling and screaming, was tucked in and secured with a strap.

"Tell Lady Gresson that I rely on her," said the old lady. "She's expecting me—Mrs. Merston Howard. Tell her that I rely on her, and that the tea must be freshly made, and China; not Indian—on no account Indian."

Chloe had gone about half a dozen yards, when Mrs. Howard called her back.

"Foster, go after her. Tell her to come here. She can back her bicycle. No, a message *won't* do." Then, as Chloe reluctantly backed, "Tell Lady Gresson that a Petit Beurre biscuit will do if she hasn't a Marie—but Toto likes Maries better. And oh, tell her, on no account more than one lump of sugar—and not a large one."

Chloe quickened her pace, and breathed more freely when she had turned another corner. As soon as she was out of sight she gave Toto a smart slap, mounted her bicycle, and rode on briskly. Toto, after one enraged yelp, fixed her with green, malignant eyes, and subsided.

Chapter Three

THE MUSIC-ROOM at Ranbourne was full of the rather raucous strains of the latest fox-trot and the sound of dancing feet. Chloe stood on the threshold with Toto under one arm, and saw Monica Gresson detach herself from her very good-looking partner and come forward a shade reluctantly. Even before she spoke, Chloe was aware that this was not one of the days when Monica was going to be "all over her."

"Good gracious, Chloe! A dog?" Her tone implied that Toto was an offence.

"He's not a dog; he's a horror," said Chloe. "And thank goodness, he isn't mine. An old lady who says she's coming to stay with you pressed him into my hand by the roadside. She said that I was to save his precious life by bringing him here and seeing that he had China tea at once, with one lump of sugar in it, and a Marie biscuit. She said her name was Mrs. Merston Howard."

"What can I do with him?" said Monica, looking helpless.

"Housekeeper's room," said Chloe. "And if we're going to dance, I want to take off my coat and change my shoes."

They disposed of Toto, and Chloe slipped out of her coat and patted her hair.

"Who is Mrs. Merston Howard?" she asked.

"My godmother. She's frightfully rich, and hasn't any relations. Mother thinks she'll leave me her money; but she won't."

"She'll probably leave it to Toto. Who's here?"

"Joyce Langholm and the brother from India; and the two Renton boys—you know them; and—and Mr. Fossetter who's staying with us."

Monica's manner became a trifle conscious. She had the largest blue eyes in the County; on the strength of them she considered herself a beauty. For the rest, Chloe's description of her as bun-faced was apt enough.

"Who is Mr. Fossetter?" said Chloe, laughing.

"We met him at Danesborough." Monica became flushed and eager. "He knows simply everyone and goes everywhere. I believe he's one of the best dancers in London—and quite too frightfully good-looking. Chloe, you won't flirt with him, *will* you?"

"I never flirt," said Chloe. "And as long as a man can dance, I don't care twopence how hideous he is, or how handsome."

Martin Fossetter was dancing with Joyce Langholm when the door opened. He looked across the room and saw Chloe Dane in a thin orange jumper and a short skirt that showed very pretty feet and ankles.

"Who's that?" he asked.

Miss Langholm froze a little.

"A girl Monica used to be at school with. She's in a shop or something now. It's awfully decent of Monica to have her here, of course; but I think it's silly myself—unsettling for the girl, you know."

Martin Fossetter had a most sympathetic voice. He smiled at Joyce and said:

"Yes, I know." Then, after a little pause, "What's her name?"

"Dane—Chloe Dane," said Miss Langholm.

Mr. Fossetter began to talk of other things. He had the knack of being personal without impertinence, and his very handsome eyes assured the woman on whom they rested of a most particular and poignant interest. One of the most courted women in England once said of him: "Martin Fossetter makes you feel that you are the heroine of some thrilling romance. I'm never quite sure though whether *he's* the hero or the villain." Miss Langholm was not so acute as this; she was merely rather better pleased with herself than usual.

Presently Mr. Fossetter asked Monica to introduce him to Chloe. They danced, and Chloe found him the partner of her dreams, with a step that suited hers to a marvel.

"How beautifully you dance," said Martin Fossetter.

Chloe nodded.

"It's about the only thing I can do decently. I do love it."

Martin's dark eyes rested on her with admiration—and something else. So this was Chloe Dane, the girl that old Mitchell Dane was coming to Maxton to have a look at. One might gamble on his being satisfied.

"Do you know, I've just been staying at Danesborough," he said.

"Have you?" Chloe's tone was indifferent.

"Yes, that's why I was so interested to meet you. They still remember you there, you know, and talk about you."

Chloe said nothing. She did not care to speak of Danesborough to a stranger. Even to Rose she hardly ever spoke of her old home— twice, or three times perhaps in their two years together; and to a stranger—no, Chloe had nothing to say about Danesborough to this stranger. He was aware at once of her withdrawal.

"I'm sorry," he said. "I thought you might like to hear about it—to know that Mr. Dane hasn't spoilt the place. It's beautiful and—"

The sympathy in his voice altered Chloe's mood. She looked up at him suddenly, and he saw that her eyes were not really black after all, but a very, very dark brown. They could look soft too, as well as bright; they looked soft now.

"I was only nine," she said—her voice was like a child's voice—"I was only nine. I did love it. There was a lily pond, and there were peacocks. I remember there was a white peacock that mewed like a cat; and I called him Henry—I don't know why, but I did." She laughed a little, and looked away. The sympathy in Martin Fossetter's eyes had brought a mist to her own. Chloe was not used to sympathy, and it touched something in her warm young heart.

"The lily pond is still there," he said. "I saw it in the summer. There was a crimson lily among the white ones. You ought to go there and see it in the spring."

"I shall never go there again," said Chloe.

Martin smiled.

"That's like saying to the fountain, 'Je ne boirai jamais de ton eau,'—you know the proverb. I think you're tempting fate when you say that you will never go back to Danesborough any more."

Chloe laughed, suddenly, frankly. Her eyes were black again, and very bright.

"It's a fate I don't mind tempting," she said, and dropped his arm.

Chapter Four

CHLOE WENT to tea with Miss Tankerville next day.

"She always asks one such ages beforehand," she complained to Rose; "and then it's ten to one she forgets you're coming. I'm bored stiff at having to go. I wonder if it's true that she's going to give the school up soon. I believe there are only about half a dozen girls left, so she might just as well."

There was certainly an air of genteel decay about the house and grounds. Chloe remembered them, if not well kept, at least in decent order. Now the whole place had an under-staffed, neglected look, and the big house echoed emptily to the feet of Miss Tankerville's few remaining pupils.

Chloe waited in the drawing-room, and thought how dreary the conservatory looked. Last winter there were still chrysanthemums there, but now a half-drawn curtain failed to conceal bare, discoloured staging, rusty pipes, and broken flower pots.

The door opened, and Miss Tankerville came in, rather flustered. She still wore the tight curled fringe and tight boned waist of the nineties, and affected a pince-nez on a thin gold chain which was always getting entangled in the old-fashioned watch-chain that clanked round her neck like a fetter.

"Chloe! Dear girl!" she exclaimed, and pecked at Chloe's cheek. The pince-nez fell off, and had to be retrieved. "Dear girl, I'm always pleased to see you; but this afternoon it just happens—yes, it just happens—now, let me see, did I ask you for this afternoon?"

"You did," said Chloe. "But it doesn't matter a bit—if you were going out or anything of that sort—I can quite easily go home again."

"Then I did ask you." Miss Tankerville looked round vaguely, as if she expected some sort of corroborative evidence to fall from the ceiling. "I did ask you then. Dear girl, I begin to remember. I met you in the High Street, and I asked you to come and have tea with me—but surely, surely it was for last Sunday."

"It doesn't matter a bit," Chloe repeated. She would have been quite pleased to go home. She wished very much that Miss Tankerville would stop holding her hand in the limp grasp that was so difficult to get away from.

"Last Sunday *surely*. I know I was expecting you then, for I know I was just a little bit hurt when you didn't come. And this afternoon— now, *this* afternoon—"

"It really doesn't matter, if you want to go out," said Chloe for the third time.

Miss Tankerville pressed the hand which she still held.

"No, no, I'm not going out, dear girl. It's just a little—just the least little bit awkward, that's all. You see, a chauffeur is a chauffeur. And though, of course, he isn't one really, I'm not even sure whether he'll come here in plain clothes or not. And I thought that if I were on the look-out for him, I might just let him in myself—on account of Susan, you know. You see, he'd be sure to leave his cap in the hall, wouldn't he? And I thought that perhaps, without his cap on, Susan would hardly notice anything when she brought in the tea. And if you don't mind, dear girl, will you just come over to the window so that I can keep my eye on the drive? Maids do gossip so dreadfully—and I can't explain to Susan that his mother is really Lady Enniston, can I?"

Chloe got her hand away at last, and said, "No, I suppose not." Then she sat down on the window seat, looked with dancing eyes at Miss Tankerville's harassed profile, and made an inward vow not to stir from the spot until she had seen the mysterious visitor who was going to make the tea-party "a little bit awkward."

"If you can't tell Susan, I think you might tell me," she said. "Who is it that isn't really a chauffeur?—and why is he coming to tea?—and do you really want me to go away? It all sounds most exciting."

Miss Tankerville adjusted her pince-nez and peered into the mist. Chloe was a dear girl, a very dear girl; but of course she was working at Miss Allardyce's; and would Maud Enniston really like dear Michael to be introduced to a girl as pretty as Chloe who was only a dressmaker's hand? Then, conversely, Michael, dear Michael, might at any moment arrive in a chauffeur's uniform and wearing that terrible cap. Chloe Dane was the grand-daughter of old Mr. Dane of Danesborough, such a very proud old man, and a regular patrician—a regular patrician. Now, how could one introduce a chauffeur in uniform to Miss Chloe Dane of Danesborough? Miss Tankerville turned from the window with nervous perplexity writ large on every feature.

"You see, dear girl," she began in her most flustered voice, "your grandfather—perhaps you don't remember him as I do, but I can never help feeling just a little bit responsible to him. And dear Michael—you see, it's so awkward, and I find some difficulty in explaining. And of course, dear girl, if you had done as I wished, and had remained with me as one of the staff, it would certainly have made a difference to your position—not, of course, that I have the slightest wish to hurt your feelings or to reflect upon your present employment; but I feel a—a—well, a certain responsibility to Michael's mother who was one of my earliest pupils—one of my very earliest pupils—and a most sweet girl. And, though I don't as a rule approve of second marriages, she was, of course, very young indeed when Michael's father died, and her marriage to Lord Enniston has been most satisfactory, most satisfactory. She was Maud Ashley-Hill, a daughter of Sir Condor Ashley-Hill's," concluded Miss Tankerville with the air of one who has now explained everything.

Chloe had begun to enjoy herself.

"Yes, that makes it quite clear, doesn't it?" she said. "I mean all the fathers and mothers and grandfathers and people. There's only one thing, dear Miss Tankerville, and that is, who is Michael?"

"Didn't I explain? Dear girl, surely I did. I met him this morning after church; and when I asked him to come to tea, he seemed so grateful, and said he had the day off because the car was out of order. And I never thought of your coming; and indeed, dear girl, if you didn't mind,—the position seems to me delicate—yes, delicate, and a little awkward. I am not used to these unconventional situations. But I feel responsible to his mother, and—and also, of course, to your grandfather."

Chloe's laugh rippled out, suddenly, irrepressibly.

"Dear Miss Tankerville, don't worry. It's quite easy, really. You can introduce the chauffeur to the dressmaker, and Lady Enniston's son to my grandfather's grand-daughter. There's nothing unconventional about that. It's only worrying when you get them mixed—I mean when I'm Miss Dane and he's the chauffeur, or the other way round. Don't send me away—I don't want to go a bit. And by the bye, you've never told me his name."

"Mr. Foster," said Susan, opening the door.

Michael Foster came into the room, a big young man in the most ordinary blue serge in the world. Miss Tankerville heaved a sigh of relief as she shook hands and ordered tea.

"And Susan—the lights. Michael, dear boy, I'm pleased to see you, I'm very pleased to see you." Then, as the room sprang suddenly into light, she turned fussily towards Chloe with a hurried, "Dear girl, this is Mr. Foster.—Michael, let me introduce you to Miss Dane, an old pupil of mine."

"We have met before," said Chloe. She put out her hand, and felt that Michael Foster's hand was large and strong.

"Before! Dear girl, you never said. I didn't know—I had no idea. Are you sure?"

"Well, it was hardly a meeting"—Chloe was perhaps a little sorry that she had spoken—"I just saw Mr. Foster yesterday when his car had broken down on the way to Ranbourne. Is she all right now?"

Michael Foster shook his head.

"I got her to Ranbourne, but she's not right yet."

Miss Tankerville broke in with a flood of questions about "Your dear mother." A little later on, when they had had tea, she remembered a photograph album "with a charming picture of dear Maud in a group," and departed to find it.

Michael Foster turned to Chloe.

"Did Toto bite you?" he inquired with much interest.

"He tried to. As soon as I got round the first corner I slapped him; then he didn't try any more. He's a little horror, but I give him full marks for brains. As a matter of fact, I wouldn't mind having Toto and training him. I believe he'd be rather fascinating if he wasn't so insufferably spoilt. I prefer him to his mistress anyhow."

Michael made a face.

"Pretty steep, isn't she? I've never been called such names in my life. Thank goodness, I've only got another week of it."

"Have you given notice?" asked Chloe demurely. "Or—or is it the other way round?"

His eyes twinkled. He had rather nice little creases round them. Chloe liked the way they crinkled up when he laughed.

"Oh, I don't belong to her," he said. "I'm driving my own car for a firm—just to get the hang of things whilst I'm marking time,—and she came in the other day, and said she'd got an impertinent nincompoop of a chauffeur who'd smashed her car and gone off at a moment's notice. She wanted us to put it right and give her another car and 'a *really* reliable man' meanwhile, because she was just going off to pay a round of visits. I'm the really reliable man, worse luck. I don't wonder the other poor chap got desperate and smashed the car."

Miss Tankerville swept back into the room, bearing a heavy Victorian album with gilt clasps. She laid it on Michael's knees, and sat down beside him.

"Dearest Maud at fourteen," she said, breathlessly. "No, not that one: that's Fanny Latimer who made that very sad marriage—but there, we won't talk about it; it's better not. And this is Judith Elliott who was your mother's great friend. She went to Hong Kong, and married an American—a very accomplished girl, though too fond of reading novels. And this—now this is a *really* good photograph, a most excellent group of our croquet team, taken in the summer of 1897. No, your mother's not in it, I'm afraid; but that girl in the middle is Emily Longwood who used to be quite a friend of hers; and the one next to her is Daisy Anderson—or is it Milly? Now, that's really very stupid of me." She turned the page to the light, and the pince-nez fell with a clatter. "Very stupid of me," she murmured as she disentangled them from the watch-chain and replaced them on her nose, "very stupid indeed; but, d'you know, I can't be sure which of the Anderson twins played in that croquet tournament. I think it was Daisy; but, on the other hand, it may have been Milly, because I think she really was the better player of the two." She turned another page.

Chloe caught Michael's eye for an instant. And a little spark of something seemed to dance between them. She looked away again at once. The interminable string of names flowed on.

Chapter Five

MICHAEL WROTE that night to his mother:

"DARLING MUM,—

"I'm feeling so virtuous that I must blow my own trumpet. Instead of skulking in byways, I boldly accosted the Tank in the High Street—absolutely walked into her very jaws and said, 'How d'you do?' And of course she asked me to tea. After a frightful struggle with myself, I went; and we looked at school albums for two solid hours, sitting side by side on the sofa. There were some perfectly appalling photos of you. My hat! What clothes women wore in the nineties! I'm glad you don't look like that now—only please don't shingle your hair, or I shall go back to Africa, and never come home any more.

"I've practically made up my mind to put Uncle Horace's money into the firm I'm working for now. I like 'em better than the other people, and you do get to know the ropes a bit when you're behind the scenes. I shall carry on as cabby for a bit longer though. As I shall probably never have any more capital than this, I'm going to be horribly cautious. It was frightfully decent of the old fellow to think of me.

"By the way, there was a most awfully pretty girl at the Tank's—an old pupil like you, but a little more recent. At present I feel as if I should fall hugely in love with her if I was to go on seeing her. Don't be alarmed. My old horror takes the road on Tuesday, so that only leaves Monday for me to get into mischief. I don't suppose I shall see her again, and perhaps it's just as well. I haven't felt so romantic since Lillah Blake gave me the chuck when I was eighteen. *There's* something for you to have heart-throbs over. Calm yourself by remembering that I shall be out of danger by the time you read this.

"Tons of love,

"MICHAEL."

On Monday evening Chloe Dane left the house with the green railings half an hour later than usual. She had stayed behind to finish a dress which had been promised without fail by Monday night. She was glad to get out into the air after sitting still for so many hours.

The shops were shutting in the High Street. That was a nuisance, because she really had planned to do some shopping. She stood for a moment, hesitating, outside Baker's. They were still open, but it was such a shame to rush in at the last minute and delay some girl who was putting stock away. Chloe knew how it felt to be kept back at the last moment after a long day's work. She moved on; and as she did so, some one behind her, said:

"How do you do, Miss Dane?"

Chloe stopped, swung round, and saw Michael Foster.

"How did you know it was me?"

"I—well, I just knew it was," said Michael.

They stood, looking at each other; Michael very angry with himself because he felt shy and tongue-tied; Chloe amused.

"I'm going home," she said.

Without a word Michael began to walk down the High Street beside her. Chloe's amusement became tinged with embarrassment. What was one to do with an almost totally strange young man who, like Felix, kept on walking?

"I'm going away to-morrow," he said at last.

"Are you?" said Chloe. She looked up at him suddenly with laughing eyes. "I do hope Toto is quite well. Why do you keep me in suspense? You must know that I'm simply longing for news of him."

"Toto will live for ever," said Michael gloomily. "And so will Mrs. Howard. However, I shan't have to live with them—that's one comfort. To-morrow I drive them to London and shed them, also, I hope, for ever. Er, Miss Dane, do you ever go to the pictures?" Michael turned bright red as he jerked out the last sentence.

"Sometimes."

There was a pause.

"Miss Dane—I say, would it be awful cheek? I mean, if you weren't doing anything else, would you—would you come to the pictures this evening?"

Chloe bowed to Bernard Austin who was glaring mournfully from the other side of the street—she had refused him for the sixth time about a week before—; then she smiled at Michael.

"I'd like to awfully. Rose Smith who lives with me is going with her fiancé. They wanted me to go too; but I was going to be tactful and mend stockings at home. I do loathe mending stockings and being tactful,—don't you?"

"I can't mend stockings—at least—well, I did in a sort of way when I was in Africa. And my mother was most frightfully rude about them when I came home, and scrapped the whole lot—perfectly good some of them were too."

"Can't you be tactful either?"

"I don't know. I wasn't very tactful just now. But I say, will you really come to the pictures?"

Chloe considered. She liked Michael Foster; she liked him a good deal; and he was leaving Maxton next day. It was perfectly safe. "Rose will probably scold, but I don't care," she thought. Then she said aloud:

"Yes, I'll come. I'm just going home to tea. You'd better come with me and meet Rose and her fiancé."

Rose did just raise her eyebrows when Chloe walked in with a strange young man; but the tea party in Mrs. Jones' sitting-room, lent for the occasion, was a cheerful and friendly one. As they walked to the cinema, Chloe asked:

"Were you long in Africa?"

"Two years. I didn't like it, and my mother simply hated my being out there. I didn't get demobbed till two years after the Armistice—I was in Palestine and Egypt. And then I was crocked for a bit; and then I went to Africa orange farming. I hated it like poison."

"Why?"

"I don't know—I did. I like people. I loathed the veldt, and Kaffirs, and waiting for orange pips to grow into forest trees. And when a great-uncle I'd never seen left me his little all, I threw my hat in the air and came home—"

"And spent it?" There was horror in Chloe's tone; she looked at him severely. "How could you?"

"I didn't—not much. I bought my car, and ran round having a good time for a bit. Then I made up my mind to go into the motor business. I like cars better than anything, really; and I've got one or two ideas of my own that I want to work out. But of course you can be most awfully had, so I thought I'd get to know the ropes a bit before I parted with any of Uncle Horace's money. I shall probably go into the firm I'm driving for." He laughed. "It's quite good fun, and I've learnt a thing or two."

"It must be lovely driving people like Mrs. Howard," said Chloe.

"They're not all like that. After all, you meet people you can't stand almost anywhere. There's a man here now that I simply bar; I'm always running across him." He broke off, and Chloe said:

"You'll be glad to leave Maxton."

"I don't know." His tone was strictly non-committal. "I shall probably butt into him in town." He frowned, and then laughed. "I can't think why I began to talk about him. It's a frightful mistake to talk about people you bar."

Two hours later they walked home together. Edward Anderson and Rose had dropped behind. Michael did not say a single word until they turned into the quiet street where Rose and Chloe lodged. Then he burst into speech:

"Do you believe in telling the truth?"

"I always tell the truth," said Chloe. She laughed because Michael was so solemn. "I was very nicely brought up—by Miss Tankerville. She'd be simply horrified at your asking such a thing."

Michael went on being serious.

"I don't mean telling lies or—or untruths in the ordinary sense. I mean, this is such a beastly conventional world, and we're all brought up to behave in a conventional way; one can't really speak the truth bang out; but sometimes one would like to frightfully. That's what I meant."

"There's a game where you have to speak the truth," said Chloe. "Last time I played it, one girl left the room in tears, and a man I used to know rather well has never forgiven me, and probably never will. It doesn't always answer." She paused. Discretion bade her pause, but curiosity urged her on. She turned innocent eyes on Michael, and added, "Of course it depends on what you want to say."

Michael said nothing. He also was wrestling with discretion.

They reached the street lamp by Mrs. Jones' door, and stood there. Rose and Edward were not in sight.

"You see," said Michael, suddenly finding words, "I've only seen you twice, and it sounds such awful cheek if I say what I should like to say." He became furiously red and plunged on. "If we weren't all so frightfully conventional, I should say I like you better than any girl I've ever met, and I'd like most awfully to be friends, and see you again; only of course you'd think it most frightful cheek if I did."

Chloe's laugh shook a little.

"You—you haven't said it, of course."

"No, but I'd like to say it. Would you—would you be angry if I did?"

"Furious!" said Chloe. "Absolutely furious, of course."

"Then I won't say it; but—I say, you'll remember that I would have liked to say it, won't you? And—and if you ever want anything done for you, or anything like that—" He broke off.

Rose and Edward came slowly into the circle of lamplight.

Chapter Six

"Chloe, how could you!"

"How could I what?" Chloe lit the gas as she spoke, and turned round laughing. She knew quite well what she would see—a serious, reproachful Rose, full of concern and good advice.

"Chloe, you know very well. How could you pick Mr. Foster up like that and bring him back to tea?"

"Poof!" said Chloe, blowing her a kiss. "Rose, you're not a chaperone yet. And if you think I'm just going to sit down and let you come being married over me, you little know your Chloe."

"It's just because I do know you," said Rose. She checked a tendency to dimple, and looked severe instead. "Chloe, you oughtn't to do things like that, and you know it."

"That's what all the sermons say. Rose, I believe one could make quite a hit with potted sermons if one was a parson. That sentence of yours would make a topper. If you come to think of it, that's all sermons ever do say: 'You know you oughtn't to.'" She made a face. "I suppose being a parson's daughter will out. After all, what have I done? Asked a perfectly nice man to tea and gone to the pictures with him, accompanied and chaperoned by you and Edward. And the Tank introduced him to me—even if she did feel rather bad about it. And—and anyhow, he goes away to-morrow, and I shall never see him again."

"You just wait and see," said Rose.

On Tuesday evening Chloe and Rose went home together. Michael Foster had left Maxton; but a man stood where Michael had stood the night before, and waited as he had waited for Chloe to come through Miss Allardyce's green door. It was an old man this time. It was, in fact, Mr. Mitchell Dane. He waited until the girls came out, and then walked behind them the length of the High Street. Scraps of conversation reached him—Rose's name from Chloe, and Chloe's name from Rose—laughter.

At the foot of the High Street he crossed over, and watched them turn into Basing Street. He stood looking after them for a moment, and then went back to his hotel.

Next day was a busy one in the work-room. Finishing touches were being given to the dresses for the County Ball which would take place that night. Miss Allardyce was much fluttered, and kept changing her mind about everything.

"The flowers higher up, Miss Smith. Oh, no, no, no, not there! Lower down, and an inch or two to the right. Miss Dane, that bodice is too low. Oh dear, oh dear, it really is too low! But the time to alter it—where is it? It can't be done—and yet—"

"I could put a fold of net," said Chloe, "but it's just as you pinned it on her, really."

"Yes, yes, put the net!" said Miss Allardyce distractedly, and then, ten minutes later, declared with her hands at her head, but it would never, *never* do, and that Chloe must take it off again. "And oh, how thankful I shall be when to-day is over!"

Rose and Chloe were thankful too when the last of the dresses had been sent off by a special errand boy. Rose was going to the ball with Edward Anderson, and was in a state of pleasurable anticipation which she tried to conceal because Chloe, who had no frock to wear, must play at being Cinderella and stay at home.

"Oh, Chloe, I *wish* you were coming," she said for about the fiftieth time.

"So do I," said Chloe frankly. "But go in a window curtain or one of Mrs. Jones' antimacassars, I won't and can't. Just think of Monica's face if I arrived in an antimacassar! I'd love to do it—just walk artlessly up to their party, and say how shy I felt, and '*Dear* Lady Gresson, I *may* stay with you, mayn't I?' Rose, I believe I really could make an antimacassar dress if I gave my mind to it."

"You haven't got a ticket," said Rose.

"It's just as well, isn't it?"

"There's a parcel for you, Miss Dane," said Mrs. Jones in the hall as they came in.

"For me?" Chloe pounced on it. Parcels were few and far between. "It's a box—a dress box!"

She ran upstairs with it, burst into their room, lit the gas, and was cutting the string before Rose overtook her.

"What is it?"

"I don't know. Cut the string! Cut all the knots! Rose, it's a dress box—but who, who on earth could possibly be sending me a dress, unless Ally's gone clean off her head and addressed one of her atrocities to me by mistake? Oh-h-h!"

The string was cut, and the paper was off. The box that was revealed was not one of Miss Allardyce's boxes. It bore the name of a famous firm—a firm so famous that Rose and Chloe clutched each other and gazed at it in petrified silence. Chloe was the first to recover.

"Either it's a practical joke,"—the words came whispering—"or else we've just walked straight through Mrs. Jones' front door into a fairy story, and at any minute—at *any* minute—the pumpkin coach may arrive."

"Open it, Chloe," said Rose.

"Perhaps it's full of old newspapers."

"Perhaps it isn't. Chloe, *do* open it!"

"One," said Chloe—she put her hands on the lid—"Two,"—she lifted it an inch—"Three,"—she flung it back. White tissue paper crossed by white ribbons. She untied them with shaking fingers; the paper crisped and rustled as she pulled it away; there seemed to be reams and reams of it. And then—

"It is the fairy story! It *is*!!" said Chloe, with the last thin sheet in her hand. The colour sprang to her cheeks. "I believe we're asleep. I don't believe it's real." She was looking with unbelieving eyes at the silver tissue of her dreams.

It was Rose who lifted the shining frock and held it up—a fairy tale dress, a dream dress, simple with the simplicity that is of great price. They both looked at it. Chloe began to laugh very softly and irrepressibly.

"How—how ripping! Rose, there are shoes to match! And the sort of stockings you read about! And—and—"

"Who *can* have sent it?" said Rose with a gasp.

Chloe snatched the frock from her, pinched it to see if it was real, and held it up against the light.

"I don't care who sent it. I don't care if it turns back into rags at midnight. I don't care for anything else in the world as long as I can just wear this lovely, lovely thing. And—and—oh, what a pity Michael Foster's gone away!"

"Chloe, here's a note."

Chloe tore it open, the silver dress over her arm, and exclaimed in astonishment:

"Lady Gresson! It can't be—it simply can't—I don't believe it."

"What does she say?"

"She says"—Chloe's voice was bewildered in the extreme—"she says:—

"MY DEAR CHLOE—

"It will give us great pleasure if you will join our party to-night. We will call for you at nine o'clock. Will you accept the frock and shoes from an old friend?

"Yours affectionately,

OLIVIA GRESSON.'

"She's never been mine affectionately since I went to work for Ally," said Chloe. "Oh, Rose, how topping of her—how simply topping! There's a postscript to say she's got my ticket." She threw the silver dress on to the bed, and hugged Rose vehemently. "I don't believe a single word of it—it's a lovely, lovely dream. And oh, ducky, ducky dear, *don't* wake me up till the ball is over!"

Chapter Seven

MAXTON IS justly proud of its Borough Hall, and of the excellence of the dancing floor in the ballroom there.

Mitchell Dane stood by one of the arched doorways at the top of the room. He looked towards the entrance with the long-sighted gaze which is unaware of nearer objects. In his case this was the result of a mental focus which was bent upon that one far doorway and excluded everything else. Miss Jones, with her red hair and brilliant rose-pink dress, passed within a yard of him, and he did not see her. He was waiting for Lady Gresson's party to arrive; waiting, with a curiosity and impatience which surprised himself, to see Chloe Dane come into the big room and stand under all those brilliant lights in the silver dress which he had sent her through Lady Gresson. It was the test that he had planned.

He had seen Chloe in coat and hat, pretty enough, holding herself well enough, talking as girls talk. England was full of pretty girls. It wasn't just a pretty girl Mitchell Dane was looking for: it was an heiress for his half million, a Dane of Danesborough who would hold up her head and smile away those whispers as to his origin and that of his money. Any pretty girl could walk down Maxton High Street and make a pleasant picture to the eye. Society is the test of breeding. Mitchell Dane wanted to see Chloe come into this big, crowded place; he wanted to see her dance, to watch her face and manner; wanted, in fact, to be sure of his ground before he took even the slightest step into the open.

Lady Gresson was late. Lady Gresson was always late; she arrived everywhere in a state of frantic haste and rasped temper, declaring that she could not imagine what had delayed her, and blaming Monica, a clock, her car, or the long-suffering Sir Joseph. She came in now, thin, worried, flushed, with a collar of diamonds high about her lean throat, and Monica just behind her, rather sulky in the pale blue which was supposed to flatter her eyes.

Mitchell Dane's nostrils twitched very slightly. He was thinking that he would have thrown his money into the sea or left it to a cat's home before he would have taken Monica for his heiress, if she had happened to be Monica Dane.

Martin Fossetter came in with the Gressons. Behind them, Jack Renton and Joyce Langham, and Tim, the other Renton boy, with Chloe. Mitchell Dane's appraising glance rested on her intently. He noted her entrance; the manner of it; her air and carriage. This was no little work-girl tricked out in a shining dress, but Miss Chloe Dane who came into the great ball-room as if it belonged to her. She was speaking as she came in—speaking and smiling. Tim Renton was asking her for a dance, and next moment she put her hand on his arm and they slipped into the crowd of dancers. Mitchell Dane turned and watched them as they came round the room towards him.

Chloe dancing was Chloe at her best; and Chloe dancing in her silver dress was a sight that might have brought softness into any man's eyes. Mitchell Dane's glance did not soften, but it approved. She passed quite close to him, and he heard her pretty laugh. Seen like that, Chloe was more than pretty; she was radiant. Her eyes shone, and the brilliant colour rose to her cheeks, that colour which nature gives so rarely, and which seems to have a life of its own—the expression of youth, warmth and joy. To-night Chloe carried with her that atmosphere of colour, joy, and youth; it made a radiance about her, and gave her beauty. The light in her eyes, the spring in her step, the lift of her head, and that geranium flush—these filled the eye and rejoiced it.

Mitchell Dane stood quite still by his archway for the next half hour. He watched Chloe dance with Martin Fossetter, and with a young man whose gloomily ferocious expression advertised a hopeless passion.

Chloe always found it difficult to decide whether it was better to refuse to dance with Bernard Austin, and to feel that he was glaring at her from a doorway, or to dance with him and be glared at at close range. In either case Maxton talked—and Chloe usually lost her temper. To-night her mood was kind enough to attempt the impossible. She smiled at Bernard as she had not smiled at him for many a long month.

"I'm so frightfully happy," she said. "Bernard, do be a dear and cheer up. I'm a person in a fairy tale—Cinderella, or the goose-girl who turned into a princess,—and I simply can't do with people being gloomy. You see, this isn't Maxton at all; it's the country East of the Sun and West of the Moon; and we're dancing in a particularly thrilling fairy story that I don't know the end of."

Bernard stared at her.

"I don't know what you mean."

"I don't know myself," said Chloe. "It wouldn't be half so exciting if I did. Perhaps my silver dress will turn into a holland overall or some other up-to-date equivalent of Cinderella's rags; or perhaps a hippogriff will come sailing into the hall when the clock strikes twelve, and carry me off no one knows where; or perhaps the Youngest Son—

it's always the Youngest Son in fairy stories—will step suddenly out from behind one of those pillars and vanish me away with a Cloak of Darkness thrown round us both."

"What on earth's a hippogriff?" said Bernard.

Chloe looked shocked.

"What an utterly neglected education you've had! And you a schoolmaster, too! It's a horse with wings *of course*. Bernard, wouldn't it be topping if it did come sailing in—the hippogriff I mean. I do adore riding; and a horse with wings—just think of it!"

"I think you're talking nonsense," said Bernard gloomily.

Chloe sighed. It was Bernard's utter inability to talk nonsense which made him so hopeless as a suitor. "Fancy *living* with a person you had to talk sense to all day long!" she once said to Rose. "I shall write a Moral Tract about it, and call it, 'Why Women Grow Old.' " She sighed, and said in a little voice:

"Of course I am talking nonsense—I always do when I'm happy."

Bernard looked loftily disapproving, missed his step, and trod on one of the silver slippers.

"Ouf!" said Chloe. "Don't do that! Bernard, I'll never dance with you again if you spoil my shoes—there's a real, solid, practical fact for you instead of the nonsense you disapprove of."

"I want to talk sense," said Bernard.

A look that Chloe dreaded came into his eye—the look, not so much ardent as obstinate, which indicated that he was about to rush once more upon his fate.

"I want to talk about you. Chloe, I must have it out with you. You went away in the middle last time, you know; and I never seem to see you alone now."

Chloe's chin went up; her eyes warned him.

"Do you call this being alone with me?" she said. "Bernard, if you dare to propose to me with eight hundred people looking on, I swear I'll never speak to you again."

Bernard relapsed into silence and inspissated gloom.

Chloe's dance with Martin Fossetter left her with a vague feeling of disappointment. He was charming, courteous, the ideal partner as far as his dancing went; but all, as it were, from a distance. "He might be doing a duty dance with Lady Gresson," was Chloe's unspoken thought. The dark eyes hardly rested upon her, or when they did, betrayed no interest. Chloe in her silver frock might just as well have been the stout Miss Jones with her red hair and the pink ostrich feather trimming sewn by Chloe's own fingers upon the garment which she declared had been copied from old Mrs. Duffy's pink flannelette nightgown.

Mr. Fossetter's talk touched lightly upon the surface of things in general. The warm sympathy that had tinged his voice the other day was absent from it now. Even whilst he danced with Chloe his eyes followed Monica Gresson round the room, and when the dance was over he rejoined her with alacrity.

It was at this moment that Lady Gresson touched Chloe on the arm.

"Here is some one who wishes to make your acquaintance, my dear—your—your cousin, Mr. Mitchell Dane."

Chloe looked up; she had to look up a long way, because Mitchell Dane was so *very* tall. She saw him standing there before her, very tall and very thin, an old man with a face that puzzled her because it reminded her of something, she did not quite know what. She thought of a splinter of ice, of a fine steel thread, and of grey snow-clouds. These three images came into her mind and brought with them a chill. Her colour changed a little. It was as if, coming out of a warm and lighted room, she had met the stab of the east wind. All this in just the second when their eyes met. Cold—that was the key-note of the impression. She thought he looked as if he had never been warm in his life: eyes a faint, icy blue; lips just a pale line.

"I'm afraid I do not dance," he said. "Can you bear to sit out whilst other people are dancing?"

Chloe smiled at him. It was rather an extra nice smile, because she felt sorry for anyone who looked all frozen up like that—this was Chloe's own way of putting it.

"I should like to talk to you for a little, if I may," said Mitchell Dane.

They went up into the gallery. From where she sat Chloe could see the swing and movement of the dance, the light and colour below. Mitchell Dane sat with his back to the room and his eyes on Chloe.

"Do you remember Danesborough?" he asked; and Chloe answered:

"Oh, yes. I was nine years old, you know; I can remember things that happened when I was four."

"It's sometimes a mistake to remember too much," said Mitchell Dane. "Half the people in the world make their own troubles by forgetting what they ought to remember; and then they keep 'em alive by remembering what they ought to forget."

"Ought I to forget Danesborough? It doesn't make me discontented, you know. It's like a nice secret that I can take out and look at."

"You liked Danesborough then? You remember it pleasantly? All the secrets that people take out and look at when they are alone are not pleasant ones, you know."

Chloe felt as if he had touched her with a cold finger. She was sorry for him, because she thought he must be very lonely. She was interested too, and a little excited.

"You liked Danesborough then?" he repeated.

"I loved it," said Chloe. Her voice was warm with memory.

"What did you love? Tell me a little about it. You see I'm interested because I live there—you know that, I suppose."

"Yes—oh, yes—Monica Gresson told me."

"Well, what did you love at Danesborough?"

"I think everything. It's being so big—that was one thing. I could get right away from everyone and play hide-and-seek. And I did love the horses, and the dogs, and all the creatures."

"Creatures?"

"Birds, and squirrels," said Chloe nodding, "and fish in the ponds—everything except the hens. I don't think I could ever love a hen; they're so stupid, and hot, and feathery."

"Would you like to go back to Danesborough?" said Mitchell Dane. He looked very directly at Chloe as he spoke, and saw her colour brighten. "You can if you like," he added without waiting for her to speak.

The brilliant colour faded. Chloe's hand tightened on the arm of her chair. Her eyes never left Mitchell Dane's face.

"What do you mean?" she asked.

"Something quite simple. I can put it into quite a few words, I think. I have a great deal of money. I have Danesborough. And—I have no relations except yourself. I think that states the facts correctly."

"*Are* you a relation?" said Chloe; and then wondered whether she had been rude.

Mitchell Dane actually smiled.

"Well," he said, "the relationship is certainly a distant one. I couldn't tell you just where my great-great-grandfather left the family tree and started a family on his own account; but we needn't bother about that, I think. Danesborough and the name make better links than any half-forgotten pedigree. I don't know if you understood what I meant just now when I said that you could come back to Danesborough if you liked. I am asking you to come back to Danesborough."

A sensation of terror passed over Chloe. It did not enter her consciousness, but it passed like a cold breath and was gone. Some reflection of it showed in her eyes, for Mitchell Dane saw it there.

"What's the matter?" he said. "I am proposing to adopt you, and to make you my heiress. I want the place to go with the name, and you're the last of the old stock. I'm not counting the Australian Danes; they'd never make roots here now. And I have a curious desire to found a family."

Chloe sat bolt upright. Her colour was all gone, but her eyes were steady. In a voice that was just over a whisper she said, "I don't know you—I don't know you at all."

He nodded approvingly.

"No, that's quite true. You don't know me; but you can get to know me. There'll have to be beginnings. As a beginning, perhaps you will pay me a visit with Miss Gresson. My secretary is married, and his wife, Mrs. Wroughton, is good enough to do the honours for me. Will you come?"

Chloe did not speak at once. Then suddenly the words came— quite simple words:

"It's so big, Mr. Dane! I'm frightened. I'm not ungrateful, but it's all—" She broke off. Her hand fell from the arm of the chair and brushed against the silver of her skirt. At the touch the colour sprang into her cheeks. She caught a silver fold and held it out.

"You—*you* gave me this. I knew it wasn't Lady Gresson, really. People can't suddenly do things like that. It was you. It *was*, wasn't it?"

"Yes, it was I. Perhaps you will not be offended if I explain a little. I wanted to see you. Well, I could have called on you in Maxton, or Lady Gresson could have asked me to meet you at Ranbourne. I wanted more than that: I wanted to see you in the sort of setting which Danesborough would give you; and I wanted to do this without committing myself. To be quite frank, I might have found you quite unsuited to my purpose. Well, if that had been the case, you would have been none the wiser; you would have had your frock and the ball, and there would have been no hurt feelings. I should have gone away and left my money to one of the many admirable institutions which are continually asking me for subscriptions." After a little pause he continued: "Will you come and spend a week at Danesborough? I daresay Lady Gresson and her daughter could be persuaded to come too. You need not make any decision just yet. Caution is a virtue which I very much approve; my experiences have taught me that most men, and all women, would be the better for a little more of it." He rose as he spoke, and Chloe got up too. She found that she was trembling a little.

"I work," she said. "I'm not free to pay visits—you know that."

"Would you like to come? I think it could be arranged very easily."

Chloe did not know whether she could say truthfully that she would like to come. She felt an unreasoning desire to run away. She felt as if she were really Cinderella, and as if the shining dress which had made her so happy had turned to rags; she wanted to take it off and never see it again. And all the time her conscience told her how ungrateful it was to have such thoughts as these. She walked silently down the gallery stairs, and was sad for her vanished fairy tale.

Chapter Eight

CHLOE DANCED again with Tim Renton, a cheerful youth with a free tongue and a good conceit of himself.

"What's happened to you?" he said. "No chit-chat, no light and airy badinage—in fact, no anything! Make a remark about the weather, there's a good soul, or the whole of Maxton will say that I've proposed to you and been turned down. I should hate that."

"Which part of it?"

Tim Renton grinned.

"Being turned down, of course. What on earth did the old buffer who looks as if he'd just come out of cold storage say or do to cast such a horrid blight?"

"I'm not in the least blighted," said Chloe.

"Well, you look it. Did he say, 'Fly with me, and with all my worldly millions I will thee endow,' or words to that effect?"

Chloe tried to look very severe.

"Tim, you haven't any manners at all. I don't know why I dance with you."

"I expect it's because I'm so beautiful," said Tim. He had the kind of ugly, flat face that goes with green eyes, freckles, and a grin.

Chloe laughed, and felt more cheerful.

"If he *was* proposing that you should fly with him, I wouldn't go—I don't believe even the millions would make it worth while. Lady Gresson says he is going to adopt you; but, personally, I should hate to be adopted by a sort of survival from the ice age. Now you go right ahead and tell me just what kind of a neck I've got to butt in on your affairs. You'll do it awfully well, and I shan't mind a bit, so we'll both be quite happy. Your lead, partner!"

The bright, angry colour ran up into Chloe's cheeks.

"How dare Lady Gresson go about talking like that! It's not her business. I should think Mr. Dane would be furious." Then, with a sudden change of manner, "Tim, why did you say that?"

"Say what?"

"You know—about Mr. Dane. If he did want to adopt me, why shouldn't I say 'Yes'?"

For once in his life Tim Renton looked serious. The ugly face showed a promise of strength and sense.

"I don't know. I was chaffing."

"But you meant something."

"I don't know what I meant. At least—"

"Tell me!" said Chloe imperiously.

"My dear girl, there's nothing to tell. I like you; and I don't like him—that's all."

The words kept coming back to Chloe then and later. As nearly as possible they defined the indefinable. There are people you like, and people you don't like. You don't always know why you like people; and you don't always know why you dislike them.

Chloe did not let her other partners find her silent; but the bloom had gone from the evening. She did not dance again with Martin Fossetter. Of course, as Chloe put it quite firmly to herself, she did not care in the very, very least whether Martin Fossetter asked her to dance with him or not. It vexed her to think how intimately she had talked to him that afternoon at Ranbourne; and of course it would have been pleasant to have had the opportunity of snubbing him a little. She had, in point of fact, made up her mind to be very distant to Mr. Fossetter, and it was annoying not to have been able to put this good resolution to the proof.

Towards the end of the evening Bernard Austin succeeded in producing his rather well-worn proposal.

"You can't say there are eight hundred people looking on now, Chloe, and I must have it out with you."

"I wish you wouldn't," said Chloe crossly. "It's not the slightest use. I can't think why you *want* to when you know it isn't the slightest use."

Chloe had been sitting out an interval with Jack Renton. She made a movement to rise, but Bernard dropped into the empty chair beside her.

"It's this way," he began. "You say it's no good; but as long as I go on seeing you I have the feeling that in the end you'll listen to me. Why shouldn't you? I'm making enough to give you a comfortable home; and a schoolmaster is like a doctor—he's bound to get married. Indeed, he's much more bound to get married than a doctor is.

As a matter of fact, and quite apart from being in love with you, I'm *bound* to get married." He brought an acquisitive gaze to bear upon Chloe, and said firmly, "I *need* a wife."

When Bernard Austin talked like that Chloe always wanted to box his ears. Having received a refined education at the hands of Miss Tankerville, she restrained herself; but the tips of her fingers tingled badly.

"I *need* a wife," repeated Bernard Austin. He was leaning forward with his elbows on his knees. "As a bachelor, I am at a distinct disadvantage. Parents expect one to have a wife. Mrs. Methven Smith told me only yesterday that she would send all her six boys to me if I were only married. The eldest is eight. She said she couldn't feel any confidence that their underclothing would be changed at the proper times in the spring and autumn unless I had a wife that she could write to about it. I told her the school matron was most efficient; but she said that a wife would take more interest. I *must* have a wife."

"You can have twenty so long as I'm not one of them," said Chloe sharply.

"I only want you," said Bernard. "Mrs. Methven Smith—"

"My good Bernard," said Chloe, "I haven't the slightest intention of marrying anyone for ages. And when I do get married, it won't be because I've got a passionate desire to talk about vests and pyjamas to Mrs. Methven Smith."

Bernard looked pained.

"A wife should identify herself with her husband's work. She should throw her whole heart into it. She—"

"Good gracious, Bernard, do stop!" said Chloe in an exasperated voice. "When you've got a wife, she can do all those things; but they don't interest me. Do you hear?—they simply don't interest me. I'm not your wife; and I'm not going to be your wife." She sprang up as she spoke. "I don't want to be anybody's wife; I want to dance." She laughed over her shoulder at him. "You dance a heap better than you make love, Bernard. Look here, I'll give you a really good tip," she added as he got up and gave her his arm. "It won't work with me, but it might with some one else. Next time you propose to a girl—no, don't interrupt; it's rude—next time, you try telling her what a lot of interest you're going to take in her and how you're going to put your whole heart into making her happy. And—don't talk so much about yourself."

Chloe got home before Rose because Lady Gresson did not stay to the end of the ball, and Edward Anderson did. Chloe was sitting up in bed when Rose came in, pretty and glowing in the pink frock that she had made herself. She flung off her coat, and sank down on the bed with an "Oh, Chloe, such heaps to tell you!"

"So have I," said Chloe.

"And you mustn't mind—Chloe darling, you must promise not to mind, or it will spoil everything."

Chloe roused herself from her own thoughts and plans. Something must have happened to make Rose look like this, so flushed and tremulous.

"What is it?" she asked. "Tell me at once, ducky!"

Rose came nearer, flung an arm about Chloe's shoulders, and hid her face in Chloe's neck.

"You mustn't mind—you must promise not to mind," she whispered.

"What is it?"

"Edward has to go out a month earlier, and—and—oh, Chloe, we'll have to be married next week; and I do so hate leaving you."

Chloe felt a hot tear go trickling down the back of her neck. She put motherly arms about Rose and hugged her.

Danesborough seemed nearer.

Chapter Nine

CHLOE STOOD on the terrace at Danesborough, and watched the sun go down into a bank of mist. Rose was married and gone, and Maxton seemed very far away. She had been at Danesborough for nearly a week. After a short interview with Mr. Dane, Ally had fairly pressed a holiday upon her, and she had gone off with the Gressons in a mood between shrinking and excitement.

Chloe saw the sun grow redder and rounder in the fog. The air was very still; the sky a faint, dusky blue, fast changing into grey; mist rising everywhere. From where she stood, the ground fell away in five terraces. The mist was rising against them like a tide. Away to the right, the great mass of leafless woods curtained by the dusk. To the left, a hazy gleam from the lake in the hollow.

Chloe remembered it all so green and smiling in the sunshine. With that child's memory which crowds all its happy recollections upon a single canvas she had pictured Danesborough as the old folk-tales picture Avalon, a place always green and always sunny, where roses, lilies, daffodils, and irises bloomed for ever, and the rosy apple-blossom broke from boughs weighed down with ruddy apples—a Danesborough that never was; a child's imagining; a child's dream. But Chloe missed her dream and was sad for it. The real Danesborough gave her nothing to take its place. The woods were leafless, and the gardens slept.

She turned and went into the lighted house, and in the house met again that something that had driven her out upon the terrace. Chloe did not know what this something was; but it met her at every turn.

Mrs. Wroughton, the secretary's wife, crossed the hall as Chloe came in—a little faded woman with hair like straw, and a mouth that was always slightly open. Chloe never saw her without wondering how the red-faced, jovial Mr. Wroughton had ever come to marry such a frightened wisp of a creature.

"Oh, Miss Dane, you've been out."

"Yes," said Chloe.

"It's—it's getting quite dark."

"Yes."

Emily Wroughton's trick of making banal and self-evident remarks had become almost as irritating to Chloe as it obviously was to Emily's husband.

"But milder—I really think it is milder—only foggy—there seems to be quite a fog—so autumnal! I believe Mr. Dane was asking for you just now. Have you seen him?"

Mr. Dane himself opened the drawing-room door as she spoke. He stood back when he saw Chloe, with a gesture that invited her to join him. When she had come into the drawing-room, he shut the door.

"Aren't you cold?" he asked. "You should have had a coat."

"I'm never cold. Rose used to get quite angry about it. She said it was dreadfully aggravating."

"Yes, I can understand that. I am a cold person myself." He paused, and then said with some abruptness, "Do you remember this room at all? I've changed it as little as possible."

"I don't know," said Chloe. "It's funny, but I remember all the outside things so much better than I do the house."

"If you come to live here, you can do anything you like with it." There was no expression in Mitchell Dane's voice.

Chloe was looking about her. She had hardly been into the drawing-room at all—they had used the library and the morning-room. This room, with its fine proportions and long windows opening upon the terrace, had the bleak, formal effect of a place unlived in; its atmosphere was rather that of a museum or public institution; everything about it was formal. The pale Aubusson carpet had a chilly look which the delicate brocade curtains repeated. The whole room was colourless without any stronger tint than the faint pastel hues afford. Old gilding; old damask; the faded water-colours of some half forgotten grandmother—everything, as it were, keyed to the lowest possible tone—, everything except the black cabinet.

"Oh!" said Chloe. "I remember that." She pointed at it and ran forward.

It stood out in the room, as it stood out in Chloe's recollection—a Chinese cabinet of black lacquer decorated in gold. She had not seen it at once because it was set in the recess beside the fireplace, and she had turned towards the windows.

Mitchell Dane smiled.

"Ah! You remember that."

Chloe was all glow and sparkle.

"Yes, I remember it frightfully well. But isn't it odd? I didn't remember that I remembered it until this minute; and now—it's just like a curtain going up. I—I can see myself standing on a chair, and trying to find out where the river came from."

She had come close to the cabinet as she spoke. It was very large. It towered over Chloe's head even now; to the child it had seemed unbelievably tall. The river began in the left-hand top corner. It was a golden river, winding its way amongst mountains and trees. Sometimes there was a boat upon it; sometimes tiny golden men stood amongst the rushes on its banks. Chloe gazed at it, fascinated.

"I remember it more and more. I always loved it."

The river wound upon its golden way. The rushes reared themselves upon the bank. Chloe put out her finger and touched the little shining waves that lapped against the rushes. She was little Chloe Dane again, escaped from the nursery and looking into a Chinese fairy-land. Three little men in the rushes. One had a hat; and one had a basket; and one had speared a fish. Their names came back with a rush, the ridiculous, make-believe names which she had given them. Timmy Jimmy, that was the one with the hat; and the fisherman was Henry Planty; and the man with the basket was Mr. Dark. The child Chloe had loved Timmy Jimmy and Henry Planty, but she had always been a little bit afraid of Mr. Dark.

Mitchell Dane saw her touch two of the little men and draw her finger back from the third. He saw the colour come with a rush to her cheek, and watched her with interest. He was always interested in people; but it was years since that interest had come so near a normal human feeling as it had during the past week. He wondered what Chloe was thinking of.

Chloe was not in the drawing-room at Danesborough at all. There was a black, muddy marsh under her feet, and tall rushes that rose between her and a night-black sky. All the light came from the golden river. Chloe stood amongst the rushes, and heard people moving. She knew who the people were. They were Timmy Jimmy, and Henry Planty, and Mr. Dark. The child Chloe had made rhymes about them. Each little man had his own rhyme, and the ridiculous jingling words said themselves over to Chloe across the forgetful years:

"Timmy Jimmy has a hat,
  Very wide and very flat.
  Oh, how I wish I had a hat
  Just like Timmy Jimmy's hat!"

That was the first rhyme. And then there was one about Henry Planty:

"Henry Planty caught a fish,
    And put it on a golden dish.
    Henry Planty's golden fish
    Gives a golden wish."

That was a perfectly thrilling rhyme. Chloe could see the golden wishes there in the dark. They were little bright things like fire-flies, and if you caught one, you could have your wish. Only they were just terribly difficult to catch.

The third rhyme rose up in her mind:

"The dogs all bark
    At Mr. Dark.
    I would not like to have to touch
    The basket he has got.
    I'd say loud out, 'I'd rather not,'
    Because I do not like you very much,
    And if I was a dog, I'd bark,
    Mr. Dark.'"

Chloe came back to the drawing-room at Danesborough with a start. Why, that was really just what she felt about Mitchell Dane. It came straight out of the silly rhyme—"I'd rather not, because I do not like you very much."

Mitchell Dane's voice sounded suddenly in her ears:

"I'll give you more than a penny for your thoughts, Chloe. What are they?"

Chloe looked over her shoulder; she had a listening, remembering look.

"I gave them names," she said very low. "I gave them names. But I never told anyone; it was a tremendous secret."

Mitchell Dane smiled.

"A secret—and you kept it?"

"Oh, yes, I kept it always. I never told anyone. I—I had forgotten; but it's all come back."

"Secrets are safest when they are forgotten. Unfortunately they have a way of coming back," said Mitchell Dane, his voice very cool and matter of fact. Then, after a little pause, "Do you suppose you could keep a secret?"

She turned towards him with a confident nod. The abstracted fit was passing.

"Of course I can."

"You're very sure. Why that 'of course'?"

Just for a moment Chloe looked rather like an impudent boy.

"Why, because I'm a woman, and women are *very* good at keeping secrets—didn't you know that?"

"That's not the general opinion, but—"

The atmosphere changed suddenly. Chloe was aware of being searched through and through, dissected. She felt extraordinarily small and extraordinarily helpless, like a fly on a pin. The impudence went out of her, and she heard herself say with a gasp, "Don't! Don't!" The sensation passed as suddenly as it had come.

"So you can keep a secret?"

This time Chloe did not laugh. She met his eyes steadily, and said, "Yes, I can."

Mitchell Dane turned round towards the fire, and began to warm first one foot and then the other.

"When I retired from business two years ago,"—his quiet, level voice seemed to continue rather than begin a statement—"when I retired from business two years ago, I had a good deal of my stock-in-trade left on my hands. It was, and is, very valuable. It needs extremely expert handling. I should never advise you to attempt to handle it. I do not suppose for a moment that you would desire to do so; but, in any case, it is a matter for the expert, and I couldn't advise you to touch it. On the other hand—"

"Mr. Dane, stop!" said Chloe. She had stood still until this moment, but now she made a quick step forward. "Mr. Dane, don't! Don't tell me anything!"

"And why not?"

Chloe was rather pale.

"Because, Mr. Dane, at Maxton you asked me—I mean, you told me—"

"I told you that I wished to adopt you. Is that what you mean?"

"Yes," said Chloe, her eyes wide and imploring.

"And to make you my heiress."

She nodded, biting her lip.

"Well," said Mitchell Dane, "what about it? Why did you stop me?"

"Because—because I can't," said Chloe from her heart.

"You don't want to be adopted?" Mr. Dane's voice was as expressionless as his face.

"No, I can't!"

"Or to be my heiress?" A spice of malice crept in.

"No, I can't—really." She put out her hand with a troubled gesture, her eyes searched his face.

"It sounds dreadfully ungrateful, but I can't."

"Why?" His voice was rather amused. "I'm not the least bit offended. But it would really interest me to know why you *can't* take Danesborough and half a million—I think I told you it was half a million."

Chloe had an impulse of anger, an impulse of pity.

"I don't know you," she said. "I shouldn't ever know you. I should feel—yes, always—that I was taking things from a stranger. You can't be a daughter to someone whom you don't know." In the end pity came uppermost with a rush. "I'm—I'm so dreadfully sorry, Mr. Dane," she said.

There was a pause. Mitchell Dane shifted from his right foot to his left, held the right foot to the fire, and said nothing. If he felt any disappointment or hurt feeling, no sign of it appeared. He seemed to be lost in thought and unaware of Chloe. She had time to find the silence oppressive before he said,

"When you interrupted me just now I was about to tell you that there are various people who would be quite pleased to have the handling of my stock-in-trade. Some of these have been associated with me in business, and I dare say they think themselves quite competent to carry it on without me. Now, Chloe, this is what I want to impress upon you—"

"Why are you telling me this?" said Chloe.

"Because I choose," said Mitchell Dane. "I ask nothing of you except that you should listen and remember what I am saying. I do not wish any of these persons to have the handling of my stock-in-trade. I trust you to see that they do not have the opportunity of doing so."

"What have I got to do with it? I can't, indeed I can't!"

"You're too fond of that word, I think. I'm really only asking you to remember what I'm saying. I won't keep you much longer. But I wish to tell you something—something rather important. When I came here two years ago, I had a safe built into the wall behind that cabinet. It's a very special safe. I had the cabinet adapted in order to accommodate and conceal it. As the cabinet has stood in this place for at least a hundred years, it would not, I think, occur to anyone that there was a safe behind it."

"But the men, the men who did the work—they would talk," said Chloe.

"Wroughton and I did the work," said Mitchell Dane. "And the cabinet is clamped to the wall and to the floor—for greater security."

"Then Mr. Wroughton knows?"

"Yes."

With the one short word Mitchell Dane left the hearth, went to the cabinet, and unlocked the doors.

The cabinet was in two parts. It was the upper doors that he flung open, disclosing a number of small drawers ornamented with fishes, dragon-flies, and birds. The gold on the drawers was much fresher and brighter than the gold on the outside of the cabinet.

Chloe remembered these drawers very well. One of the uncles had collected butterflies when he was a boy, and his collection had occupied the whole top of the cabinet.

"Are the butterflies still there?" she asked. He pulled out a drawer and showed her a slightly damaged peacock butterfly, rather jostled by a large stag-beetle.

"Yes, they're here—a little the worse for wear. That's time, not me; I haven't disturbed them." He looked at the draggled peacock wings with something that just fell short of being a smile. "Broken butterflies, eh?" he said. "I've seen a good many in my time. The collection struck me as being appropriate—quite appropriate. Now, Chloe, look! This is new since your time."

He opened two drawers, one on the right and the other on the left, pulling them right out. Then with either hand he reached into the space left by each drawer, and Chloe heard a click. He stepped back, and said,

"It's quite simple—just a little spring catch on either side. Put in your hand and feel for yourself."

"Why? What is it?" said Chloe. She felt along the side until her fingers touched the catch. It lay about a foot in. When she pressed it, it ran smoothly down and fastened with a click.

Mitchell Dane nodded.

"The one on the other side is just the same. Now open it again."

Chloe did so.

"But what does it do?" she asked a little breathlessly.

"This," said Mitchell Dane. He took hold of the middle partition and pulled. Quite smoothly, and without making any sound at all, half of the upper part of the cabinet slid forward. It was like pulling out a drawer, only the drawer was three feet high, being in fact a whole section of the cabinet with its block of shallow drawers intact.

He lifted the section out and laid it on the floor. The middle of the cabinet was now only a hollow shell. He took a small torch from his pocket and threw its beam into the dark interior. Chloe saw the black lacquer on the inner side of the back. He shifted the light to the left and then to the right, and she caught the gleam of metal.

"Two more catches there; then that section at the back opens towards you like folding doors."

Chloe came closer, looking hard into the darkness, not looking at Mitchell Dane.

"But why?" she said, speaking under her breath. "Why?"

"I'm going to tell you why. Behind the door there's a safe built into the wall. The cabinet is clamped to the floor so that it can't be moved—I think I mentioned that. Now, please remember this. Wroughton knows that the safe is here; but he doesn't know how to open it. It's a combination lock; and he don't know the combination, and never will. No one else knows anything—at least I shouldn't think they did. Wroughton wouldn't talk for his own sake. And Stran—no, Stran don't know anything."

"Who is Stran?" said Chloe, still in that whispering voice.

Mitchell Dane gave a short laugh.

"A young devil—and don't you trust him a yard. I've got him in a cleft stick because I always made him give me receipts—they're in there by the bye." He flashed the torchlight into the darkness like a pointing finger. "And if he ever gives you any trouble, there's your remedy."

Chloe drew back with a shiver.

"I don't understand. What do you mean? I don't understand a bit. Why do you tell me all this?"

Mitchell Dane dropped the torch into his pocket, and fitted the missing section back into the body of the cabinet.

"You're not wanted to understand. But I'm telling you what'll be useful to you some day. I want you to listen, and not bother about whether you understand or not. The lock behind there is a combination. We'll go into my study after this, and I'll show you the sort of thing, and how it works. You can't open it unless you've got the right word. If I ever want you to open it, I'll send you the word. But you're not to pass it on to any living soul. Do you hear? Don't trust anyone!"

"Oh!" said Chloe. "That's horrible!" Mitchell Dane was Mr. Dark— the someone whom you didn't like and couldn't bear to touch. There was all the child's instinctive repulsion in Chloe's voice.

He replaced the drawers which hid the side catches, and closed the cabinet, locking it with a key which had a twisted handle and hung from a fine steel chain. When he had put the key in his pocket, he turned and looked at Chloe with a little glint in his cold eyes.

"Horrible, is it?" he said. "Yes, I suppose you would think that. Let me give you a very serious piece of advice—if everybody acted on it, there wouldn't be nearly so much trouble in the world. It's just this. Don't love anyone, because if you do, sooner or later you'll get hurt. Don't trust anyone—most people'll let you down, if they get the chance. And never put anything on paper that you don't want the whole world to know."

Chloe's chin went up.

"I never take advice!" she said vehemently. "And I'd rather be hurt a hundred times, and let down a thousand times, than not be able to love people and trust them. If you can't love people you're dead—just dead!"

Mitchell Dane looked at her with a good deal of admiration and just a very faint stirring of something else—pride, affection, a sense of kinship. He found Chloe very much alive, very young and certain of herself.

"So I'm dead, am I?" he said, smiling a little.

"I think you are," said Chloe with the scarlet in her cheeks and the ring of defiance in her voice. She felt as if she was up against something that she hated but was not in the least afraid of. She was exultant and angry.

"And that's why you won't come and live with me?"

"Yes, I think it is."

Mitchell Dane nodded.

"Perhaps you're right," he began. "Perhaps—"

The door opened and Mr. Wroughton came into the room.

Chapter Ten

CHLOE WENT back to Maxton next day. A fortnight later she wrote to Rose:

"It's dull without you, but of course I knew it would be. I shan't stay here. I should like to try London, only everyone says it's so desperately hard to get a job.

"Ducky, I'm a blighted being. You'll never guess what's happened. How can I break it to you? Get the sympathetic tear ready, and I'll do it as gently as I can. Yesterday being Saturday, I went for a walk, and in Halfpenny Lane I met Bernard Austin and a damsel—a strange damsel. She wore tortoiseshell spectacles and a blush. Bernard blushed too. I, of course, turned pale and clutched my heart. Then Bernard introduced us. Her name is Penelope Jackson, and she looks nice. They are engaged. And I gather she has money. She adores Bernard, and he just lets her and looks silly. I wanted to slap him all the time, but thought I'd better not, in case he should misunderstand and think I wanted him back. He always did seem to feel encouraged by the things which would have snubbed other people. It's a blessed relief to have him off my hands."

Here the letter broke off, to be found and finished by Chloe three days later.

"Rose darling, I feel exactly as if I'd got into a dream and just anything might happen. Oh, I do, do, *do* so wish that you were here. I'm bursting to talk to someone, and have been within an ace of flinging my arms round Ally's neck and saying 'Let me confide in you.' This will show you what I've come to. So far, I've stopped myself doing it. I'm going to confide in you instead. But you're such thousands of miles away.

"I wrote all the first bit of this letter on Sunday, and I can't remember why I didn't go on with it on Monday, but I think it was because we had a busy day. It all seems like the year before last.

"On Tuesday I was sewing black sequins on to a dress for the thin Miss Fellowes, when Ally came in frightfully flustered, and said that a gentleman wanted to see me, and would I go down into the parlour, and if I liked, she would come too. I said 'No,' quite firmly, and went down. And there was a little oddment of a grey man who said that he was Mr. Dane's solicitor, and that Mr. Dane had died suddenly and left me everything.

"I sat down on the nearest chair and said, 'Nonsense!' And he said, 'Not nonsense: a solid legal fact. May I enquire if you are of age? And I said, 'Not till February.'

"Rose, why did he leave it to me? I told him I wouldn't have it. And I told him he was dead, and that that was why I wouldn't go and live with him. I never would have believed that I could have said such dreadful things to anyone—and I didn't mind a bit; I just said them. And he only smiled. The dreadful part is that I can't feel sorry about his being dead now, because I think that what I said to him was quite true, and that he has really been dead for years and years and years. You can't be sorry about a person you only met after they were dead, can you? That sounds mad, doesn't it? I think it's all rather mad. Why should he leave me Danesborough and a most frightful lot of money, when he'd only known me for a week? And I was probably ruder to him than anyone ever had been before."

There Chloe was wrong. Many people had spoken their minds to Mitchell Dane in the past, and more than one woman had said harder things than Chloe had said. Tears, threats, prayers, and curses had all alike failed of their purpose. Chloe's little outburst had been very mild indeed compared with some others. Chloe, however, was not to know that.

She finished her letter to Rose at Danesborough on the day of the funeral.

"It's all over, and everybody has gone. That sounds as if there were crowds, which isn't true. The little, grey solicitor man came—his name is Hudson,—and two or three other people from London—men. But there were no relations, and no one who cared at all. Mrs. Wroughton cried all the time, but that's because she's the sort of woman who cries when things happen. I should think three pocket handkerchiefs was her allowance for weddings, christenings, and funerals. She isn't really sorry, nor is Mr. Wroughton, though he has been with Mr. Dane for fifteen years. No one minds—and it makes me feel as if I must howl."

There was a blotted signature and a rather smudgy postscript:

"Rose, I would mind if I could; but I did only know him for a week."

Chloe had just addressed the letter, when Blayne, the butler, came into the room.

"Dr. Golding would be glad if you would see him for a moment," he said; and Dr. Golding himself, spruce, bluff and rosy, came in behind him as the words were spoken.

"I won't keep you, Miss Dane." He shut the door on the butler and came over to her, fumbling in his pockets. "Trying day, and you must be glad it's over—bitterly cold too. Now, where did I put the thing?

Too many pockets, that's about the size of it. But I've got it on me somewhere, and I promised to give it into your own hands."

"What is it?" said Chloe.

"A letter. Ah, here it is. No, that's income tax. But I'm sure I've got it. Yes, now this really is it—a letter that I promised Mr. Dane I'd give you. He pushed it into my hand when the nurse was out of the room—about the last sensible thing he did—and made me promise to give it to you when you were alone." He laid a large, crumpled envelope on the table in front of Chloe. "And I was to ask you to read it in my presence, and to burn it as soon as you had read it. Some sick man's fancy, I expect; but perhaps you won't mind carrying out your part of the bargain."

Chloe took up the envelope and turned it over. It was sealed in three places. She broke the seals, and took out a sheet of strong linen paper.

Dr. Golding had gone over to the fire, and stood there, rubbing his hands and talking cheerfully.

"Bitter cold day, I must say. But I'm off out of it to-morrow, thank goodness. Taking a two months' holiday, and very glad to get it, I can assure you. Algiers; Morocco; Egypt—doesn't that make your mouth water? My locum, Jennings, by the way, is a friend of Wroughton's, so you're sure to meet him—but not professionally, I hope." He gave his short, bluff laugh.

Chloe had unfolded the sheet of paper, and was looking at the single line of writing upon it, a single line of four words in Mitchell Dane's hand—four words, and one of them her own name. She read them carefully:

"The word is Chloe."

That was all. There was no signature. Nothing but the four words.

Chloe walked over to the fire with the paper in her hand, and pushed it down on to the red embers with a quick thrust. The edge of the paper caught and curled back upon itself; a little spurt of flame, a few sparks, and Mitchell Dane's message was gone.

Chapter Eleven

CHLOE WAS still thinking about that message next day. She understood it very well. The word that would open Mitchell Dane's safe was "Chloe." It was quite simple, she had only to set the combination lock so that the letters spelt her own name, and the safe that lay behind the black cabinet would open to her. Every time her thought reached this point she felt the same thing—a quick recoil from the bare idea of opening that safe.

Danesborough, which had been the house of her childish dreams, a centre of pleasant memories, had become the setting of something which she could not define, but from which she shrank. As a child, Chloe had often played a game called "Hotter and Colder." Something was hidden and had to be looked for. When you came near the hidden thing the person who had hidden it called out "Hot," "Hotter," "Burning," "Scorching"; and when you wandered away you were recalled by the warning "Lukewarm," "Colder," "Freezing." Chloe felt as if she were playing this game again. Danesborough held a hidden thing. It was that hidden thing which had changed the house.

The hidden thing was in the safe. Chloe pictured it as something burning, white-hot, not to be touched. Every time she passed the drawing-room door she felt the nearness of this hidden thing. It was just as if a voice out of the old game was calling to her and saying, "You're getting hotter; you're getting hotter all the time."

On the day after the funeral she opened the door and went in. The voice said, "Burning hot," and Chloe shivered and stood still a yard from the door, looking across the pale, frigid room to where the black cabinet filled the whole of the recess on the right of the fireplace. She could see the golden river and the little men: Timmy Jimmy, and Henry Planty—and Mr. Dark who had always frightened her. He stood a little apart from the other two, and looked down at the shut basket in his hand. He had a secret too.

Chloe turned with a jerk to find herself face to face with Mr. Wroughton. He seemed more like a farmer than a secretary, with his breadth of shoulder, florid face, and deep, jovial voice.

"Hullo!" he said. "I was looking for you. You'll want to do this room up, I expect. Were you planning it all?"

"Not exactly," said Chloe. And then she said what she had not meant to say. "Where are Mr. Dane's keys, Mr. Wroughton?"

She thought he looked surprised. Just for a moment his manner seemed to accuse Chloe of a little undue haste. She felt rebuked; but he answered her at once and very pleasantly.

"I have them, of course. Was it some special key you wanted? Or shall I hand them all over to you? Perhaps you wouldn't mind coming into the study."

Chloe followed him like a school-girl. And then all at once her spirit asserted itself. After all, Danesborough was hers; the keys were hers; she had a perfect right to ask for them.

"I wanted the key of the black cabinet. It has my uncle's collection of butterflies in it, and I'd like to look at them again."

Mr. Wroughton lifted a dispatch box, set it on the littered study table, and opened it.

"There are a great many keys here. Would you know the one you want?"

He was watching her as he spoke, and a little flare of resentment rose in Chloe. "Why does he look at me like that? Why does he ask if I should know the key?" She remembered that he had come into the room when she and Mitchell Dane were talking; but the cabinet had been closed and locked by then.

"Don't trust anyone." That was what Mitchell Dane had said.

"Do you know the key?" he repeated.

His eyes were not in keeping with the rest of his face. As she met them, Chloe realized with a start that they had something of the same cold quality as Mitchell Dane's—yes, cold, light eyes that gave the lie to that ruddy face.

"I expect you know it," she answered quickly, and put out her hand.

He picked up a large bunch of keys and let it hang jangling from his thumb.

"Are you going to take all these over?" he asked. "I've really wanted to have a talk with you, you know,—about my position. Mr. Dane left most things in my hands; and I thought perhaps you would be glad of my services for the present at any rate."

"Yes," said Chloe—"yes." She spoke in a gentle, considering fashion. If Mr. Wroughton had known her better, he would have thought it very unlike her usual manner. As it was, he experienced some relief.

"It's a pity you're not of age—it complicates things. But if you will accept my help, I think Hudson and I can save you a lot of trouble. You will, of course, make your own arrangements when you come of age; but meanwhile"—he laughed pleasantly—"I'm here to do the donkey work. Now is this the key you want?"

He picked up the thin steel chain which held the key of the black cabinet. Chloe looked at it, and gave no sign.

"We might take the keys into the drawing-room and see," she suggested, and once again was aware of scrutiny.

It was when they were in the drawing-room again, and the key with the twisted handle had turned silently in the lock of the black cabinet that Mr. Wroughton asked with startling suddenness:

"Did Mr. Dane show you his safe?"

"He told me where it was," said Chloe.

"And did he tell you how to open it?"

"He told me no one could open it," she said, and saw him frown.

"Did he tell you that it was a combination lock—the sort that needs a word to open it?"

"Yes, that's what he said. He said no one could open it without the word."

Mr. Wroughton looked at her very intently, very insistently.

"Did he tell you the word? Did he?"

"No, he didn't," said Chloe. She was shaking, and not quite sure whether she had told a lie or not. Mitchell Dane had not told her the word—not then. But the message which she had burned rose up before her accusingly.

"I hate the whole thing!" she cried suddenly. "I hate it, and I don't want to talk about it!"

"I asked," said Mr. Wroughton, "because I know the safe contains some very important papers. I think it really ought to be opened, if you don't mind my saying so."

Chloe looked down, bit her lip, and tapped the floor with her foot.

"Very well—open it." Her voice was low and suppressed.

"My dear Miss Dane, that's easier said than done. No one can open it without the word. I was hoping very much that Mr. Dane had told you what the word was. If he didn't, I'm afraid we're hung up."

"Perhaps it's amongst his papers," said Chloe. She took the key out of the cabinet door as she spoke, and pulled out one of the drawers at random.

Mr. Wroughton stood by and watched her, his hands in his pockets. He did not talk, and he did not move, but just stood there—a big man in rough clothes, who looked a good deal out of place in the pale, faded room.

Chloe did not allow her Uncle Walter's collection to delay her for very long. It was, to tell the truth, a sufficiently depressing spectacle. There was moth in some of the drawers, and a general air of decay. The bright colours that had pleased her so much as a child were dull and lifeless in this November light. She felt no desire to linger under Mr. Wroughton's eye, gazing at these mouldering relics. After a very brief inspection she locked the cabinet and turned away.

"I'm going out," she announced; and five minutes later she banged the front door behind her and began to skirt the house.

It was a blowy, blustery day, but she was in shelter until she turned the north corner and met a great buffet of wind that beat the colour into her face and made her laugh and gasp for breath. She swung round and raced before it down the gravelled path that led past the stables to the walled garden. The wind ran with her like a noisy, shouting companion, past the walled garden—she had no fancy for enclosed spaces to-day—, and on over rough grass to a little spinney of larches all bare and delicate against a lead-coloured sky.

Chloe flung her arms about one of the trees, and turned to face the wind, glowing and happy. The depression which clung about the house like a mist was all gone. She wondered at the Chloe who had stood so meekly before Mr. Wroughton with hardly enough spirit to ask for her own keys. She whistled this Chloe down the wind with a scornful toss of the head, and leaning there with her arms about the swaying larch, she began to make plans.

There were no horses at Danesborough. She must have a horse. Not this week, but surely next week she might buy a horse and have riding lessons without being considered hard-hearted. She must learn to drive a car too. There were at least three to choose from—the big Daimler limousine; the Napier touring car; and the little A.C. two-seater—that was the one she had set her heart upon. But there seemed to be a tendency to regard it as Mr. Wroughton's car. Not for the first time, Chloe had a sudden, vivid feeling that Mr. Wroughton was too much in evidence.

"When I am of age——" she said to herself, and leaned her cheek against the rough bark of the little larch tree. She began to make pleasant plans.

When Mr. Wroughton had seen Chloe leave the house, he went into the study and asked for a trunk call. Whilst he waited for it to come through he stood looking down into the fire with a heavy frown on his face. He did not look jovial any more.

As he stood there the door opened, and Emily Wroughton hesitated on the threshold.

"What is it?" said Wroughton over his shoulder, his voice rasping on the words. "Come in or stay out—I don't care which, but for heaven's sake, make up your mind!"

"If you're busy——" said Emily, "I mean—I don't want to interrupt you."

"Well, don't do it then! I'm expecting an important call."

She backed out of the room, half closed the door, and then opened it again.

"It was about the servants, Leonard. I mean—that is—perhaps another time—I didn't know you were busy."

Wroughton swung round, the telephone bell rang, and Emily shut the door in a flurry. Wroughton was scowling as he picked up the receiver. Through his "Hullo!" he was aware of Emily slowly and cautiously releasing the handle of the door. He said "Hullo!" a second time, and then, "That you, Stran?"

The voice that answered him was familiar.

"Yes. What's up? You sound peeved."

"No, it's nothing—Emily fussing round the door like a hen, that's all."

He listened, and heard her withdraw on tiptoe. At the other end of the line Stran laughed.

"I was afraid the heiress had cut up rusty."

"Not exactly."

"Bordering on it?"

"No. But I can't quite make her out. One minute she's as frank and open as a child, and then shuts down like a clam."

"As how?"

"She told me to-day that she knew where the safe was—said he'd told her, and asked me for the thingummyjig key. And then when I tried to find out whether she knew the word she shut down and talked about her Uncle Walter's butterflies."

"Do you think she knows anything?"

"I don't know."

"No idea?"

Wroughton hesitated.

"I believe she does know," he said at last.

"Well, if she does know, she'll be using what she knows. The woman doesn't live who could keep her hands off a secret that she's got the key to. That's where you come in, old thing. You'll have to do a good deal of sitting up and taking notice. Speaking for myself, I really can't afford to let the lady get going. The old man kept what he was pleased to call 'my receipts,' and everything else apart, I'm bound to get 'em back. So look lively."

"Suppose you come down and take a hand."

"Next week." Stran's voice was very cool and easy. "I'll give her time to get thoroughly bored, and then roll up casually and renew our acquaintance."

"All right. She's pretty well fed up already. Emily's not exactly a gay companion."

"Not exactly! Well, so long."

Wroughton replaced the receiver, rang off, and went to the door. "Emily!" he shouted at the top of his voice.

Chapter Twelve

BREAKFAST WAS apt to be a silent meal at Danesborough. Mr. Wroughton, coming in late, was sufficiently occupied with the important business of eating; and Emily, nervously busy with the tea things, had learned in the course of years not to risk a snubbing. She made one remark every morning to Chloe:

"You should pour out, you really should, Miss Dane. I don't feel I ought to be doing it."

"I hate pouring out," said Chloe on the morning after the little scene about the key. "I simply hate pouring out. Let's make Mr. Wroughton do it for a change if you're tired of it."

"Oh, no!" said Emily, in a frightened whisper. "Oh, dear no! Oh, please, Miss Dane, you won't suggest such a thing, will you?" She very nearly dropped the milk-jug in her fright as Leonard Wroughton came into the room and shut the door noisily behind him.

Chloe felt amusement pass into pity tinged with scorn. To be so much afraid of a man—of any man! It was pitiable. Emily Wroughton wanted shaking. Why didn't she stand up to the man, and bite him when he snubbed her? Chloe looked at her shrinking behind the tea-cups—the wispy hair; the nervous gestures; the unbecoming black jumper, far too low in the neck. She looked away with a frown.

Mr. Wroughton was at the side table, helping himself to kidneys and bacon. The silence irked her. She reached for the marmalade pot, and innocently cast a bomb into the stillness.

"Who is Stran?" she said, and helped herself to marmalade.

The question was addressed to Emily, and Emily began to answer it, but got no further than a repetition of the name.

"Stran—," she said, and then Mr. Wroughton came forward and set down his plate with a clatter.

Chloe repeated her question.

"Yes, Stran. Who is Stran?" And this time Leonard Wroughton took up the word.

"Why, what made you ask that?" he said.

"Mr. Dane spoke of him," said Chloe. "Just mentioned him, you know; and it's such an odd name."

"Stran is short for Stranways—not so odd really."

"Who is he?"

"Just an acquaintance of Mr. Dane's. You're not very likely to come across him. What did Mr. Dane say about him?"

Chloe's eyes had a sparkle in them; Mr. Wroughton's domineering stare had roused her temper. He had no business to look at her, or at any woman, like that.

"Oh, he just mentioned him," she said, and went on eating toast and marmalade.

Something about this little encounter made her better pleased with herself. She had stood up to the Wroughton man and seen him subside into flushed silence. It helped to obliterate the memory of her meekness the day before. Chloe was not at all accustomed to being meek, and she had no intention of letting Leonard Wroughton bully her.

She had her first driving lesson later on that morning, and came home fairly intoxicated with the air, the speed, and the new sense of power.

"It's like having wings almost," she said to herself as she ran up the steps and into the hall. And there, just by the study door, she heard her own name:

"No, Miss Dane is not in, I'm afraid."

Chloe ran into the room, and saw Leonard Wroughton at the telephone.

"I'm just back. Glorious! Is that some one for me?"

He handed her the receiver, and she asked,

"Who is it?"

A man's voice came to her:

"Oh, is that Miss Dane?"

"Yes, it is. I've just come in."

"It's Michael Foster speaking."

"Oh, how nice!" said Chloe with naïve truthfulness. After the funerary gloom of the last ten days, how nice to hear Michael's cheerful voice, how nice to speak to somebody young! She looked up from the instrument and gave Mr. Wroughton a cool little nod of dismissal.

"It's a friend of mine. Perhaps you wouldn't mind shutting the door."

"That's ripping of you," was Michael's answer. "I—I went down to Maxton two days ago, and you weren't there."

"No, I was here."

"They told me that—I saw your Miss Allardyce, and she told me. And the reason I rang up—"

There was a pause. It lasted such a long time that Chloe said, "Are you there?", and said it twice.

"Yes, I'm there—I mean, I'm here—I mean the reason I rang you up—"

There was another pause.

"I do wish you wouldn't keep going away," said Chloe. "It's perfectly horrible when you don't know whether there's anyone at the other end of the line or not—I simply hate it. Do go on."

"I am going on," said Michael. "What I'm trying to say is this, only I don't know if you'll think it awful cheek—"

Chloe gave a little gurgle of laughter.

"Do tell me what it is. If you only knew how deadly, deadly dull I've been."

"Have you?" Michael sounded rather hopeful.

"Bored stiff," said Chloe succinctly.

"Then perhaps—well, what I mean to say is, I may be down in your direction next week. I think I'm booked for a job that'll take me past Danesborough, and—and I was wondering whether you would let me come and see you."

"I should love it," said Chloe.

"May I really?"

"Yes, of course you may."

Chloe went to her room singing. She had snubbed Mr. Wroughton; she had driven a car for twenty miles; and Michael

Foster was coming to see her next week. The gloom that brooded over Danesborough lifted.

It was as she passed the drawing-room door on her way down to lunch that Chloe decided to open the safe.

"I've just let myself get silly about it," she said. "I don't expect there's a thing inside it except stocks, and shares, and bonds, and fusty, mouldy business sort of things like that. I'll just open it and have done with it. I didn't know I could be such an idiot about anything; and if I can't pull myself together, I'll just grow into a trampled worm like that poor, wretched Emily."

At this point the poor, wretched Emily joined her. Chloe slipped her hand inside Mrs. Wroughton's arm and spoke warmly, impulsively:

"Why didn't you come out this morning? It was simply ripping. Why don't you drive?"

"I—I shouldn't care to—I haven't got the nerve."

Chloe gave the thin arm a little squeeze.

"Why are you frightened of things?" she said. "I hate to see people frightened."

Emily Wroughton looked nervously over her shoulder; they were in the hall, and Chloe's voice carried so.

"My dear Miss Dane, please, *please*!" And then, as they came into the empty dining-room, she asked in her quick, jerky way:

"Aren't you frightened sometimes?—when people are vexed—when you can't please them? When one tries very hard to please people, and they are never quite pleased, quite satisfied, it gives one such a terribly fluttered feeling—at least that's what I find."

"People," of course, meant Leonard Wroughton. Chloe accepted the faint attempt at camouflage.

"I wouldn't try so hard if I were you," she said with a little glow of indignation in her voice.

Chloe might resolve to open the safe at the earliest opportunity, but that opportunity was not easy to come by. For one thing, Emily Wroughton was for ever at her elbow. Or if by chance she disappeared for an hour, it seemed impossible to cross the hall without encountering Mr. Wroughton. It was, of course, quite open to Chloe to tell either Leonard Wroughton or his wife that she wished to be left alone in the drawing-room in order to go through Mr. Dane's private papers. There were moments when she thought of taking this course; and there were other moments when she was upon the point of wiring to Mr. Hudson to come down and open the safe with her. Reason suggested one of these courses. But stronger than reason was the instinct that held her back—Mitchell Dane's face; Mitchell Dane's voice; fragments of his talk.

Chloe knew at last that she could force herself to open the safe. But she must be alone and secure against interruption. She must be alone because she was afraid—in spite of everything she was afraid—of what that safe might contain. She would open it. She would make herself open it. But she must be alone.

Three days slipped away, and the safe remained shut. To get away from the Wroughtons Chloe had to leave the house. Leave it she did, and drove herself for mile on glorious mile, forgetting everything in this new, vivid delight. But when the drive was done, there was Danesborough to come back to—Danesborough and the Wroughtons. Each day as she came back into the hall she felt that clinging something close in about her like a mist and chill her glowing thoughts to greyness.

On the fourth day she saw her opportunity. Leonard Wroughton went to town by the twelve-fifteen. He took a suit-case with him, and Emily explained that he was going to stay at his club:

"I don't suppose he'll be back till late to-morrow, or perhaps not till next day. Leonard does so hate to be asked questions."

"Yes, I've noticed that," said Chloe.

Emily made a nervous movement.

"Oh, men are like that. Lots of women are so silly—they will ask questions, and expect a man to tell them where he goes, and what he does, and just when to expect him back. It's very foolish indeed—it really is. Leonard simply can't bear to be asked questions. And I never dream of asking him what he's going to do, or when he is coming back, though it's dreadfully awkward sometimes—about meals, you know, or if anyone wants to see him. I just have to say that I've no idea when he'll be back."

Chloe laughed a little indignantly.

"And what happens when you go away? Do you just drift off into the blue, and let him guess when you'll be back?"

A singular look crossed Mrs. Wroughton's face—a momentary eagerness passing into terror.

"Oh, of course not. Oh, my dear Miss Dane what things you say!"

Chloe laughed again.

"Try it!" she said, and ran upstairs.

In her own room she sat down and made a plan. Here was her opportunity of opening the safe and getting it and its tiresome contents off her mind. She decided to wait for the night. Emily would be sure to cling to her like a burr all day, with just that timid persistence which it is so hard to rebuff without actual brutality. The fact that Leonard Wroughton used this brutality towards his wife a dozen times a day made it impossible for Chloe to be otherwise than gentle. No, she would wait until the house was quiet, and Emily and the servants asleep. Then she would go down to the drawing-room, open the safe, and dispose once and for all of her own ridiculous fears and fancies.

Chapter Thirteen

CHLOE SAT UP in bed, lit a match, and looked at her watch for the sixth time. It was only half-past eleven. She blew out the match with an impatient puff. Never, never, never in this world had time crawled so. Every hour of the long day, every dull minute of a dull evening, added to Chloe's feeling that an intolerable stretch of time lay between her and the moment when she had made her plan that morning. It *was* only that morning, but it felt like years, and years, and years—the sort of years that prisoners endure when they haven't even got oakum to pick and are driven to tame rats and spiders. With a whimsical twist of her thought Chloe regarded Emily as, not a rat or a spider—imagination baulked at that—but as a prisoner's mouse, a thin, anxious mouse, with beady eyes and an air of having been half-starved for years. Poor Emily! It would be dreadful to be like that.

Chloe slipped an inch or two deeper into the drowsiness which waits on those who sit in the dark defying sleep. She was awake—yes, of course she was awake—but all the same she distinctly saw Emily Wroughton with a pink, pointed nose and large mousy eyes through which the light shone with a red glare. She woke with a jerk, and lit another match. It was a quarter to twelve.

"I won't go down till twelve," said Chloe to herself. "I said I wouldn't, and I won't."

She twirled the match between her fingers, and let it burn down, down until the flame scorched her hand. Then she blew it out, shook up her pillows, and began to think how quickly a quarter of an hour can pass when you don't want it to.

"Now, if I was at a dance, with a really thrilling partner like— oh, well, like that Mr. Fossetter. Yes, he *was* rather thrilling; there's something romantic about dark eyes, and he's a dream to dance with. Yes, if I was dancing with him, or with anyone else I liked,"—Chloe's chin lifted a little—"why a quarter of an hour would be gone before it had begun. Zip! Oh, how I wish I was going to a dance to-night in my darling silver dress instead of having to creep and crawl in a black house as if I was a burglar or a ghost, with that beastly, beastly safe waiting for me to open it! And if there are only stocks and shares in it, I suppose I shall be thankful. But oh, what a colossal fool I shall feel!"

The thought pricked deep. Chloe struck a match with such a vicious jerk that the head flew flaming on to the floor and sizzled there. She dropped a book on it and tried again. The match flared, and the little white circle of her watch showed her the two black hands together at twelve. With a sigh of relief she lit a candle and flung the bed-clothes back.

The coast should be clear enough now. It was two hours since she had said good-night to Emily, and at least an hour since she had heard any stir in the house. She made her preparations in a little glow of excitement. To have come at last to the point of action was like being suddenly freed from a heavy weight. She put on a dark blue dressing-gown and blue felt slippers, picked up and tested her bicycle lamp, blew out the candle, and opening her bedroom door, stood there upon the threshold.

The passage was quite dark. All the house was dark, quite dark and still. Chloe stood listening until it seemed to her that the silence was rising about her softly, insistently, beating in upon her thoughts as waves beat. And now it was no longer silence, but fear—that chill, unreasoning fear which saps the power to act. Chloe knew that if she stood there much longer, the fear and the silence would overmaster her and turn her tamely back into her room again.

With a sudden movement she crossed the threshold and took a couple of steps forward. Then, as suddenly, she turned back again, took the key from the inside of her door, closed the door, locked it on the outside, and slipped the key into her dressing-gown pocket. She drew a little sigh of relief as she turned away. She had not thought of locking the door when she had planned what she would do; and suppose Emily had come to her room while she was away. There were a thousand chances against it; but the instinct that had turned Chloe back was afraid of the one dim chance that lay beyond the thousand.

She set her left hand on the wall and felt her way past the right-angle turn into the broad corridor, and so to the head of the stairs. She took the first step hesitatingly and moved along it until her groping fingers touched the balustrade. That would be easier than feeling her way down by the wall. It was quite easy really; the steps broad, shallow, and softly carpeted, and the hall itself not dark with the absolute blackness of the closed in passages behind her. She came down into the hall, turned to the left, and opened the drawing-room door.

All her movements up to now had been slow and steady, but a sudden breathless sense of hurry came on her as the door opened. She slipped into the dark room and shut the door, and felt her heart beat and her hand tremble. She would have liked to switch on all the lights in the big cut-glass chandeliers, set all the rainbow colours dancing in the lustres, and flood the room with brilliance. Quite suddenly she hated the darkness so much that she could hardly bear it. She took her bicycle lamp out of her pocket and turned it on. The little lane that it cut through the black room seemed only to make the surrounding gloom more intolerable. Chloe gave herself a little shake.

"You're making a most abject fool of yourself. Do you hear? Stop dithering at once, and attend to business!"

The first thing to be done was to lock the door. That one chance in a thousand clamoured insistently. She felt for the key. No, of course it would be outside; a careful housemaid would have locked the door before she went to bed. But the door had not been locked: it had opened to Chloe's hurried touch without delay. She opened it now, found the keyhole empty, and closed it again, frowning deeply. She had passed that door dozens of times a day on every day since she had come to Danesborough. She had never passed it without being conscious of it, without some shrinking or defiant thought of what lay beyond it. As she looked back upon those many times of her passing, there was always a key in the picture; she couldn't see the door at all without a key. Then who had taken it away? A little anger rose up in Chloe; but if she had not been angry, she would have been afraid. Why should the key have disappeared?

She walked across to the alcove beside the fire, and turned on the shaded reading lamp which stood on a table in front of the cabinet. The shade was faintly rose-coloured, and the light came through it just tinged with a sickly pink.

Chloe put out her bicycle lamp, set it down on the table, and turned to the cabinet. It looked very large, very tall, and very black. The golden river flickered in the pinkish light. The little golden men stood rigidly amongst the golden reeds. Chloe put the key in the lock, turned it, and opened the folding doors. Now that the moment had come, anger and fear, dread and suspicion, were all gone. She was intensely, vividly herself, quick of thought and hand, working to a methodical plan.

She touched the springs as Mr. Dane had touched them, and by stretching her arms to the widest possible extent she was able to draw out the middle section of the cabinet as he had drawn it out. It was quite light—Uncle Walter's butterflies were insubstantial enough—; but the width made it awkward to handle, and she was glad to set it down. The gaping space which it left behind shaded away into blackness. Chloe looked at it, and then looked down at the section which she had withdrawn. If anyone came—nonsense, there was no one to come. But if anyone did come, why, there would be this awkward thing to advertise Mr. Dane's secret.

Chloe picked the section up. Clear of the cabinet it was easier to manage. She crossed with it to the nearest window, and set it down behind the pale, heavy curtains. Then she stepped back, arranged the folds a little, and came again to the cabinet. Her feet made no sound at all on the thick carpet; it was like walking on moss—queer, light-coloured moss with a straggly pattern on it. Chloe shook off the thought as she would have shaken off a wandering puff of thistle-down. Then with a steady hand she picked up her bicycle lamp and turned off the pink electric light.

The new-come dark was very black indeed. She turned on her lamp, and pushed it far back into the cabinet. Then she set her knee on the edge of the opening and crawled forward into it, turning half-way to reach the outer doors and partly close them. She was now half sitting, half kneeling in a space about four feet six inches wide and something under three feet high. The depth might have been three feet or a little less.

Holding the lamp in her left hand, she felt for and found the little spring on either side which released the folding doors in the back wall of the cabinet. With the last click the doors sprang an inch apart. Chloe opened them widely, and saw before her the door of the secret safe. The door was painted red, bright red like sealing-wax. The lamp made a circle of light upon it, so brilliant that it looked like fire. Chloe saw this brilliant circle, and with her mind's eye she saw two other things as well—Mr. Dane's odd smile as he showed her how to manipulate just such another lock as this: "Only of course the combination is a different one—you understand that"; and the note which she had burned in kind Dr. Golding's presence, the note with her name in it—just her name, her own name—"Chloe. The word is Chloe."

She shifted the circle of light until it fell upon the lock, then propped the lamp a-tilt against her knee, and used both hands to set the combination. With a click the door of the safe swung in towards her. She had to shift her position and press up against the left-hand wall of the cabinet to give it room. Then slowly, reluctantly, without excitement, she lifted the lamp and turned the light upon the open safe.

Papers. There were only papers. Packets, and packets, and packets of papers.

"I said it would be only stocks and shares, and fusty old mortgages and things," said Chloe. And then something came, as it were, behind her formulated thought and struck it dumb. Quite suddenly, quite unexpectedly, she was afraid. Kneeling there with the lamp in her hand, looking at those piled up shelves, she was horribly, unaccountably afraid.

Those harmless-looking bundles of papers frightened her more than anything had ever frightened her in her life before. They were not stocks and shares, or parchments, or business papers: they were letters—packet on packet of letters, two together, three together, half-a-dozen, all neatly tied up with red tape. Chloe felt as if she had been turned to ice. Everything seemed to stop in that cold atmosphere of dread. Thought stopped, feeling stopped. There remained a mechanical impulse that made her set the lamp at a convenient angle and reach for the nearest packet. It slipped as she touched it, and she picked it up with the pink knot uppermost. It was loosely tied and came undone easily enough.

There were three letters in the packet, two of them without envelopes. Chloe picked up the first of these and opened it. Her hand did not shake, but it was cold and stiff. She read:

"My own darling, darling boy," and was touched with an odd emotion. Had anyone really ever written to Mr. Dane like that? She turned the sheet over and saw that it was signed "Judy." She did not read the letter, but picked up the second loose sheet. It was very much blotted and quite short. It began abruptly:

"You mustn't come again. I believe he knows. If he doesn't know, he suspects. You mustn't come.

"Your broken-hearted

"JUDY."

Chloe took up the third letter. It was in an envelope addressed to Mr. Dane. She took out the enclosure, and found that it was in the same handwriting as the other two letters; but it began, "Dear Sir." Chloe held it nearer to the light. The writing was so hurried, so agitated. It ran:

"I can't pay what you ask—I can't indeed. I'll do what I can. Haven't you any pity at all? What good will it do you to ruin me? I'll do what I can if you give me time."

It was signed "J. St. Maurice."

That was the last letter in the packet, but there was an endorsement on a loose half sheet of paper. The endorsement was in Mr. Dane's handwriting: "Two letters from Lady Alexander St. Maurice to Mr. Ralph Baverstock, and one which she very foolishly wrote to me. Nothing has yet been paid. She has expectations from her godmother, Lady Hilldrington. From Stran."

Chloe tied the letters up and put them on one side. She was capable of this, but not of any mental activity. Her mind did not move; her thoughts did not move. The contents of the three letters remained with her as something which she saw quite clearly, but which meant nothing. It was as if she had opened a book beautifully printed in some unknown language; there was no meaning; to her frozen consciousness the letters had no meaning.

She took a second bundle of letters, and found the endorsement uppermost: "Three letters to Sir Gregory Slade Moffat from his eldest son—November, 1920. From Stran. N.B. Sir Gregory received his baronetcy January, 1921."

A faint, dull wonder stirred in Chloe's mind. She opened the first letter, glanced at it, and let it fall. It seemed to be an answer to some inquiry about a cheque. She unfolded the second letter, and found it in the same vein—bravado tinged with uneasiness. The third letter was different:

"I've been a damned fool. But for God's sake pull me out of
the mess. You stand to lose as much as I do if there's a scandal.
There are ways of shutting people's mouths."

There was more in the same strain. All three letters were signed "Jack." Chloe put them down and stared at the unopened packets which lay, some in the track of the beam of light from her lamp, some in the greyness beyond the beam, some scarcely seen, but guessed at in the far, dark corners of the safe. They were all letters; letters that should never have been written. She remembered Mr. Dane's face when he said, "Don't love anyone. Don't trust anyone. And don't put anything on paper that you don't want the whole world to know."

Kneeling there and remembering, she opened three more packets. Each one held its secret, its shameful secret. Chloe did not read the letters through. It was terrible to her to read them at all. Each packet was neatly and succinctly endorsed in Mr. Dane's writing, and two of the endorsements bore the words "From Stran."

The unknown language changed slowly into words of terrible plainness. Blackmail!—the word seemed to start up in letters of fire in the midst of her cold, watching thoughts. Blackmail!—the word burned white hot. Blackmail! Everything became most terrifyingly clear and distinct. The marketing of these wretched, pitiful, shameful letters had been Mr. Dane's business and the source of his wealth. There were people who did such things. It was horrible—like the Day of Judgment; only this was the Judgment of Evil instead of the Judgment of Good. For an instant Chloe had a vision of a Judgment Day in which the hidden evil and darkness of the world came out into a great light and was burnt up, melting and shrivelling into nothingness. That was the Judgment of Good. But this—this was the Judgment Day of Evil; all this sin and shame, these tears and terrors, dragged out and gloated over until the darkness was tenfold dark and the terror tenfold terrible.

The letters that she had opened lay by themselves where she had piled them against the left-hand wall of the safe. They were just ink and paper with a few dark blots where the anguished hand had betrayed its owner—just blots, and ink, and paper.

Chloe put out her hand and picked up a long envelope that threatened to fall from the main pile which she had not touched. Her curiosity was faintly awakened by the fact that this did not seem to be a letter, and she had the impulse to move, to do something, anything, that would break the pictures that were forming in her mind. She was like a man sinking into some terrible dream, who feels that at any cost he must stir, shake off his drowsiness, and awake.

The envelope was one of the usual stout manilla envelopes of the size to take foolscap. It was endorsed in very large, clear letters,

"Stran's receipts. On *no* account destroy." Chloe remembered with dazzling distinctness words which had meant nothing to her when Mr. Dane had spoken them: "Don't trust Stran a yard. I've got the whip hand of him because I've made him give me receipts for every penny. If he's troublesome, you may find them useful."

A good many of the letters she had opened had been marked "From Stran." Stran, then, was Mr. Dane's jackal, or one of his jackals—one of the creatures who collected, *stole* this merchandise which he had described as his "stock-in-trade."

Chloe turned the envelope, and was about to open it, when a faintness came on her. The walls of the safe, the walls of the cabinet, seemed to be pressing in on her. There was no air to breathe. She dropped the envelope and turned, blindly groping for the half-closed doors and pushing them outwards. The air of the drawing-room, cold, still and faintly musty, was grateful to her. She crouched there drawing long breaths.

And then she heard the sound.

Chapter Fourteen

The sound roused Chloe more effectively than any amount of fresh air would have done. It set her heart beating, and shocked her into need for action.

Some one was coming downstairs.

Even as she formulated the thought, the sound changed. The footstep had left the carpeted stair, and fell now upon the parquet floor of the hall. With instant quickness Chloe reached behind her and put out her lamp. Then she caught at the doors of the cabinet and drew them close. It seemed all to happen in a moment, the sound and her instinctive movements. As the doors of the cabinet closed, the drawing-room door was opened, and through the last chink, Chloe saw a candle flame flickering upon Leonard Wroughton's flushed and frowning face.

Next moment, with a click, the light in the three great chandeliers lit the drawing-room from end to end, making the brilliance which

Chloe had longed for. It came to her now as a burning wire between the doors of the cabinet. She pulled them closer, and the burning wire was gone.

The key—what had she done with the key of the cabinet?—where had she put the key? If she had left it sticking in the keyhole, Leonard Wroughton would see it there. No mere accident or coincidence had brought him to this room at such an hour. If he was here at all, he was here to visit the cabinet; and the key—where had she put the key?

There was a little wooden catch on a pin that fastened the right-hand door. She felt for it, snibbed it, and groped along the floor of the cabinet with her other hand. Her faintness was all gone. She remembered now that she had taken the key out of the lock and laid it against the wall of the cabinet away on her left. She could hear Mr. Wroughton moving in the room outside. Her fingers clutched the key.

The key-hole showed like a little shining star in the darkness. As she put the key in softly, softly, she tried with all her might to remember whether it had grated as it turned, whether it had made any sound at all. Very steadily and slowly she began to turn the key, and as she began to turn it, she felt the door touched from outside—a hand on the handle, moving it, shaking it.

Chloe turned the key right home. It made a little click which was lost in the rattle of the wrenched handle. She held her breath, and gripped the key till it cut her palm.

The lock held. The doors held. Unless he was prepared to force them open, and meet discovery in the morning, Chloe was safe. The missing section behind the curtain scarcely troubled her. He wouldn't look behind the curtain because there would be nothing for him to look for. There was nothing to suggest to Leonard Wroughton any need for further search or suspicion.

Chloe crouched there, perfectly still in the dead darkness, and felt the air grow heavy, heavy, heavy. How long would he stay? And how long could she hold out? He had moved away from the cabinet and gone to the far end of the room. What was he doing there? What was he waiting for? Suppose, after all, that he were to go to the window. The fear that she had dismissed became suddenly clamorous. Why, any one of half a dozen things might take him to the window. He was moving again, coming back to the cabinet. This time he did not try the handle; but Chloe could hear his heavy breathing not more than a foot away.

A horror of Leonard Wroughton, a horror of being caught like a creature in a trap, came over her. She couldn't bear it; she felt as if she couldn't bear anything more at all. Then, just as she came to the very edge of endurance, she heard him swear softly to himself and turn away.

A moment later the door opened and shut again; the heavy step receded; she heard him mount the stairs. Each smallest sound seemed loud, and thrummed in her ears. She was really near to fainting as she pushed open the door of the cabinet and crept out into the dark, deserted room.

A minute passed—two, three, five. Chloe, sitting in a heap on the floor, raised her head and began to think coherently again. The house was dead still. Leonard Wroughton, having made his tour of inspection, would not return; she felt sure of that. Thank goodness she had locked her door. If he tried the handle, or sent Emily to try it, they would only think that she was inside, asleep.

As these thoughts went through her mind, there emerged more and more clearly the conviction of a plan, of a mind moving according to plan, anticipating her own movements and bent on countering them. It was according to this plan that Leonard Wroughton had given out that he would be away for at least one night. He had not intended to be away; she felt sure of that. When he went off that morning with his suit-case and his talk of dining in town he had meant to return silently and unnoticed, as he had returned. Why?

Chloe answered the question easily enough. Those letters, Mr. Dane's stock-in-trade, were as valuable now as in the days when Mr. Dane carried on his business and made the fortune which had bought Danesborough. There was another fortune in the safe for anyone who knew the ropes and had neither heart nor conscience.

Chloe went on thinking quite quickly and calmly. Wroughton had tried to trap her. He had made sure that she knew how to open the safe, and that she would use her knowledge on the first opportunity. He meant to have the letters. Chloe stiffened. Nobody should have them;

she would see to it that nobody should have them. Danesborough was hers; and the cabinet was hers; and the safe was hers; and the letters were hers. A sort of shudder came over her. The money was hers—this horrible money, wrung from terror and shame and crime. It was hers!

She got on to her feet and leaned against the cabinet with a sense of having lost her way and blundered into some horrible place full of slime and fetid odours that rose from it and choked her. The money—Danesborough—they were hers. They were most foully tainted; and they were hers.

A dreadful pang of resentment shook Chloe. Anger against the dead shook her to the depths. He had brought this dishonour upon Danesborough; and he had brought it on her. Danesborough, where her people had lived for uncounted generations—he had dared to put this disgrace upon it. She felt as if she would never be clean again.

She set her teeth, and wondered how soon she could be gone. She was living on this money, using it. She must get away at once, back to Maxton, out of it all. Yes, that was it, she must get away. People couldn't make you take money that you didn't want and wouldn't have. She would write at once to Mr. Hudson and tell him that she refused Mr. Dane's legacy.

"I won't take it, and they can't make me. Oh, how did he dare to think that I would?"

Hot tears rushed to her eyes. She made a sudden movement, and struck her hand against the open door of the cabinet. What was she going to do about the cabinet? What was she going to do about the letters in the safe? The answer came as quick and hot as her tears:

"I must destroy them. I can't go away until I have destroyed them."

She turned, felt for her lamp, and put on the light. The beam slanted across those many, many packets of letters, written for the most part on the thick, expensive paper which does not lend itself readily to destruction. Chloe knew something about the time it takes to burn papers. Letters take longer than anything; they will not burn in their envelopes; they must be taken out and unfolded. The destruction of the letters in this safe would take many hours.

She climbed into the cabinet again, and took out the letters she had read and a few still unopened packets. Then she shut the safe.

The rest would have to wait. She must have time to think. Just now she only wanted to fling herself down on her bed and cry her heart out in the kind dark that would not see how ashamed she was.

She piled the letters on the floor, and slowly, haltingly, she crossed the room and fetched the section which had to be fitted again into the cabinet to mask the safe. When the doors were locked upon it, she filled the lap of her dressing-gown with the letters and slipped her lamp into her pocket.

At the door she switched on the light in the chandeliers for a moment, and looked down the room to make sure that she had left no trace. Everything was as cold, prim, and orderly as its wont. Her fingers jerked the switch; the brilliance died; a little red glow, and then blackness. She went slowly, very slowly, through the hall and up the stairs, feeling her way and making no sound.

When she came to her own door and unlocked it, the faint grating of the key seemed to her like an alarum that must rouse the house. She stood listening for a full minute before she dared lock the door on the inside.

The sounds of her own making died and were lost in the general stillness. The locked door, the feeling of being in her own room again, gave her confidence. She no longer wanted to throw herself down on the bed and cry her heart out; she wanted to deal with the letters and destroy them.

She made her way to the bed, tipped all the letters out of the skirt of her dressing-gown, and switched on the light in the small shaded reading-lamp which stood on the table near the head of the bed. The letters lay in a heap on the bright blue eiderdown. Chloe turned from them and looked towards the fireplace. There had been a fire there when she came to bed, but it had burnt itself out. She picked up a box of matches, and then put it down again. If anyone were to pass her door and see the light. She decided that there was no need for them to see it, and before she did anything else she pushed a piece of tissue paper into the keyhole and laid a coat across the bottom of the door. Then she carried the letters over to the hearth and, crouching there, realized that she was cold—she who was never cold. The embers in the grate were black, but a very faint warmth still came from them. Well, the letters would burn all the more easily for that.

She took the first letter out of its envelope, unfolded it, and held a lighted match to its lower edge. The flame caught in a thin blue line, and then ran upwards with a rush. She threw the envelope with its cynical endorsement into the flames and watched the whole die to a black film that could no longer yield its secret to anyone.

She lit the second letter; and so burned them one by one. It took a long time. Sometimes an edge curled over and showed a word or two before the flame and the blackness took them for ever. Once a name stood out, writhing in the fire; Chloe was glad when it was gone.

When all was done, and the grate full of the thin black ash that slowly turned to grey, she got up stiffly and stood looking down at her handiwork. The ash would fly about all over the room. She pushed it down with the shovel and put one or two lumps of coal upon it. Then she washed her hands, took the paper out of the keyhole, unlocked the door, and picked up her coat.

She wondered if she would sleep. She thought that she would like to sleep, to let a curtain fall upon all that she had done and felt that night. She did not feel ready to think of it, or to decide what she must do next. She wanted to let that curtain fall, and to sink behind it into a dreamless rest.

She slept until the maid drew up the blinds in the morning and let in the cold November light.

Chapter Fifteen

EMILY WROUGHTON seemed more than usually flustered and breathless at breakfast. At the moment of saying good-morning to Chloe she managed to upset the milk, and sat uttering little deprecatory exclamations and dabbing at the spilt milk with her table-napkin.

"I should leave it alone if I were you," said Chloe.

"Oh, no! Such a mess—and the servants—and you know Leonard likes things just so. I can't *think* how I came to do it." She sniffed, dropped her table-napkin, and began to rub the tip of her nose with a wispy handkerchief. She made it very pink, and some of the colour spread suddenly and unbecomingly to her cheeks as she said, "I told you I could never depend on him. Just fancy, after all, he came back late last night. But, there, I never know; I can't depend on him a bit."

Chloe's tongue ran away with her under the sharp spur of indignation.

"I should hate to have a husband that I couldn't depend on," she said.

Emily Wroughton laughed nervously.

"Oh, Miss Dane, how that sounds! But you know what I mean. He—he didn't disturb you last night, did he?—coming in, I mean. Did you hear him?"

"I heard some one," said Chloe shortly.

Mr. Wroughton had not hurried down to breakfast. He came out of his room at about the same time that Emily spilled the milk. Instead of going downstairs he strolled along the corridor, turned to the left, and passed the door of Chloe's room. The door stood open, and a hard-featured, middle-aged housemaid was coming out with a dust-pan in her hand.

Mr. Wroughton stopped, and looked curiously at the dust-pan. It was full of a thin grey-black ash, so light that, as the woman moved, a particle or two floated off into the air.

"Hullo!" said Wroughton in a jocular tone. "Miss Dane been trying to burn the house down, Jessie?"

"It's a wonder if she hasn't," said Jessie crossly, "seeing there's nothing like paper for setting a chimney on fire. Why, the grate's just fair stuffed with it. What in the world a young lady like her wants to sit up half the night writing letters and burning 'em, when she's got the whole blessed day to do it in, beats me."

The woman's tone and manner were familiar; but Wroughton did not appear to resent them.

"Writing letters, eh? What makes you think that?"

"I suppose I can use my eyes," said Jessie. "Half a wastepaper-basket full of tore up bits besides this mess in the grate."

"Well, well," said Wroughton. "Cheer up, Jessie."

He passed on, and Jessie flounced off in the opposite direction. As soon as she had passed the corner and was out of sight, Wroughton turned and came back astonishingly lightly and quickly for so large a man. He entered Chloe's room, spread his handkerchief on the floor and tipped the contents of the wastepaper-basket on to it.

Jessie had made the most of her grievance. The basket held a few torn sheets and no more. Leonard Wroughton gathered them up in his handkerchief, and went back to his own room whistling. Arrived there, he locked the door and spread the pieces of paper on the writing-table. He was glad to see that they were not torn very small. Most of them were blank, with no writing at all on either side. It did not take him long to determine that Chloe had begun and torn up three letters, and that they were all to Mr. Hudson. When the sheets were pieced together, one of them read:

"Dear Mr. Hudson,

"I can't—" and there broke off. The rest of the sheet was empty.

The next was in four pieces. It read:

"Dear Mr. Hudson,

"I want to see you at once. Can you come down here, or shall I come to town? I—"

There was a blot after the "I," but no more writing.

The third sheet ran:

"Dear Mr. Hudson,

"I have found out something that makes it quite impossible—"

Chloe had stopped there and torn the sheet into half a dozen pieces.

Leonard Wroughton sat and looked at the three sheets for about five minutes. Then he tore them into much smaller bits, and pushed them down to the bottom of his own wastepaper-basket, which was tolerably full of circulars and bills, most of the latter being unopened.

So she had dodged him and opened the safe. The fragments which he had just disposed of meant that or nothing. Whilst he was congratulating himself on his precautions, she had slipped through them and done him down. She had certainly opened the safe. As certainly, she had taken out and destroyed letters whose value it was impossible to estimate. The question was, how many of them had she managed to destroy? He thought not so very many. He had had a look at the grate when he emptied the wastepaper-basket in Chloe's room. It was clear; the contents of Jessie's dust-pan represented the whole of the débris. The safe, with its piled up shelves, rose reassuringly before him. Chloe could have made very little impression, really, on Mr. Dane's stock-in-trade. There was still a fortune left for anyone who could lay hands on it. One thing was certain, he must see the letter to Hudson, the letter which Chloe must have written; he was convinced that she must have completed a letter to Hudson. And he couldn't be sure of Hudson. Hudson was too damned cautious; he wouldn't put anything on paper. And he fussed like a hen if you used the telephone—as if the operator at the exchange hadn't something better to do than to sit eaves-dropping all day. Even if you went to see him, he'd hedge, be non-committal, and behave as if Scotland Yard had its ear to the keyhole. He must see Chloe's letter for himself before it went to Hudson at all.

He glanced at the hall table on his way to the dining-room. Emily had put a letter there for the post, but it had no companion.

In the dining-room he found Emily and Chloe just finishing breakfast. Chloe felt his eyes rest searchingly upon her face, and knew that, in spite of much cold water, she was pale and heavy-eyed enough. She bit her lip, and looked back at Wroughton with a spark of anger in her eyes.

For a moment there was that tension under which self-control is strained to very near breaking-point. Chloe's look was an open, angry challenge; but Wroughton avoided it. With his usual "Good morning," he passed to the side table and stood there helping himself.

Chloe pushed back her chair and got up. She was furious at her own self-betrayal, but for the life of her she could not keep her dislike of Wroughton out of her voice. She stood with her hand on the rail of the chair and spoke to his back.

"I should like the Napier in half an hour."

Wroughton finished cutting a slice of ham before he turned round.

"The Napier?" he said. "I'm afraid—didn't you know?—didn't Emily tell you?"

"I don't know anything. What is it?" said Chloe.

"Well you know the Daimler has been away to be painted—Mr. Dane made the arrangement and I let it stand. The Napier was to go as soon as the Daimler came back; but there seems to have been some misunderstanding, and they fetched her yesterday whilst I was away."

Chloe's colour rose brightly.

"I should have been asked" she began, and then stopped.

There was a little pause. Emily Wroughton said, "Oh, dear!" just under her breath, but her husband said nothing at all. He had seated himself, and was spreading a roll with butter.

"I'll have the A.C. then."

Wroughton looked up with a smile which Chloe thought insolent.

"Sorry, but the A.C. is out of action too. I had a slight mishap with her last night."

"A slight mishap! What did you do?"

"I'm not quite sure. Bell is going to overhaul her this morning."

Chloe turned away sharply. Her temper strained at the leash; she was afraid of letting it slip, afraid of what she might say if she did let it slip. She was mistress of Danesborough, but she could not order Wroughton out of the house. If she were of age—if she were only of age! If she let her temper go, this impossible situation would become more impossible still. She could not order Wroughton out of Danesborough, and she was firmly determined not to go herself until she had destroyed the rest of the letters.

She turned away and spoke to Emily:

"I shall walk down into the village, I think."

For once Emily earned her husband's gratitude. "Oh, my dear! In this rain? You mustn't think of it!"

"I want to post a letter," said Chloe. "And I want some air."

"But Leonard or any of the servants would post your letter."

"I'm sure they would," said Chloe at the door. She flashed a look at Wroughton, and saw with pleasure that her tone had stung him. "I'm sure Mr. Wroughton would love to post my letter; but—I think I'll post it myself."

Leonard Wroughton finished his breakfast rather hastily. He was in the study when Chloe came downstairs. As soon as the front door had shut behind her he went to the telephone, waiting in frowning impatience for the click of the receiver at the other end. A voice said "Hullo," and his features relaxed a little.

"That you, Jennings?" he said eagerly.

Chloe tramped along in the wet. The rain was coming straight down; there was no wind. The sky was one even grey. All the trees dripped, and the grass squelched under foot. She took a short cut across it to the gate, and came out upon a very muddy road. It was a relief to be out of Danesborough even for half an hour. She tramped on, and found herself presently wondering at the heat of her own temper a little while back.

"I'm becoming a perfectly hateful person—bad-tempered, and suspicious, and altogether horrid."

Her suspicions of Wroughton—was there any foundation for them really? He might have had half a dozen good reasons for last night's unexpected return. And if, by any chance, he had heard a sound in the house, it was no less than his duty to come down and make sure that all was in order.

"The fact is that I simply loathe him, and that makes me suspect everything he does. It shows what a beast I'm turning into. I never used to loathe people and suspect them. It's this horrible place and those horrible letters—they're like poison. Why—why—why on earth couldn't I have been born in September or October instead of February?"

Chloe fell into a pleasant dream of herself of age, fully mistress of the situation, dismissing Leonard Wroughton with dignified hauteur, and then making a glorious bonfire with the contents of Mr. Dane's safe.

"I'd do it too, if I could only stick it out till February. But *I simply can't.*"

She fell to thinking of how she could get hold of the other letters. After all, Wroughton must leave the house sometimes; and if the worst came to the worst, she must simply get rid of Emily by telling her that she wanted to be alone. Open defiance was about as likely from Emily Wroughton as from an earwig. Chloe laughed all to herself. She didn't know why she had thought of an earwig, but, once thought of, there was certainly a likeness.

"The—the sort of pointedness, and always being in a fuss," she explained to herself.

She passed an outlying cottage or two, skirted the vicarage garden, and turned into Two Man Lane.

It was just at the bottom of the lane, where it came out at the end of the village street, that she heard herself hailed, and turned to see Dr. Golding's locum emerge from a cottage garden on her right. Chloe did not very much like Dr. Jennings. In the capacity of Wroughton's friend he had been at Danesborough several times, and each time she had liked him a little less. Dark, good-looking, clever, and more than a little underbred, he did not improve upon acquaintance.

"Hul—lo, Miss Dane! What luck! I was just thinking it never does anything but rain in this damn climate, and—er, there you were—a regular sun-burst, so to speak!"

Chloe said "How do you do?" in rather frigid tones. To her annoyance, Dr. Jennings continued to walk beside her, turning when she turned, and producing half a dozen letters, which made it quite evident that his objective was the same as her own.

"I forget—did you know Golding at all? Worthy old chap of course, but frightfully behind the times."

"I met him," said Chloe. "I liked him awfully."

"Worthy," said Dr. Jennings in a patronizing tone. "Of course, a practice like this is absolute stagnation. Except for one thing, I shall be glad enough to get back to town."

If he intended Chloe to ask what the one thing was, he was disappointed. She said nothing. As they came in sight of the post office she took out of her pocket the letter which she had written to Mr. Hudson, and prepared to cross the road.

A car had stopped in front of the little post office, which was also a general shop, and two of its occupants had got out and were deep in conversation with a couple who had just emerged from the shop. Chloe looked at these people, wondering who they were. It came over her with a sudden pang of loneliness that she didn't know them, that she didn't know anyone, and that it was strange—surely it was strange—that no one had been to call. Those women looked nice. One of them was quite young.

Just for the moment that these thoughts passed through her mind, Chloe stood still on the edge of the path. She was about to move, when, with a quick "Allow me," Dr. Jennings took the letter out of her hand, and, putting it with his own, walked briskly across the road to the post office. The car hid him from view for the briefest possible space. Chloe saw him emerge from behind it, greet its occupants, and push the whole batch of letters into the slot in the post office wall.

He was back again in a moment, and was instantly made aware of her sharp annoyance.

"Why did you do that?" Her tone was biting.

To her surprise, he looked at her gravely.

"I'm awfully sorry—it must have seemed rude. I'll explain if you'll let me walk a little way with you. Really, Miss Dane, I had a reason."

"A reason?" (What an extraordinary thing to say! What did he mean?) "What reason?"

"I'll tell you—I'm really sorry if I seemed rude. Here, just let's get round the corner into the lane, and I'll tell you why I did it."

They walked in silence to the corner. Then Chloe spoke stiffly:

"Well, Dr. Jennings?"

Again that odd, grave look.

"Well, Miss Dane, the fact is the whole household at Danesborough is in quarantine, and I oughtn't to have let you come into the village at all. I didn't think there would be anybody about on such a wet day, and I chanced it. But I really couldn't let you go across and post your letter, with Lady Adderley sitting there in her car, and Miss Adderley and her cousin standing talking to the Goddards just where you'd have to pass right through them to get to the letter-box—now, could I?"

"Quarantine?" said Chloe.

"Yes. We didn't want to frighten you, so you weren't told."

Chloe's head lifted and her eyes flashed.

"I'm not easily frightened. And I ought to have been told. What is it?"

"One of the housemaids—she was removed in an ambulance the day before yesterday whilst you were out in the car."

"What is it?" said Chloe again.

Dr. Jennings looked still more gravely concerned. She would hardly have known the rather facetious young man who had compared her to a sun-burst.

"I'd rather not say. I may have my own opinion; but I'd rather not say what it is until I get confirmation. Meanwhile, I'm afraid—I'm afraid I must be very strict about the quarantine. It's really necessary and serious. Nobody at Danesborough ought to leave the grounds until we know a little more. I don't want to frighten you, but, as I said before, I've got my own opinion."

"Thank you," said Chloe, "I'm not in the least frightened. I think it would have been much better if you had explained all this before. I'm not a child, and I ought to have been told. Good-bye, Dr. Jennings."

Dr. Jennings reverted to the manner of gallantry.

"Not so easily rid of me, I'm afraid!" he said, with the rather conscious laugh which Chloe disliked so much. "It's my lucky morning, you know, because I've got to go up and see Wroughton about this business, and was expecting a dull tramp, instead of which I get the chance of a walk with you."

Chapter Sixteen

DR. JENNINGS was easily satisfied if he derived any pleasure from his walk with Chloe. He had, to be sure, the opportunity of learning her profile by heart; but the profile of a coldly monosyllabic damsel is an unsatisfactory thing to contemplate for any length of time. By the time they arrived at the house Dr. Jennings' gallantry had worn thin, and his temper rasped. He shut the study door behind him with something of a bang.

Wroughton pushed back his chair and started up, flushed and anxious.

"Well—well—did you get it?"

Jennings gave a half shrug of the shoulders, took a letter out of his pocket, and tossed it to Wroughton.

"Of course I got it. There it is."

"How did you manage? She didn't suspect?"

"No, of course she didn't. I'm not that sort of mug. If I can't do a thing without bungling, I don't do it at all. As it happened, it was child's play. I had my own letters in my hand, and I took hers to post them with. The Adderley crowd were blocking the road in front of the post office, and I came the heavy professional manner over her and worked off that quarantine stunt which we agreed upon. It came in very handy, and she lapped it all up."

Wroughton turned the letter over, breathed heavily on the flap, and with care and patience got it open. It was quite short, almost as short as the fragments which Wroughton had read that morning:

"Dear Mr. Hudson,

"I want to tell you that I can't take Mr. Dane's legacy. I know I can't do anything legally until I'm of age; but I wanted to let you know that as soon as I possibly can I shall refuse it.

"Yours sincerely,

Chloe Dane

As Wroughton exclaimed, Dr. Jennings came and looked over his shoulder. He emitted a long whistle, and then said:

"What rot!"

Wroughton was swearing. Chloe, Mr. Dane, and the maker of the safe behind the black cabinet seemed to share his invective pretty equally between them.

"If there were any way of getting into the damn thing without blowing up the house with dynamite, I'd chance it and snap my fingers at her," he said furiously.

"Steady on. You're making rather a noise, you know, Len. Dynamite's a bit drastic. But I seem to have heard of safes having holes drilled in 'em."

"Not this one. It's the new Baker—Bernstein patent. I was with the old man when he saw it put through all the tests. Can't do a thing to it without blowing the house up too."

"All right. Don't crumple that letter; it's got to go on to old Hudson by the next post."

"Why?"

"You make me tired. I'm a law-abiding citizen and don't you forget it. Reading a letter's one thing, and suppressing it's quite another. Old Hudson's got to get this precious twaddle by the morning post."

"I don't trust Hudson an inch. I know those cautious men; they'll go back on you every time they get rattled. That's why I had to have the letter."

"Well, you've got the letter. What about it?"

Wroughton came closer, dropped his voice to an angry whisper, and said:

"That's where Stran comes in. She opened the safe last night, took out some of the letters—I don't know how many—and burnt them"— his colour deepened almost to purple—"burnt them! And if she gets a chance, she'll burn the whole lot. With the letters burnt and the old man's fortune gone into the Treasury, where do you and I come in?"

"Well," said Dr. Jennings, "I should still be a rising young professional man, but you, I expect, would be in Queer Street."

"It's up to Stran. If he can't come over a little milliner girl out of a raw provincial town, well, he's more of a fool than I ever took him for. He's got the field all to himself; and if he can't marry her, and get her to change her mind about the money before February, well—The bother is, she can't stay here till February, or we lose the letters. I thought I had her watched day and night, but she got away with them once, and she may again. I must get her out of here."

Dr. Jennings folded up Chloe's letter, replaced it in its envelope, and stuck it down.

"I've thought out quite a good dodge for that," he said. Then he laughed. "Stran's going to earn his money hard. I swear I don't envy him his heiress. He's welcome to her for me."

Wroughton shot a glance of sudden suspicion at him.

"Have you been having a shot at her yourself? That's not in the bargain."

"Oh, she's not my style," said Dr. Jennings easily.

Chloe heard the telephone bell that afternoon, and got to the instrument before Wroughton did. She heard him come into the room behind her and say, "It's almost certainly for me." With the receiver at her ear, she threw a smilingly defiant look over her shoulder.

"Now why should it be? I *have* got some friends, you know, Mr. Wroughton." Then, as a voice on the line reached her, she turned, nodded to him, and added, "This happens to be one of them; so if you wouldn't mind—"

As the door closed, she spoke into the telephone:

"Yes, I heard you—and I recognized your voice too. I just had to get rid of some one who was in the room. When are you coming to see me?"

Michael Foster at the other end of the line hesitated, and then said,

"I—well—I'm not sure."

To Chloe's horror, she felt something like a lump rise in her throat. She wanted to see Michael—she wanted to see him very much indeed—not only because he came from right outside this horrid circle of suspicion and ill will. He stood for the old, light-hearted life in Maxton. Chloe thought of Maxton with yearning.

"You're not coming?" The dismay in her voice startled her as much as it pleased Michael.

"I—I—well, you must know that I'd come if I could. I've been counting on it most awfully. But I'm not on the job I expected to be on, and—and—"

The tears rushed hot and stinging into Chloe's eyes. With a jerk she pushed the receiver back on to its hook, rang off with energy, and then stood there, biting her lip and feeling as if her last friend had forsaken her. She was furious with Michael for not coming, furious with herself for caring whether he came or not, and most furious of all with the little solacing whisper that said, "Perhaps—perhaps, after all, he'll come."

On her way up to dress for dinner that evening, it occurred to Chloe that she would ring up Miss Allardyce and ask her whether she had filled her place. She didn't mean to stay in Maxton all her life, but she might do worse than go back there while she looked about her. At the moment Maxton stood for home and safety.

She opened the study door without any thought that Wroughton might be there—he usually went to dress early and came down late; but as the door opened she heard his voice within and drew back quickly. The door shut without any sound, but just before it shut she heard him say, "Stran rang up,"—just those three words and no more.

Chloe ran upstairs, glad to have avoided an awkward encounter. She had a passing wonder as to whom Wroughton had been telephoning to. So "Stran" had rung up that afternoon! Chloe began to be rather intrigued about Stran. It would have been curious if it had been his call that she had answered instead of Michael Foster's. "How wild Mr. Wroughton would have been!" she reflected with a spice of malice.

Chapter Seventeen

CHLOE BEGUILED the evening with some serious plan-making. She would ring up Ally in the morning, and find out whether she would take her back.

"As a matter of fact, I expect she'll simply jump at me."

She would also ring up Miss Tankerville, and ask to be put up for a night or two while she looked for a room.

"No. Bother! I can't do that because of this wretched quarantine. How stupid! I wonder how long it lasts—I ought to have asked."

Dismay took hold of Chloe. She did not feel as if she could bear to stay another forty-eight hours at Danesborough. She had planned it all so nicely. Somehow she must get the remaining letters out of the safe. But she couldn't burn them here. She realized that the servants would talk if her grate continued to overflow with masses of black ash. As a matter of fact, they were talking already, for she had heard Jessie say something to the under housemaid when she ran upstairs to put on her hat that morning. It wouldn't do, it wouldn't do at all. No, she would get out the letters, take them down to Maxton with her, and burn them there, where it would be nobody's business but her own. She would have to watch her opportunity of course.

She went upstairs early; but she did not undress. There was a comfortable fire in her room, and she took a book and sat down by the shaded reading-lamp.

An hour passed. And then, just as she was getting sleepy, there came a tapping on the door, and the handle was turned gently.

"Thank goodness I locked it. Now who on earth—"

There was another tap, a little louder; and then Emily Wroughton's voice, raised in a timid whisper:

"Miss Dane—Miss Dane—"

Chloe yawned of design.

"What is it?" she said in startled tones. She hoped she sounded sleepy enough.

"I saw a light under your door; it looked—it looked like fire."

Chloe permitted herself a sleepy giggle.

"Dear Mrs. Wroughton, do go to bed. I was only reading a little."

"You're sure you're all right?"

"Yes, of course."

Emily stood another minute at the door. In sudden exasperation Chloe snicked the light out, yawned again, and said good-night in the drowsiest voice she could manage, after which she heard Emily move, and caught the sound of her slow and faltering retreat. She waited in the dark for perhaps half an hour, and then went downstairs to the drawing-room, locking the bedroom door behind her.

She had no intention of being caught by Wroughton to-night. If he came down—and Emily's visit convinced her that he meant to come down—, she was not going to be caught at a disadvantage, as she had so very nearly been caught last night.

She slipped through the drawing-room door, closed it behind her, and found her way to the middle one of the three long windows which faced the terrace. Here she sat down on the broad window-seat and waited. She was exactly opposite the cabinet. The curtains screened her admirably. If Leonard Wroughton had not looked behind them last night, he was not at all likely to do so to-night. Then, when he had been and gone, she could clear the safe at her leisure. She hoped that he would come quickly, for the room was cold, and she wished now that she had slipped on a coat before coming down. She was still in her black velvet dinner dress. In her own room she had been more than warm enough, but here the cold and silence crept in on her.

She moved presently, turning to the window and pressing her face close to the glass in an attempt to see out; but she could distinguish nothing. The night was dead dark, and a thick mist hung upon the pane. Chloe thought longingly of Maxton High Street, with its lamps and its lighted shops. An affectionate memory of the new cinema, with its double arch of little, brilliant, vulgar lights, and its three hideous arc lamps, very nearly brought tears to her eyes. She turned impatiently from the window, and heard what she had been waiting for—the sound of the opening door.

Instantly she was a-tingle with excitement. It was Wroughton of course; but she must see him and watch what he would do. She leaned forward, parting the curtains by just the smallest space imaginable, and saw Leonard Wroughton stand in the door-way, his hand on the switch of the electric light, the room brilliant before him under the sudden glare of all the chandeliers. He spoke over his shoulder to some one behind him.

"All right," he said, and came into the room followed by Dr. Jennings.

They crossed to where the black cabinet stood in its alcove. And then Jennings said something in a low voice. Chloe strained, but could not catch a word. She saw Wroughton take a pair of fine steel pliers out of his pocket and fiddle with the lock of the cabinet. He had it open in a trice.

"And not for the first time," thought Chloe to herself.

Jennings stood aside whilst Wroughton lifted out the middle section and laid it on the floor. Then Jennings spoke:

"Aren't you going to lock this door? It'd be a bit awkward if she came in."

"I've left Emily on guard," said Wroughton, taking off his coat. "Now you'd better hold the light whilst I have a shot at the old man's notes."

"Think they're any good?" Dr. Jennings' tone was tinged with sarcasm.

Wroughton turned on him with sudden anger:

"What a wet blanket you are! Why shouldn't they be good? Why shouldn't they be the real thing? Do you suppose a man like old Dane makes a list of words of five letters and locks it away in the back of his own private drawer just for the sake of amusing himself? When I found it this afternoon I could have shouted the house down."

"All right, go ahead," said Jennings. "After all, the proof of the pudding's in the eating. Give me the lamp and the list, and you go ahead and see whether any of the words'll move that damn lock."

Anger and excitement together rose in Chloe to boiling point. So they had found a list which might, or might not, contain the word that opened the safe! Supposing it did. Supposing they opened the safe before her very eyes, and began to take out the letters. Chloe made up her mind that the very moment the safe door swung open she would make a dash for the hall and rouse the house. She could scream, and she could beat the great bronze gong. It would be a bold measure; but she thought Leonard Wroughton would find himself in an awkward position. After all, people can't open safes that don't belong to them with impunity.

She watched Wroughton crawl painfully into the middle of the cabinet whilst Jennings directed the ray of an electric lamp so as to light up the door of the safe. Then Jennings began to read out words from a paper which he laid on the edge of the cabinet. They were all quite ordinary words: "Dream," "Table," "Motor," "Coals"... and so forth.

In the pause between each word Leonard Wroughton's fingers fumbled with the lock. At each failure Dr. Jennings' cool voice became a little cooler, and Wroughton's comments more heated. Half way through the list he backed out, and stood mopping a scarlet face and swearing.

Dr. Jennings relieved him. He handled the lock with nimbler fingers than Wroughton had done, but with no better result. As word followed word, Wroughton's suppressed fury threatened his self-control more and more. His voice rose, and when the last word proved to be as complete a failure as the first, he tore the paper across and stamped it under foot in an outburst of uncontrolled rage.

"Well, that's that," said Dr. Jennings, dusting his hands as he emerged. "My good Len, what a waste of energy! I told you all along that it would be a wash-out. And what I want now is a drink."

He replaced the missing section as he spoke, and carefully picked up all the torn paper. Wroughton, still raging, manipulated the lock of the cabinet, and they went out together, leaving the room to darkness and Chloe.

As soon as their footsteps had died away, Chloe sprang up and stretched herself. For nearly half an hour she had not dared to move, and hardly to breathe. Excitement; burning indignation; a tense watching of the fingers that fumbled with the lock; and now and again a sharp, stabbing fear when they paused—these things had been her portion. At the outset her plan of rousing the house had seemed good enough; but as the half hour passed, she began to realize how plausible a front Wroughton would be able to put upon the business. The servants were practically his servants; they might even be his creatures, part of the horrible organization which Mr. Dane had controlled. As this thought rose up before her, Chloe's courage wavered, and she felt that she was only a girl of twenty, alone in a house full of horrible things.

She had not liked Dr. Jennings, but it was a shock to find him in Wroughton's company at this hour, endeavouring to open the safe. She wondered how much he knew of its contents. To think a man rather ill-bred and familiar is one thing; but to judge him to be one of a blackmailing gang is quite another. If he were really in the conspiracy, the whole affair became much more menacing. This quarantine—was it all part of the game—part of a plan to seclude her until she did what they wanted her to do? Oh, if only kind Dr. Golding had never gone away! Chloe had only seen him twice, but she had felt instinctively that here was one of those people whom one can trust and lean upon. Well, it was no good wishing for him or for anyone else. When there's no one to help you, you must help yourself.

She parted the curtains, and went over to the cabinet.

"I hope to goodness he hasn't messed up the lock with his wretched pliers," she thought as she pushed her key home. The catch went smoothly back, and the doors opened.

Chapter Eighteen

CHLOE WASTED no time. She got the safe open and began to clear the shelves, taking the piles of letters as they came. There were, besides the letters, some account books and one or two packets of what looked like ordinary business papers. There were also three long envelopes endorsed respectively, "A.J's receipts", "Stran's receipts", "Mrs. V.H's receipts." Chloe left these with the account books, and got all the letters out. There were more than she could carry upstairs at one time, and she stacked half of them behind the cushions on the sofa which stood in front of the fire-place. Then she shut the safe, leaving the receipts and the account books inside it, turned her skirt up all round, and crammed in as many of the letters as the fold would take.

She stood for a moment by the half-open door, listening, before she ventured out into the hall. One hand held up her loaded skirt, with the other she felt before her in the dark until her fingers touched the balustrade of the stairs.

"It's a frightfully good thing that I'm nearly as quick as a cat at finding my way in the dark," she thought as she went on and up the stair, moving almost as easily as if she had a light.

She reached her room, turned back the eiderdown on her bed, and tipped out the letters. When she had pulled the eiderdown over them, she looked about her at the fire-lit room, and wished very much that she did not have to go downstairs again for the rest of the letters. It struck her suddenly that, for all she knew, Wroughton and Jennings were still in the study. Suppose the door were to open just as she crossed the hall. Then there was Emily; Wroughton had said something about Emily being left on guard. She wondered whether, after all, she had been seen or heard when she came upstairs just now.

"Well, the more I think about it, the less I shall like it," said Chloe at the door. Next minute she had locked it behind her, and was moving noiselessly to the head of the stair. She had nearly reached it when she saw a light; it shone from below, from the hall. And there were footsteps, heavy footsteps like Wroughton's. At the same moment she was aware of a faint, warm glow on her left. Some one with a candle must be coming down the passage which ran into the main corridor a few yards farther on.

The glow, faint as it was, served to show Chloe her whereabouts. There was a door on her right leading into one of the spare rooms. Chloe had it open, and was in the room with what seemed to her to be only one movement. She closed the door almost as quickly, leaving the least scrap of a chink through which to hear and, if possible, to see.

For a moment the candle-glow brightened the chink; then it was swallowed by a brighter, whiter light. She heard Wroughton stumble at the top step and mutter, "She hasn't passed?", and Emily's fluttered answer, "No—no, she hasn't."

The lights, the footsteps, and the voices receded. Chloe whisked out of her hiding place and ran downstairs without giving herself time to think.

The letters were just where she had left them behind the cushions on the settee. She bundled them into her skirt and began again the cautious, dark ascent. It was when she was nearly at the top of the stairs that her knees began without warning to shake beneath her.

There was neither light, nor step, nor movement in the house; but a cold terror came upon her and shook her from head to foot. If Wroughton should be there in the black corridor above. He might be there; and if he were, if her groping hand were to touch him unawares—

Chloe sank upon the stair and leaned her elbow on the step above. Everything rocked about her.

It was the sound of a closing door that roused her, a door away on the right—Wroughton's door? Chloe sprang to her feet, took the last two steps together, and ran down the corridor until her fingers, brushing the wall, turned the corner. There she checked herself, and went softly along the side passage to her own room.

When her door was locked and she had turned on the light, the relief was so great that she could have laughed aloud. She had done it; she had beaten Wroughton; she had got the letters! She was safe!

Safe! Her exhilaration died slowly. She stripped back the eiderdown and piled the second batch of letters upon the first. What in all the world was she to do with them? If she tried to burn them here, she would probably rouse the house, and very likely set the chimney on fire. She couldn't risk it. You can't really burn much paper in an old-fashioned bedroom grate.

No, she must get away with them—to Maxton if possible, but at all costs away from Danesborough. If only the Daimler had come back, or the Napier had not gone. That was the first time it occurred to Chloe that the absence of both cars was not just the result of carelessness—the A.C. too—all three cars laid up. No car; and the house in quarantine.

"Well, thank goodness there's the telephone," thought Chloe, and then gave her mind to the question of what to do with the letters meanwhile.

She crossed the room and opened the door of a large cupboard built into the wall. It had been a powdering closet once, and one went down into it by two steps. It had hooks all round the wall now, and Chloe's garments hung upon the hooks. Chloe did not look at them. She pulled out the small, shabby black box which she had taken to school with her as a child, and which was still her only bit of luggage when she returned to Danesborough as its heiress.

She switched on the light in the cupboard, propped up the lid of the box, and packed all the letters into it. She folded a dress or two on the top, and locked and strapped the box. To-morrow she was going to leave Danesborough; to-morrow she would be penniless Chloe Dane again, as free as air, and as light-hearted as an April day. Now she was going to bed.

Chapter Nineteen

CHLOE RESISTED an inclination to lie in bed next morning. She must get down before Wroughton did, and telephone to Ally. She heard the big clock strike nine as she ran downstairs, and felt sure of having half an hour to herself.

On the bottom step she paused, looking towards the drawing-room door. It was open, three parts open; and there was some one in the room, for she could hear movements. She took a few quick steps to the left, stood on the threshold, and pushed the door a little further. Leonard Wroughton was standing in front of the cabinet with a letter in his hand. As the door moved he swung round sharply, and he and Chloe faced each other. There was such rage in his look that all Chloe's spirit rose to resent it. She held her head high, and looked at him with both anger and pride in her black eyes. For a moment, as his colour deepened dangerously, she wondered whether he would break all bounds and offer her some actual violence.

Then something happened that frightened her: he controlled himself, with a great and obvious effort he controlled himself, took a step towards her, and held the letter out.

"Yours?" he said. Even on the one word his voice shook.

Chloe took the letter and looked at it. It was one of the letters which she had taken from the safe last night. She must have dropped it. Wroughton, finding it, could not fail to know that she had opened the safe. She gave him one defiant glance and said,

"Yes, it is." Then she turned and went along the hall into the dining-room without looking back. She did not need to look, for Wroughton made no attempt to follow.

Emily was in the dining-room, but before so much as replying to her "Good-morning," Chloe went over to the hearth and burned the letter which she had taken from Wroughton's hand. Then she stood with her back to the fire and waited for him to come in. When he came in he took no notice of her.

Chloe's voice cut into the silence, very clear and cool:

"Is the Daimler back yet, Mr. Wroughton?"

He looked at her with open insolence.

"I've no idea."

Chloe bit her lip fiercely. She supposed he was trying to make her lose her temper.

"What about the A.C.? Has Bell put her right?"

"I believe not."

Chloe walked out of the room and went straight to the telephone which communicated with the garage. When a man's voice said "Hullo," she said, "Miss Dane speaking. Is that Bell?"

Bell's "Yes, miss," sounded surprised.

"Is the Daimler back?"

"Oh, no, miss."

"What about the A.C.? Can you have her ready for me this morning?"

"Oh, no, miss."

A faint snigger came along the line to Chloe. It was not the man at the telephone who laughed, she thought, but some one standing farther off behind him. With her temper at boiling point she hung up the receiver and went back to the dining-room.

While she ate a hasty breakfast she made up her mind to telephone to Daneham station for a taxi. Not another meal would she eat in Leonard Wroughton's company. After all, what was there to stay for? She had the letters, and the sooner she got them away the better. Her spirits rose, and she went to the study telephone with a lighter heart than she had had for days. She rang the exchange, and waited impatiently for an answer.

"They're pretty sleepy in these country exchanges," she thought as she rang again, and yet again. There was no reply; the line felt dead. She was jerking the hook of the receiver, when Wroughton spoke just behind her:

"Telephone gone wrong, eh?" There was more than a suspicion of a sneer in his voice.

Chloe flung round furiously.

"You *knew* it was out of order!"

"I guessed that it would be out of order," said Leonard Wroughton. Chloe stamped her foot.

"Will you please send a man at once on a bicycle to tell the Daneham exchange that the telephone is out of order."

Wroughton actually smiled.

"It's unfortunate, isn't it?" he said. "Gives you a cut-off sort of feeling, eh?"

She was on the edge of angry tears, but she gathered up her dignity as well as she could.

"I should like a man to be sent at once!" she said, and left the room.

In the hall she turned blindly to the front door, pulled it open, and ran out, banging it behind her. It was good to come out into the wind—Chloe loved the wind. She ran with it now, down the drive until she was warm and glowing. She thought she would go down into the village and telephone from the post office; she supposed they kept a telephone there. Of course she ought to have put a hat on. She wondered if the village was very particular about hats. She couldn't go back for one now, she really couldn't; time was too precious. As it was, it would take her half an hour to walk into the village; and she had left the letters unguarded behind her. Of course the housemaids would be in and out; that made it safer.

At this moment she came in sight of the iron gates at the entrance to the drive. They usually stood wide open, but now they were shut. Chloe came up to them, tried them, and found that they were not only shut, but locked. She went to the door of the lodge and knocked, but got no answer. She peered in at a window, and saw an empty room stripped of furniture. The day before yesterday there had been a man here, and a woman and two children. She looked through another curtainless window. The lodge was certainly empty.

She did not go back along the drive, but skirted the high brick wall which enclosed the Danesborough grounds. Any idea of climbing it receded; but there was a door into Langton Lane of which she had some hopes. She came to it, and found it locked. It was stoutly built of oak, and had a new heavy iron lock as well as the two bolts which she remembered. She left the wall and cut across to the kitchen garden, which was screened from the rest of the grounds by a tall beech hedge to which the leaves still clung in brown and orange patches. The beech hedge enclosed three sides of the garden, and the outer wall the fourth. Against the wall there were fruit trees closely trained, and it was in Chloe's mind that she had climbed to the top of the wall for fruit many a time when she was a child; she had to dodge the gardeners of course. And then it came to her as a most singular thing that she had not set eyes on a gardener for days.

She chose a stout pear tree, and reached the top of the wall with a pleasant sense of achievement. On its outer side the wall dropped to a bank, and the bank sloped steeply into Langton Lane. Chloe looked at the drop, and didn't like it very much. And as she sat there, looking down and whistling softly to herself, a car came up the lane. It was driven by a young man.

Chloe flung convention to the winds and hailed the car. Any human motorist would send a telephone message for her, or order a taxi. Young men, especially, were wont to be obliging. The car slowed down and stopped; the young man looked up and uttered a very surprised "Hullo!"

"Oh," said Chloe faintly. The young man was Mr. Martin Fossetter. "Oh," said Chloe again. The colour rushed into her face. She looked very pretty. The dullest young man in England would have grasped the fact that she was exceedingly pleased to see him; and Martin Fossetter was very far from being a dull young man. He got out of his car, and climbed up the bank.

"I say, what luck—what amazing luck!" he said.

"Yes, isn't it?" said Chloe. "I mean"—she laughed a little breathlessly—"I—I'm most awfully glad to see you."

Dr. Jennings would have considered Mr. Fossetter sadly wanting in gallantry. He did not speak at all, but put up his hand to meet Chloe's. She felt a warm, strong clasp for a moment. Then she laughed and pulled her hand away rather quickly.

"If you were marooned on a desert island, I expect you'd be glad to see some one too," she said.

Martin Fossetter tapped the wall, smiling.

"Is this a desert island?"

"The whole of Danesborough's a desert island," said Chloe—"the sort where you never see a passing sail. That's why I'm so pleased to see you."

"I see. And what can I do for you now I'm here?"

Chloe hesitated.

"Why is Danesborough a desert island?"

"The cars have broken down; and the telephone is out of order; and we're in quarantine—"

"Quarantine! What for?"

"I don't know."

Chloe found herself looking into a pair of very sympathetic brown eyes, and spoke what was in her heart.

"I don't believe in the quarantine—not really."

"What makes you say that?" said Martin Fossetter quickly. "Look here, you're not serious, are you?"

"Yes, I am." Chloe was rather pale.

He put up his hand again, and she laid hers on it just for an instant, and then withdrew it hastily because the friendly touch brought a rush of tears to her eyes.

Martin Fossetter looked at her with deep concern.

"Chloe, what is it? What's the matter? Won't you let me help you?"

She nodded.

"I want you to. I want to get away—to go back to Maxton."

"But surely you're free to go?"

"No cars; no telephone; the gates all locked; and this sham quarantine set up as a bug-bear—it isn't very easy, is it? I mean to get away somehow though."

"What makes you think it's a sham?"

"I'm sure it's a sham. I can't tell you why I'm sure; but I am sure. I—I've got some papers that they don't want me to have, and I think they're trying to keep me here." She laughed a little shakily. "It sounds mad, doesn't it?"

"Who's they?" said Martin. "Is it that man Wroughton who's annoying you? I never liked him."

"Yes," said Chloe. "He wants the papers. Mr. Dane didn't mean him to have them; he—he gave them to me. But Mr. Wroughton is trying to get hold of them. He thinks they're worth a lot of money, and he knows that I'm going to burn them."

"Burn them! Why, what are they?"

Chloe shivered and looked away.

"They're things that ought to be burnt," she said in a low voice.

When she looked back again, it was to find Mr. Fossetter regarding her with a sort of tender bewilderment. She had already told him a great deal more than she had meant to tell anyone, and she had a feeling that if she went on talking to him, she would probably end by telling him all that she knew, or guessed, or feared.

"I must get away—I must get back to Maxton. Please, Mr. Fossetter, will you do two things for me?"

"Two hundred, if you like."

"Two will do to begin with. Will you go to the Daneham exchange, and tell them to come at once and put our telephone right? And will you, at the same time, order a taxi to come and fetch me to the station?"

Martin looked down. An expression of doubt crossed his face. After a little pause he lifted serious eyes to Chloe's.

"Has it occurred to you that if you're really in quarantine—"

"We're not—I'm sure we're not!"

"It might be made an excuse. I mean the lodge-keeper might have orders not to let anyone in."

"There isn't any lodge-keeper," said Chloe in a startled voice.

"What!"

"The lodge is empty. The people are gone. The gate is locked."

Mr. Fossetter whistled.

"I say, that sounds bad."

"I *must* get away—I *must* get back to Maxton."

"Yes, yes, of course. But—look here, I'll do anything to help you, but I want to make a good job of it. You see, there's a lot to be thought of. I don't believe it's any use ordering a taxi, for instance—not if there's anything in this quarantine stunt."

"I'm *sure* there isn't."

"Will you trust me to make inquiries? I can easily find out what's being said in the village. And at a pinch, you know, you can always drop over the wall and let me drive you anywhere you want to go. Would I do instead of a taxi, do you think?"

"You really mean it?"

"Of course I do. I only wish—Chloe, how many times do you suppose I've thought of you since we danced together?"

"I shouldn't think you've thought of me at all."

For the first time Chloe remembered that she had just cause of offence against Martin Fossetter. He had asked for two dances at the County Ball, it is true; but whilst he danced with Chloe, he had looked at Monica Gresson—"Pouf!"

"You're wrong," said Martin; and he said it very nicely. He had the most charming smile that it is possible to imagine. It flashed at

Chloe now, and was gone. His eyes said the rest. After a little pause he spoke again:

"You'll leave it to me then?"

"But how shall I know?"

"Will you come back here and meet me this afternoon—say, at four o'clock?"

"I don't know," said Chloe. "I'll try. Emily Wroughton sticks like a burr."

"Well, I'll be here at four, anyhow; and I'll just wait until you do come."

"Are you sure?"

"Yes, of course. Chloe,—"

But Chloe had slipped down on her own side of the wall, and was gone.

Chapter Twenty

Mr. Fossetter got into his car and drove into Danesborough village. As he came slowly through the village street he saw, emerging from the post office, Miss Adderley, first cousin once removed to Sir James Adderley of Daneham Manor, and the most accomplished gossip in three counties. He stopped at once, got out, and was very warmly greeted.

"Good gracious, Martin, where did you come from? Where are you staying?—not at Danesborough this time, I suppose."

Miss Adderley had a very sharp nose and little, pale grey eyes that saw everything; her streaky hair floated in wisps under a magenta felt hat that was at least three sizes too large.

"Why not at Danesborough?" said Martin with his charming smile.

Miss Adderley laid her hand on his arm.

"I want to look at your car," she said, and propelled him across the street.

"Why?"

"Nonsense!" said Miss Adderley. "I don't really in the least—you know as well as I do that I don't know one end of the murdering things from the other—; but that post office woman can hear flies walking on the ceiling, and—"

"And you were going to be indiscreet."

"How dare you, when you know I'm the soul of discretion? But if *half* one hears is true about Danesborough and the heiress,"—she dropped her voice to a stage whisper—"well, it naturally surprised me to hear you were staying there."

"I'm not," said Martin.

"Then why did you say you were? That's the way things get about. One can't be too careful. And goodness knows there are stories enough already."

"How intriguing!" said Martin. "Do go on. What are the stories?"

"I *never* repeat gossip," said Miss Adderley. "But of course everybody's saying—by the way, have you met Miss Dane?"

"I have."

"Have you really? Then you can tell me—is it very obvious?"

"Is what very obvious?"

Miss Adderley looked all round her and dropped her voice a little more:

"Her being odd—queer in the head, you know. Did you notice anything?"

"I noticed that she was very pretty," said Martin, laughing.

Miss Adderley tucked a long grey wisp behind one ear.

"That's all a man would notice," she said with biting scorn. "Poor thing, I'm sorry for her, with all that money and no sense."

"No sense?" said Martin.

"No—*really*. It's safe with you, I know, or I wouldn't say a word. But she really is"—she shook her head expressively, and the magenta hat slipped forward over one eye—"quite touched; quite, if one may say so, *peculiar*." She pushed back the hat and again took Martin by the arm. "The head housemaid is a friend of my Mrs. Jones, and she says the poor thing sits up all night, writing letters and burning them. *There*, what do you think of *that*?"

Martin detached himself, still laughing.

"Didn't you ever write love-letters and burn them?" he asked impudently. "It's much the safest thing to do with them, really." He got into the car as he spoke, and started the engine.

Miss Adderley was not in the least offended; she was much too full of her subject to take offence. She continued to talk, with one hand on the side of the car: "Temper too—outbreaks. And such queer ways. She's sent all the cars away because she doesn't like the smell of petrol, and discharged all the gardeners because she doesn't like to see men about the place. Even poor Bucket at the lodge has had to turn out; and I do call *that* a shame, if you don't. And the latest, the very latest,—what do you think the *very* latest is?"

"I don't know, I'm sure. I'm afraid I must be getting on, Miss Adderley."

The car began to move; but Miss Adderley was not to be done out of imparting her choicest bit of gossip. She kept her hand on the side, and actually ran with the car a yard or two, taking quick, trotting steps.

"The latest is—she's had the telephone disconnected because the bell disturbs her! There, what do you think of *that*?" She let go on the last word, and fell back, panting, but triumphant.

"Dreadful!" said Martin over his shoulder. "See you later on."

Miss Adderley clutched at her hat, which was now resting upon her left shoulder. She thrust it back on her head, and saw the car recede. Then she returned to the post office and told Mrs. Brent what a charming man Mr. Fossetter was, and what a pity it was that there were so many stories about him, to which Mrs. Brent replied darkly that it wasn't always the 'andsome ones that was the worst. "There's some that's as ugly as sin, and not a good word to say for no one," she continued, and met the little grey eyes with an innocent stare. Miss Adderley's armour was of triple brass; she gave no sign.

Chloe ran up to her own room, looked in the glass and was grateful with all her heart that she had not met anyone as she came upstairs. This flushed, bright-eyed Chloe could not have escaped a very unwelcome notice. "You can pinch your cheeks to make them pink; but how on earth am I to get pale enough to pass muster with the Wroughtons? It's dreadful—I look happy, and I've got no earthly business to look happy." Then she laughed and tossed her head a

little. "You needn't think that it's *you*, and be conceited about it."—
She was apostrophizing the absent Mr. Fossetter—"It isn't you in the
least, so there! It's just the desert island feeling, and seeing a sail on
the horizon—that's all it is."

If Chloe was right, the "all" still included a good deal. She had
been so starved of common kindness and ordinary friendly ways since
she came to Danesborough; and she was by nature the friendliest
creature in the world. She had not known how lonely and starved she
was until Martin Fossetter looked up from his car and said "Hullo!"
The reaction was one which might carry her far, especially when
stimulated by tender glances, a voice that said her name as no one
else had ever said it, and the prospect of a romantic deliverance.
Martin Fossetter certainly had a good deal in his favour.

Quite suddenly, in the midst of her high spirits, Chloe remembered
the letters. She had locked them last night in the black box; and this
morning, before leaving her room, she had turned the key in the
cupboard door. She locked the door of her room now, and went to
the cupboard a little anxiously. The housemaids must have been
about, and surely even Wroughton would draw the line at forcing the
cupboard door and the lock of her box.

She drew a breath of relief when she found the letters as she had
left them. But the moment's fright made her cast about for a better
hiding place. After racking her brains she could think of only one that
was at all likely to baffle a real search. She unpacked the letters and
carried them into the bedroom. Then she rolled back the mattress and
bedding from the foot of her bed and spread the letters on the spring
mattress beneath.

When the bedding had been tidily replaced, Chloe packed the
box with her clothes and locked it again. Then she went downstairs.
The letters, she thought, would be quite safe now until she had seen
Martin Fossetter. She must of course put them somewhere else before
the housemaids did the room next morning; but in her heart Chloe
hoped ardently that she had slept her last night at Danesborough, and
that by next morning the letters would be out of harm's way for ever.

Chapter Twenty-One

MR. FOSSETTER waited in Langton Lane from four to five with exemplary patience. The sky was dark with clouds, and the light failed rapidly. At five o'clock a rustle, a scramble, and a little gasp announced Chloe's arrival. She became visible as a black shadow on the top of the black wall.

"Mr. Fossetter, are you there?"

Mr. Fossetter climbed the bank.

"Of course I'm here," he said.

"I couldn't get away before, and I simply daren't stay. Emily's been sticking like the worst sort of glue. Well?" The last word was breathlessly eager.

He hesitated, and Chloe beat her hands together.

"Have you done anything? What have you done? Did you go to the telephone exchange? Did you order my taxi?"

"Well, as a matter of fact—"

"Haven't you been? Haven't you ordered it?" Her voice was sharp with dismay. "You don't know what it's like, being cut off like this, and every minute like the longest possible sort of hour."

"Chloe, listen. I went to the exchange at once; and they'll send up a man to-morrow."

"Not to-day?"

"They're short-handed. Then about the taxi—I thought I'd better just see you first. Have you any plans?"

"Yes," said Chloe. "Yes, I'm going back to Maxton—I told you so this morning."

"Chloe, don't be vexed. The fact is—well, I was wondering whether Maxton was the best place for you to go to."

"It's the only place where I've got any friends," said Chloe a little piteously. "I thought I would go and see the Gressons at once, and tell Sir Joseph what has been happening—he's a kind old thing, and I thought he would advise me and be a sort of stand-by."

"The Gressons are abroad," said Martin Fossetter quickly.

"Are they? Are you sure? When did they go?"

"I met them a couple of days ago on their way through town. They've gone to Mentone."

"Well, it can't be helped," she said. "Will you please order that taxi."

"Yes, I'll order it." His tone was a dubious one. "But Chloe, have you thought? Supposing they play this quarantine stunt and won't let it in?"

"It's worth trying. Please, please order it, Mr. Fossetter."

"And if it doesn't come?"

"Then you'll take me to the station, won't you?"

"I'll take you anywhere you want to go—Maxton, London—" He broke off, and then added rather vehemently: "I wish you'd make it London."

"Why?" said Chloe in a very innocent voice.

"Guess!" said Martin. The word shook a little.

Chloe thrilled; and the thought of Maxton became less attractive.

"I must get some work. And I don't know anyone in London; I shouldn't know where to go."

"Work?" said Martin in a puzzled voice. "Why must you get work?" He was aware of Chloe leaning nearer to him. Her words came on a quick, whispering breath; they tumbled over one another a little:

"I can't keep Mr. Dane's money. I can't take it, or keep it, or use it. And I've only got about two pounds of my own; so I must get some work at once, you see,—at once."

"But, my dear girl—"

"There aren't any 'buts'—there aren't really. It's horrible money that I couldn't touch if I were starving."

"Chloe!"

"I can't explain. But there it is—I can't touch it. So you see, I must have some work at once."

"I see." He dropped his voice to a quietly meditative tone. "Now, if you were coming to London, I think I might be useful. My aunt, Lady Wenderby—you've heard of her—, well, she runs all sorts of hostels and girls' clubs, and all that sort of thing, and she'd get you a job in no time. She knows all the ropes, and she could tell you where to go, and the right people to see, and all that."

Everybody in England knew Lady Wenderby's social activities. Chloe was certainly allured.

"I didn't know she was your aunt."

"Well, as a matter of fact she's cousin; but I've always called her Aunt. I wish you'd let me take you to her instead of going to Maxton. I wish—"

But Chloe drew back.

"No, I'll go to Maxton first. But if you'll give me an introduction to her later on, I'd be ever so grateful. Mr. Fossetter, please, *please*, will you order that taxi?"

"And if it doesn't come?—you know, Chloe, I'm afraid it won't come; they won't let it in." He heard her draw her breath in sharply. "Could you be here early, quite early in the morning?"

"Yes, of course. I could get out at six before anyone's about. Could you be here at six?"

"I would stay here all night if it would be any good," said Martin Fossetter in the voice which made Chloe's heart beat. She prepared for flight.

"I must go."

"Chloe," said Martin quickly. "Come with me now! I can't bear your going back. Come with me now!"

Chloe was kneeling on the wall; her hands held the brick coping tightly.

"No, I can't," she said very quickly. "I must bring the letters—I can't leave the letters behind."

"Chloe!" said Martin in the darkness.

"Good-bye," said Chloe. "Six o'clock to-morrow morning—if the taxi doesn't come. If—if it does,—"

"Oh, I'll be at the station," said Martin. He heard her drop down on the other side of the wall.

Chloe ran all the way back to the house, and then had to stand on the terrace to get her breath before going in. There was a little wind that came in gusts, a cold damp wind that promised rain.

She went in reluctantly, and sat in the drawing-room, her ears strained for the sound of wheels, and her fingers busy unravelling a tangle of silks for Emily Wroughton's interminable embroidery.

She was at present engaged in working bright pink flowers, hybrids mercifully unknown to nature, upon a black satin ground. The silks on Chloe's lap were of every shade imaginable. She pulled out strand after strand, and sometimes said "Yes" or "No" when Emily paused in her prattle; but all the time she was listening, listening, until the strained sense mocked her by simulating each expected sound in turn. It was long before she gave up hope. But when the dressing bell rang, and no taxi had arrived, she turned resolutely to her plans for getting out of the house in the darkness next morning.

She went up to bed early, and considered very seriously the question of how to get the letters away. She could get out of the house herself, but she couldn't possibly carry her black school box as far as the kitchen garden; something smaller and handier must be found. There were some suit-cases at the back of her cupboard. They would be better.

She went into the cupboard and switched on the light. The suit-cases were marked with Mr. Dane's initials, and she would not have taken them if she could have thought of any other way of getting the letters away. She chose two of good size, and, by dint of squeezing, got all the letters into them. She couldn't lock the cases, of course, but she fastened the spring catches and did up the straps. Then she stood up and looked about her.

"I must have some clothes, but they'll just have to go in a parcel." In the end she found a small cardboard dress-box which she filled with things that she really could not do without. All the rest of her clothes she packed in the old black box. Then she went to bed, and was asleep almost before she had finished saying to herself, "Five o'clock—I must be sure to wake at five."

It was really on that last word that she passed into sleep, because in the middle of saying it, she saw herself standing in front of an avenue of enormous 5's, hundreds of feet high and glittering like icicles in the sun. She had to walk down the avenue to reach the bottom of Maxton High Street, where she would be quite safe. She began to run, and as soon as she came into the avenue she found that the 5's really were made of ice; a wind blew between them and shook the frost from them in flakes that cut her hands. She was carrying the suit-cases that held the letters, and they got heavier every moment. It was most frightfully cold. She wanted to leave the letters and run away, but she knew she mustn't. If she could only reach the very bright light at the end of the avenue, she would be safe. The light was the arc light outside the railway station at Maxton, and Chloe wanted to reach it more than she had ever wanted anything. She tried to run faster, but her feet would not do what she wanted them to; they stopped and would not move. And just behind her she heard Mr. Dane say in his soft, cold voice, "Don't love anyone. Don't trust anyone. *Never* trust anyone, Chloe."

"Oh!" said Chloe in her dream. It was not a scream, but a struggling, sobbing cry. "Oh!" she said again between sleeping and waking. And then the dream was gone; everything was gone except darkness—and some one moving in the darkness.

Chapter Twenty-Two

CHLOE LAY on her bed in the dark, quite rigid. The fire was out; all the bed-clothes had slipped off on one side, leaving her uncovered. That was why she was so cold. She had had a dream about being cold, and about Mr. Dane. She must have dreamt that some one had moved just now. It couldn't be true, because she had locked her door and put the key under her pillow.

In the darkness by the door somebody moved again. Chloe heard the sound of a quick breath that was very nearly a gasp, and then, in an uneven whisper, her name:

"Miss Dane! Miss Dane!"

Chloe bounced up in bed, full of righteous indignation. All that agony of fear for Emily—Emily who wouldn't scare a fly.

"What on earth—", she began, and made a dive for the lost bed-clothes.

"Ssh," said Emily. "Oh, *please*. Oh, Miss Dane, I must speak to you!"

Chloe put up her hand and switched on the light in the little reading lamp beside her. A rosy glow showed the incongruous figure of Emily Wroughton standing just inside the door and leaning back against it. Her mouse-coloured hair hung down in tightly braided plaits. She wore a dressing-gown of purple ripple-cloth trimmed with cheap Nottingham lace of a yellowish shade. Her face came very near the lace in colour, and her knees shook under her. Quite obviously she was very much frightened.

"Mrs. Wroughton, what is it?" said Chloe. "Are you ill?"

"No—n' no," said Emily. She put her hand to her throat as if she were strangling, and came forward with slow, tottering steps until she reached the bed. She sank upon the floor beside it.

"The light!" she whispered. "Put it out!"

"Mrs. Wroughton!"

"Put it out! He'll see it. He mustn't, *mustn't* know."

"Who'll see it?"

"Leonard," said Leonard's wife. With a sudden spasm she reared herself up, snatched at the switch, and gave a gasp of relief as the glow faded into blackness. "I must speak to you—I simply must." Terror seemed to flow out from her in waves. Chloe felt the touch of it, and shivered a little.

"What on earth's the matter? Has anything happened?" She felt Emily come a little nearer, and knew her to be half kneeling, half crouching against the side of the bed.

"I couldn't bear it any longer—I had to tell you—I *had* to! He'd kill me if he knew, but I couldn't let you—let you go on, and not warn you."

Chloe began to feel afraid.

"What is it?"

Emily sniffed.

"Why—oh, why didn't you open the safe?" she wailed. "They only wanted the papers; and really, you know, they were Leonard's just as much as they were Mr. Dane's. Why didn't you let him have them?"

Chloe put out her hand and took Emily firmly by the shoulder.

"Do you know what those papers were?" she asked in a sort of cold rage.

"No—no. Oh, you're hurting me!"

Chloe actually shook her.

"Then don't, *don't* talk such utter bunkum! And for goodness sake tell me what's upset you so."

Emily drew away, sobbing.

"Oh, how dreadfully unkind you are!—and I'm doing my best, my very best, to help you."

"I'm sorry," said Chloe with sudden repentance. "Look here, I'm most *awfully* sorry if I was rude or hurt you just now. But if you *would* get on with it, and just tell me why you're so upset—"

"Oh, Miss Dane,—" said Emily. She paused, sniffed, and blew her nose. Then, with another gasp, "It's such a dreadful thing, and I don't know how to say it."

"Nonsense!" said Chloe. "I suppose they're not going to murder me?"

"No, no," said Emily, in a quick, scared voice.

"Well then, what is it?"

"It's—it's a plot," said Emily Wroughton under her breath.

"Yes?" said Chloe. "Please go on."

Emily went on in a flurried whisper:

"Leonard thinks that Mr. Dane showed you how to open the safe. And he thinks you've opened it and taken out papers that really belong to him. And—and he thinks that you've burnt some of them; and he wants to stop your burning the rest of them. You see, they really belong to him, and he says they're worth a great deal of money. And, oh, my dear Miss Dane, he means to get hold of them somehow—he does indeed."

"All right," said Chloe, "let him go on and get hold of them."

"Oh, my dear, don't, *don't* talk like that. You're so young, and you don't *know*. That's why I couldn't bear it any longer—I felt that I had to warn you."

"Look here," said Chloe, "don't you think it's time you stopped hinting at all sorts of dreadful things, and just told me straight out whatever it is you've come here to tell me?"

"It's—it's so difficult to begin," said Emily. "I don't think you know what danger you're in."

"Danger?" said Chloe. "Nonsense! What on earth's to prevent my walking out of the house to-morrow and going back to Maxton?"

Emily seemed to choke for a moment.

"Leonard would prevent you—and Dr. Jennings would prevent you," she whispered.

"They couldn't—they wouldn't dare."

"You don't understand. It's so hard to tell you. But I must tell you. Everybody—everybody all round—believes that you're queer in the head. It would be quite easy to stop your getting away."

"What utter rubbish!" said Chloe in angry, heartfelt tones. "How could anyone believe such nonsense?"

"They do," said Emily with trembling insistence. "They all think that you're not—not responsible, and that Leonard and I are looking after you. They think that it's you who has been dismissing most of the servants, and getting rid of the cars, and having the telephone cut off. They think that you've got a craze about infection, and that you believe the house is in quarantine and won't see anyone. Surely you must have noticed that no one has been here—none of your grandfather's old friends or—or even the Vicar. Surely you must have noticed it and thought it very odd?"

"I thought it was because they didn't like Mr. Dane."

"No—no," said Emily, "it's because they think you're mad. Leonard and Dr. Jennings have made them think that you're mad. There isn't anybody who doesn't believe it; and there isn't anybody who would help you to get away."

A very, very comforting vision of Martin Fossetter, and Martin Fossetter's car rose at this moment in Chloe's mind; but even this did not keep her heart from beating rather hard.

"But it's such nonsense—such nonsense," she whispered, and heard Emily's sudden, protesting movement, Emily's quick answer:

"Perfectly sane people have been shut up in asylums before now, Miss Dane."

Chloe's heart beat faster still. It was true; there was a case last year; everybody in Maxton was talking about it. She clutched the bed-clothes about her and fought with panic. Emily was speaking again:

"I had to warn you. Oh, my dear Miss Dane, there's only one thing for you to do, there is indeed."

"What is it?" said Chloe, and hoped her voice was reasonably steady.

"If you could get away at once before they've finished making their plans, and if you could hide, really hide yourself until you're of age—"

"Yes?"

"If they couldn't find you, they couldn't do anything. If you could get away to London and hide, just for two months until you're of age."

"I could go to Mr. Hudson," said Chloe, speaking more to herself than to Emily.

"No. *No!* He's in it too—you mustn't do that. Miss Dane, don't you see that they're all in it together? You must get right away, and hide until you're of age." Emily steadied herself by the edge of the bed, and got to her feet. "I had to tell you. But Leonard would kill me if he knew," she said in a low, hopeless voice. Then she blew her nose violently, bumped against the table, and began to feel her way to the door.

Chloe heard her open it with a last sob. She listened till the door was shut again and she heard the sound of a key withdrawn fumblingly—another key. So that was how Emily had got in. The thought just came and passed as Emily's steps receded. When she could hear nothing more Chloe flung herself down upon her pillow and cried her heart out.

Emily Wroughton went back to her own room with a slow, dragging step. She felt very unhappy indeed. "How wicked I am—how wicked!" she kept saying to herself.

Her room was warm and brightly lighted. Leonard Wroughton stood before the fire in his dressing-gown, waiting. For once his look approved her, and as soon as she had shut the door he laughed and said:

"Bravo, old girl! That was a top-hole performance, and it ought to do the trick."

"Leonard, you listened!"

"Naturally. I couldn't afford to leave anything to chance. I really had no idea that you would be such a star performer."

For an instant Emily sunned herself in the unaccustomed smile. It was such years since Leonard had seemed to like anything that she did. Then that dreadful feeling of wickedness swept over her again.

"Leonard! Leonard, you're not going to harm her! You promised. I wouldn't have done it—you know I wouldn't—if you hadn't promised me that."

Leonard Wroughton laughed again.

"My good Emily—" he began; and then with an ugly sneer, "Why, she stands to get what fortune-tellers promise as their choicest plum."

"What's that?" gasped Emily; her pale eyes widened.

"Why, a handsome husband and ten thousand a year," said Leonard Wroughton.

Emily began to cry.

"It frightens me," she said. "It frightens me dreadfully, for you, and for us all. Leonard, what—*what* will you do if she goes on saying that she won't take the money?"

"I think," said Leonard Wroughton, "that you may trust the handsome husband to see to that. And there are always the letters. I don't mind saying that it was a considerable relief to my mind to know that she's got the bulk of them safe."

Chapter Twenty-Three

CHLOE DID NOT have to wake herself at five after all, because only the most fitful snatches of sleep came to her after she heard Emily lock the door and go away. Her dream, the darkness, and Emily's revelation had shaken her. With the cumulative pressure of lonely days behind them, they had shaken her almost to the point of panic. Time and again she woke from a half doze to find fresh tears upon her cheeks, and a dreadful feeling of fear at her heart.

"Martin—Martin will take me away. They can't do anything, really, because Martin's going to take me away." The thought beat panic back. If it hadn't been for Martin,—no, she mustn't think of that, or the terror would sweep over her again. Martin wouldn't fail her. Only just a few hours, and he would be waiting in the dusk of Langton Lane.

"Oh," said Chloe from the very, very bottom of her heart, "Oh, Martin, I do bless you and bless you."

At five o'clock she decided that the night was really over, and got up. It was, of course, pitch dark—the coldest, darkest hour of all the twenty-four. She dressed quickly, and put on, not the black she had been wearing for Mr. Dane, but her own clothes that she had had at Maxton—the tan woolly jumper, a dark brown coat and skirt, and a long tweed coat to go over all. It was going to be cold in an open car, cold and windy. She found an old brown scarf, and crammed a close-fitting felt hat well down on her head; it was old too, but its bright tan colour suited her.

It was when she looked in the glass that the lurking fear began to pass away and her spirits to rise. And yet the really difficult and dangerous part of her escape was still before her.

At a quarter to six she opened the door, slid the two suit-cases into the passage, and went back for the cardboard box which held her clothes. Then she came out of her room, locked the door, and put the key in her pocket.

The suit-cases balanced each other very well, but the cardboard box was awkward. In the end she tied it to one of the suit-cases with her scarf, and made her way very, very cautiously to the head of the stairs, and from there down into the hall, feeling before her with her foot at every step. She had made up her mind not to attempt to open the front door—"Too many bolts, and bars, and jangly chains and things"—; one of the study windows would be ever so much easier to manage. And manage it she did, with as little sound and as much haste as possible.

From the moment that she got out of the house and into the dark garden with its smell of wet earth, all Chloe's fear left her; she didn't care a bit how dark it was, or how cold. There was an up-rush of hope in her heart as she made haste to meet a new day, new ways—and Martin waiting in the lane.

From the top of the wall she peered down into a pit of gloom; and, before she could speak, Martin spoke from just beneath her:

"Hullo—that you?"

"Yes," said Chloe breathlessly. "Me, and two suit-cases and a cardboard box." She heard him laugh softly.

"What a little brick you are! Here, let me have them."

Chloe handed down the precious suit-cases, dropped the cardboard box, and then proceeded to get over the wall herself. She hung by her hands, Martin steadying her, and then came down with a rush into his arms. Just for a moment she stood there leaning against him, and felt his clasp tighten. Just for a moment the darkness and the silence were full of warmth and light, and the sound of Chloe's beating heart. It was over. She was safe; she had got away. Martin would take care of her now.

"Chloe," said Martin Fossetter. "Chloe!"

But Chloe laughed, slipped away, and scrambled down the bank into the lane.

There was a keen, tingling sense of adventure in the air; the darkness was full of it; the wind that presently blew in their faces was full of it. The car slipped down the lane, swung round two crooked corners, and came out upon the London road. Chloe spoke then:

"I'm not going to Maxton—I'm going to London. But—how did you guess?"

Martin laughed just under his breath.

"I wanted you to so much."

"But how did you know?"

"How does one know anything?"

The car sprang forward as he spoke, and the wind took Chloe's answer away. They were driving straight into the wind, and straight into the dawn. In the dusk the hedge-rows began to show like black walls, and the sky seemed to lift above them. Martin turned the lights off. The long, straight road lay white and empty between the hedges, and away on the horizon pale lines of gold showed like cracks between the grey, low-hanging clouds.

Chloe's heart sang in her as she watched the daylight grow. Neither she nor Martin spoke; but a sense of things unspoken and imminent was upon them both. Presently Martin would make love to her—and if Chloe was not in love with Martin, she was very much in love with love, and youth, and the morning; she was aware of something in her, poised, balanced, waiting for a touch, a breath.

Martin, for his part, was silent because his instinct told him that Chloe needed this silence. He had made more or less serious love to a good many women. To Chloe he made love with a difference. Like the skilled musician who for the first time touches the strings of an instrument finer than any he has yet known, he felt at once expectancy and triumph. Her frank look and confident air; the eager warmth; the sudden, proud withdrawals—these were Chloe. Quickness; simplicity; ready tears and ready smiles; a child's courage and a child's terrors—these were Chloe too.

He sat silent beside her, and thought strange thoughts.

Chapter Twenty-Four

THEIR EARLY START did not land them very early in London. They had breakfast at a road-side cottage which advertised "Cyclists' Teas," and had to be coaxed a good deal before it would rise to eggs and bacon. It was a delicious breakfast, like a breakfast in a fairy tale. Chloe's cheeks were glowing from the wind. She had the brilliant look that some flowers have when the bud is just opening. Martin could not keep his eyes from her, nor hide the spark in them—perhaps he did not try very hard.

"I suppose your aunt *is* in town?" Chloe said suddenly.

"Oh, yes. I saw her a couple of days ago."

"You're sure she wasn't going away?"

"Yes, quite sure."

"You see," said Chloe, "I don't know another soul in London—of course, I don't know her. But—I say, you're sure she won't think it very odd?"

"Why should she?"

Chloe laughed.

"It depends on how well you've brought her up. Of course, if she's used to your just blowing in out of the blue with a stray girl who hasn't got anywhere to go, it's all right; otherwise, you know, she might think it a little odd." One of those April changes came over her face. "Martin, I'm really a little bit frightened."

"You needn't be."

It was an hour later that the car began to labour. Martin got down, fiddled with things that Chloe didn't understand, and presently started her again. She ran draggingly for the couple of miles which took them to the outskirts of Frambleton and a garage.

Martin heaved a sigh of relief.

"I thought we were going to get stuck by the road-side."

"What's the matter?"

"Don't quite know."

Ten minutes later he was being very apologetic: "I'm most awfully sorry, but I'm afraid it means two or three hours. We'll have to have lunch here and push on afterwards."

They touched London at four o'clock; but it was nearly half-past when Martin stopped before an imposing house in a quiet square.

Chloe fought against an overpowering rush of nervousness.

"I won't get out till you've explained," she said, and sat there very upright, waiting for the door to open.

The interminable minute passed; the door opened. Martin stepped inside. Chloe stiffened her back and waited. Idiotic to feel nervous. Nothing to be nervous about. One old lady was very much like another, and she always got on beautifully with old ladies. She had got as far as this in self-admonishment, when Martin ran down the steps. The door of the house shut behind him.

He came round the car, leaned on the side of it close to her, and said in a low, agitated voice:

"Chloe, there's some awful muddle. I feel I've let you down most awfully."

"What is it?"

"She isn't here. I can't understand it at all. I think she must have been called away to one of her daughters—she seems to have gone off quite unexpectedly. The wire that I sent from Frambleton was lying unopened in the hall. The butler thinks she may be back to-morrow. He said they weren't forwarding anything."

Leaning there so close to her, he felt, rather than saw, the quiver that shook her. A street lamp half a dozen yards away made the dusk light enough for him to see her face, all white like a face in a bas-relief, only the eyes very black, and looking at him.

"What shall I do?" she said in a little voice. They might have been on a desert island, the square was so empty.

"Chloe, don't look like that! It's all right—it really is."

Chloe's eyes never moved from his face.

"What shall I do?" she repeated. "Perhaps—perhaps—I'd better go to Maxton after all. I meant to—you know I meant to. But last night—I wasn't going to tell you—Emily Wroughton came into my room, and she frightened me." The pressure of the thing she had not meant to tell him became intolerable; the words came fast on a whisper of sobbing breath. "She *did* frighten me. She said they were going to try and make out that I was mad. She said everybody in Danesborough believed it already. She said"—her hand caught suddenly at his arm—"Martin, they couldn't really, could they?"

He gave a long whistle of dismay.

"So that's it!" he said.

"Do you think they could?—do you think they really could? Emily said I'd better go away and hide till I was of age." She drew her hand away. The relief of speech had been great. "Martin, they couldn't! I think I was silly to be frightened. I think I'll go to Maxton. What do you think?"

Martin spoke gravely, very gravely:

"Chloe, I don't want to frighten you, but I think Mrs. Wroughton gave you pretty good advice—I do really. If you go to Maxton, you're asking for trouble. They'll find you at once, and—you're not of age, you see."

He heard her take a quick breath of dismay. He leaned over the side of the car.

"Chloe, if you'll trust me—." There was a note in his voice that called to her.

She said "Yes"?—and then she shivered because her dream came back, and Mr. Dane's voice saying, "Never trust anyone, Chloe."

Martin's hand came out towards her. She made the first beginnings of a movement. The sense of being alone together, quite alone, deepened. She heard him say her name. And then a taxi swung by, and stopped just ahead of them. Half a dozen children poured out. There was a chatter and clatter of tongues; last directions to the driver from a fussy governess. Chloe drew back and sat up straight, hands clasped about her knee.

Martin's moment had passed. He was too wise to attempt to recapture it. He said instead, "I've got a plan."

"What is it?"

He made a gesture with his right hand.

"We can't talk here. I know a very nice, quiet hotel—the sort of place one's aunts and cousins go to. If you would let me take you there—"

Something in Chloe said "No." Her lips repeated the word just audibly.

"Chloe, why?"

She had to find reasons for what had been purely instinctive; and she had to find them for herself before she could set them up between herself and Martin. Hotels cost money; she hadn't much money. She didn't want to go to an hotel. She didn't quite know why, and came back to the thought of the money. It would cost too much; only she couldn't say that to Martin. The something that had said "No" shrank proudly from the thought that he might offer to lend her money. She gave herself a little shake, and seemed to wake up.

"I don't want to go to an hotel; but I do want a wash, and my tea, and a little time to think. And—aren't we near a station?"

Martin straightened himself.

"Not frightfully near. Why a station?"

Chloe's spirit was coming back.

"I told you why. I want a wash; and I want some tea; and I want to think. Take me to a station, please,—a good big one where they'll be sure to have real hot water."

"Victoria's the nearest," said Martin. "I could take you there. I shall have to garage the car."

He got in as he spoke. That it was quite useless to talk to any woman who confessed to wanting her tea was a fundamental fact brought home to him by an experience that had not lacked variety.

He drove Chloe to Victoria without further protest, merely inquiring what she proposed to do about her luggage.

"I shall put it in the cloak-room; and then, you see, we shall be quite free. I've got just the beginnings of a plan myself—I'll tell you presently."

They fixed a meeting place, and Chloe, standing by her suit-cases, watched the car move out of sight.

The cloak-room first. She made her way there, deposited the suit-cases, hesitated a little over the cardboard box, and finally kept it with her.

A little later she leaned back on the sofa in the ladies' waiting-room, and with the passing reflection that it was nice not to feel so gritty any more, she began to develop the infant plan of which she had spoken to Martin.

Old Nurse had lived in London till about two years ago, when she went out to her son in Australia; she had lived with a married niece. If the niece could be found, and would take Chloe in, it would be much, much cheaper than an hotel. The bother was that she couldn't remember the address. The niece's name was Harriet—Harriet Rowse—and the number was 122. But she couldn't, for the life of her, remember the name of the road. She strained thought to the breaking point, and then suddenly relaxed.

"No good doing that. Perhaps it'll come if I leave it alone. And supposing it doesn't—"

Chloe became aware that she desired intensely to produce a plan of her own. Martin's plan—no, she *didn't* want it; she wanted a plan of her own.

She leaned back, shutting her eyes, letting her thoughts drift. If she couldn't remember the name of that wretched street,—what then? There must be places for girls who had to work;—of course there were places, like Lady Wenderby's hostels. Martin wouldn't know; but they might have asked at the house; someone in the house would have been sure to know. That's what happens when you're frightened—you don't think of things till afterwards, when it's too late.

Then quick as light she thought:

"But it's not too late at all. I can telephone to the house and ask now."

"Now!" Chloe was on her feet at the word. She would just have time to telephone before Martin came back. She crossed the station, entered a telephone box, and looked up the number. Her pennies rattled through the slot, there was a click, and a man was saying "Hullo."

Chloe had decided that her visit to the house with Martin had better be ignored. She asked casually:

"Is Lady Wenderby in?"

The answer came in tones that betrayed surprise:

"Her ladyship is abroad." The last word stood out from the rest of the sentence. Mentally, Chloe stared at it.

"Do you mean that she went abroad to-day?"

"Oh, no, madam. Her ladyship left for the Riviera quite a fortnight ago."

The receiver in Chloe's hand seemed suddenly to be as cold as ice and as heavy as lead. There must be some mistake. There *must* be some mistake.

"You say Lady Wenderby went to the Riviera a fortnight ago?"

"Yes, madam,—to Mentone."

Chloe spoke once again very slowly; her voice seemed to have turned cold and heavy too:

"Do you know when she is coming back?"

"No, madam,—but it won't be for a month or two."

"Thank you," said Chloe. She hung the receiver up, took her cardboard box in her left hand, and walked out upon the platform again.

A train had just come in, and a black stream of people came flowing past. Caught in the swirl of it, she moved on, because just for the moment she had lost the power to think or act for herself. The stream carried her on. It was really only a minute later that she found herself noticing that the girl in front of her had a brown velveteen skirt that draggled at the back and a silk stocking with a hole in it. Chloe saw this, and went on following the girl until she found the outside air blowing cold in her face, and realized that she had come out of the station and was standing on a crowded pavement past which a continuous line of traffic surged.

She stood on the kerb with the string of the cardboard box cutting her wrist, and stared at the traffic—such bright lights, and such a noise; three buses in a string; cars without number; a boy on a bicycle whistling—he had red hair and freckles; another bus, rather empty. It was like watching pictures on the screen at the cinema. Then the policeman on the island in the middle of the street was holding up his hand, and immediately Chloe felt herself pushed forward.

She reached the island, stood still, and became aware that she was trembling from head to foot. Slowly, very slowly, the sensation of being in a dream was passing away. She began to think and to formulate her thoughts in odd, jerky sentences. She must get away. Martin mustn't find her. Martin had told her lies. Why? It didn't matter why. She must get away. She must go to Harriet Rowse. No she couldn't, because she had forgotten the address. It was 122 something. Old Nurse's letters—c/o Harriet Rowse—no, one didn't put that on an envelope—c/o Mrs. Rowse, 122 Hatchelbury Road! Chloe drew in a long breath of damp, petrol-laden air, and found it purely sweet. The horrible dream feeling was gone. And she had remembered Harriet's address.

She turned, and spoke to the big policeman.

"Please, can you direct me to Hatchelbury Road?"

Chapter Twenty-Five

"Is Mrs. Rowse at home, please?" said Chloe. Hatchelbury Road was very dark and very dingy. The open door of No. 122 disclosed worn yellowish linoleum on the floor, and steep stairs that ran upwards into darkness. A little girl in a dingy overall stood on the linoleum and peered up at Chloe. The only light came from the half-open door at the end of the very narrow passage. There was a heartening smell of cabbage, onions, oilcloth, and herrings.

"Is Mrs. Rowse at home?"

"Ow, yes."

"Can I see her?"

The little girl fidgeted from one foot to the other, sniffed, and looked back over her shoulder.

"Mrs. Rowse, 'ere's a lidy to see yer."

The half open door opened a little wider. A large woman appeared, wiping her hands on her apron. The little girl vanished, leaving Chloe with the impression of a piercing voice and a high, bony forehead. Mrs. Rowse came forward, ponderous, breathing heavily.

"Mrs. Rowse," said Chloe in a quick, timid voice, "I've come to you because I don't know anyone else in London."

"You've come to the wrong shop if you want money," said Mrs. Rowse, still drying her hands.

The brutal directness of the words brought Chloe's head up.

"It's not a question of money," she said quietly. "Your aunt, Mrs. Beeston, must have spoken of me."

"Mrs. Beeston is in Australia," said Mrs. Rowse in the same hard, unmodulated voice which she had used before. "She's in Australia, and if she owes you money, you must write to her about it, for I'm not responsible for other folks' debts."

Chloe could have slapped her. It was, in fact, a temptation—those huge bare arms, those large pale cheeks, so eminently slapable.

"It's nothing to do with money." She raised her voice as if she were speaking to somebody who was deaf. "It's nothing *whatever* to do with money. It's—it's—Mrs. Rowse, I'm Chloe Dane. You must have heard Nurse speak of me."

"Mrs. Beeston is in Australia," said Mrs. Rowse without moving.

Chloe lost her temper.

"Of course she's in Australia. What's the good of keeping on saying so? What I want to know is, can you give me a room?—can you take me in for the night? I can pay," she added with a tap of the foot that was nearly sharp enough to be called a stamp.

Mrs. Rowse went on looking at her, and just as Chloe was about to burst into speech again, she said:

"You'd better come in. I dunno about a room; but you'd better come in." She wheeled round, opened a door which Chloe had not noticed, and led the way into a dark room, where she presently lighted a singly noisy gas-jet.

The room was the regulation parlour, or, as Mrs. Rowse called it, "me droring-room." There was a pair of blue and gilt vases on the mantelpiece. They appeared to be like trees growing up from a dense undergrowth of photographs, amongst which Chloe with a curious sensation recognized one of herself taken nearly three years before; it was encased in a frame of massive gilt. Mrs. Rowse picked it up, held it to the light, looked broodingly at it, and then turned her dark, protruding eyes on Chloe. After a moment she nodded.

"Yes, it's you," she said. "And you'll please to excuse me for being pertickler. She left it behind by mistake; and half a dozen times I've meant to send it off. When I had the money, I forgot it; and when I remembered it, I hadn't got the money." She gave a short, hoarse laugh. "Lucky I didn't send it, seems to me." She put it down, and once more fixed her eyes on Chloe. "What's a young lady like you want with a room in a house like mine? You're Miss Dane right enough; and if you're Miss Dane, you know as well as I do that this isn't no place for you."

Chloe met the look with a smile.

"Oh, Mrs. Rowse, you're going to take me in, aren't you? I came to you because Nurse used to talk about you such a lot, and I knew I'd be safe here. And—and you will take me in, won't you?"

"There isn't nobody in London that can say that I'm not respectable. I'm a respectable woman, and my house is a respectable house, and no one can say different—you're right enough there."

Chloe smiled again; it was the coaxing smile of a child.

"Yes, I *know*. That's why I came. You'll take me, won't you?"

Mrs. Rowse folded her arms and stood like a rock.

"If you can pay," she said—"cash down, and a week in advance."

"How much will it be?"

Mrs. Rowse considered. Chloe's shoes were old, her hat shabby, her tweed coat by no means new. She pressed her lips together for a moment, then licked them and said, "Fifteen shillings, Miss Dane."

From Danesborough to Hatchelbury Road was a long, strange step. On the whole, Chloe preferred Hatchelbury Road. If the physical atmosphere was a trifle heavy with cabbage and gas, the mental atmosphere was a good deal less oppressive.

Mrs. Rowse disclosed herself as "not a bad old sort." She was grasping, but she was strictly honest, and she worked very hard. Mr. Rowse was a porter at Victoria. A son of nineteen, the joy and pride of Mrs. Rowse's heart, was also a porter. The other occupants of the house were the little girl, Maudie Marsh, and her mother, a wispy widow who went out charing and was in some inexplicable manner related to Mr. Rowse's step-mother, a lady often referred to but never seen.

Chloe had a little room, and a bed so hard that it would have been a trial to one of the Seven Sleepers. The bed had greyish twill sheets and two very thin, frayed blankets. Chloe slept in it with a sense of safety which Danesborough had not given her. She was ready enough to sleep when night came, for her days were spent walking about all over London looking for work. She went from agency to agency, applied for innumerable situations, and at the end of a week had spent time, money, and energy, all to no purpose. The time and energy did not matter so much, for she had plenty of both; but the money began to matter most dreadfully. Fifteen shillings paid in advance for the first week, and a second fifteen shillings for the week to come—that was thirty shillings gone from her two pound ten, without reckoning food and fares. The fifteen shillings included breakfast, but there were other meals. Naturally she walked as much as she could; but walking made you so desperately hungry, and she had only one pair of shoes. The question of how much shoe leather a penny bus fare might be expected to save occupied her a good deal. Then there was the question of the suit-cases which she had left in the cloak-room at Victoria. Those horrible letters—what was she to do about them? Useless to bring them to Hatchelbury Road, where she had no means of destroying them. Chloe blenched at what Mrs. Rowse would say if she asked permission to burn several hundred letters in the kitchen fire. On the other hand, were they safe at Victoria?

She sought counsel of Mr. Rowse, a burly, kindly soul, and enquired anxiously whether a box would, in any circumstances, be given up to anyone who could not produce the receipt for it. Mr. Rowse was comfortably definite on the subject; his considered opinion was, "Not much, it wouldn't; but you'll have a deal to pay if you leave it there long."

Chloe decided to leave the cases where they were. She also decided to stop thinking about them.

A thick curtain seemed to have come down between her and all the world that she had known before. She tried not to look behind the curtain, because Martin Fossetter was there, and the day that she had driven with him from Danesborough. She could not always help looking back. All that day Martin had made love to her, not in words, but with every look and every inflection of his voice. All day Chloe had trembled on the edge of response. When she reached this point in her thoughts, there came up from the very bottom of her heart a most fervent "Thank God I *didn't* care." She had so nearly cared, so very nearly; and he had lied to her.

Emily Wroughton's words came back. "Oh, Miss Dane, can't you understand that they're all in it together?" Was that the explanation? Wroughton, Jennings, Hudson, and Martin, all in it together. No good thinking of it. Drop the curtain and look on to the fifth of February when she would be twenty-one—the fifth of February more than two months off. And her money would last a week with care!

Chloe tackled Mrs. Rowse.

"Mrs. Rowse, there must be jobs to be got. I've got to *have* a job, you know. Don't you know of anything I could do?"

They were in the kitchen; Mrs. Rowse was mending socks with astonishing rapidity; Chloe was sitting on the edge of the kitchen table swinging her feet.

"Gracious, how awful my shoes are getting!" she thought, and repeated, "Mrs. Rowse dear, I simply *must* have a job."

"Not many jobs going for a young lady like you," said Mrs. Rowse. "My heart alive! Albert do come heavy on his heels!"

The sock into which she had rammed her enormous fist certainly showed more fist than heel.

"Mrs. Rowse *dear*, I'm not a young lady. It's a most frightful handicap to be a young lady. I'm just a girl, a poor, plain, ordinary, honest, respectable girl."—Mrs. Rowse made the sort of snorting sound which is usually written "Umph."—"Do just glue tight on to that, and tell me what an ordinary, respectable girl can do to earn an honest living."

"Gels," said Mrs. Rowse, "used to go into service—it's gone out of fashion, but they used to. The point is, what about a character?—excusing me for naming it, Miss Dane."

"I *know*," said Chloe. "I've got a lovely character. But I told you I don't—I don't exactly want anyone to know where I am just now; so I can't very well *produce* the character, can I?"

Mrs. Rowse's needle went in and out, in and out.

"Then service isn't any good. Those that'll take a gel without a character hasn't got too much character themselves. A gel's got to be careful where she goes—especially a pretty one." She looked severely at Chloe for a moment, and added, "If you was plain, it'ud be a lot easier."

"I should hate to be plain," said Chloe with a beaming smile. "Dear Mrs. Rowse, *do* think of something. You see if I don't get a job, I can't pay you after this week—and I know you're much too kind-hearted to turn me out into the street."

Mrs. Rowse snorted again.

"You ought to go back to your friends, you ought," she said. "I don't hold with young gels running away and hiding. And what's the use of your saying you're not a young lady, when anyone can see the length of Hatchelbury Road in the dark that you are? If you was really a plain, ordinary gel, why I suppose there's a job you could have to-morrow. But you're not, and you couldn't do it."

Chloe slipped off the table.

"Mrs. Rowse, how frightfully exciting! What is it? Tell me at once! It's no use saying I couldn't do it, because I'd do *anything*."

Mrs. Rowse looked up. The heavy creases round her mouth conveyed an impression of amusement touched with scorn; there was class-consciousness in the air.

"You wouldn't go out charing," she said in her heavy, decided voice.

Chloe stamped.

"Wouldn't I just? I should char beautifully."

"What?—scrub?" said Mrs. Rowse. "Boiling water and soda in a bucket, and you on your hands and knees with a scrubbing brush?" She gave the short, hoarse laugh which reminded Chloe vaguely of a motor omnibus starting up.

Chloe gurgled.

"But I should love it—I really should. What does one get paid for doing it?"

"Tenpence an hour. You couldn't do it, I tell you."

"You don't know what I can do. Tell me—tell me more at once! Tenpence an hour sounds lovely."

Mrs. Rowse hesitated, caught Chloe's eye, and was lost.

"Mrs. Marsh is took bad, and can't go to the lady that she obliges regular three times a week. To-morrow's one of her days."

"Joy!" said Chloe. "I don't mean about poor Mrs. Marsh. Of course I'm frightfully sorry if she's ill; but I *do* so want a job." She clapped her hands and laughed.

Mrs. Rowse looked at her with disapproval; her eyes fairly bulged with it.

"I could lend you a napron," she said.

Chloe kissed her.

Chapter Twenty-Six

AT NINE O'CLOCK next morning Chloe rang the bell of Miss Marcia Hayman's flat, and had it opened to her by the kind of cook who is nearly extinct.

"Good morning," said Chloe; and instantly a high, worried voice called from somewhere inside the flat:

"Mrs. Western, is that Mrs. Marsh? Tell her to be sure not to tilt my mirror like she did last time."

Mrs. Western nodded the head with the neatly parted grey hair.

"We was expecting the charwoman," she explained.

Chloe dived at the opening.

"Yes, I know. But she's ill—she can't come. I've come instead. I've got a note from her."

Mrs. Western's round, rosy face took on a subtle change of expression.

"Step inside," she said. Then, taking the note, she left Chloe standing in the hall and disappeared through a half open door on the right.

Chloe heard voices; Mrs. Western's and the high, worried one; snatches of words, "In the hall—I'd better see her—hope she won't break things—so careless"; and on the last word Miss Hayman came out from what was evidently the dining-room. A table-napkin hung down over one arm, and she had the pinched features and the worried look which went with the worried voice.

"Oh, good-morning," she said, and blinked at Chloe out of pale blue eyes that had pink rims and sandy lashes. Her bobbed hair, a couple of inches too long, was grey, with sandy streaks in it. "Er—good-morning. Are you—er, experienced, and—er, very careful? I hope—I mean, things do get broken so dreadfully, and—er, the paint is all quite new." She paused with a bewildered look, rubbed her pale, thin nose with her forefinger, and without waiting for an answer to any of her questions, half turned and began to call, "Mrs. Western! Mrs. Western!"

Chloe said firmly, "I'm very careful."

But Miss Hayman only rubbed her nose again, and, murmuring "Mrs. Western will show you what to do," drifted back into the dining-room, dropping the table-napkin as she went.

Chloe plunged into the mysteries of charing.

It is a fact that some women really like housework. Chloe discovered herself to be one of them. So nice to see things coming clean; so nice to find confusion, and leave order in its place; so really amusing to polish beautiful furniture until it shone like dark water. It was hard work of course; but Chloe's youth and strength, which had fretted in idleness, rejoiced at the very hardness.

There was a half-way break when she and Mrs. Western drank tea and ate bread and cheese in the spotless kitchen. Mrs. Western ate the cheese from the point of a knife: Chloe took it in her fingers. Each had a secret thought on the subject. Chloe's, "How dangerous. I've never seen anyone do it before"; and Mrs. Western's, "A likely girl; but, lor, what a bringing up, to eat cheese with her fingers!"

Chloe was very grateful for the cheese, and polished with new zest and efficiency. At one o'clock Mrs. Western paid her half-a-crown, and she put on her coat and hat.

When she emerged into the hall, she was aware of Miss Hayman at the telephone. As it had been fitted into the angle of the wall between the hall door and the dining-room, it was impossible for Chloe to leave the flat without disturbing a lady who looked as if she would be rather easily disturbed. She drew back into the kitchen therefore, and waited whilst Miss Hayman's high-pitched voice made every word of her conversation audible.

"No! Not really?" she was saying with almost tearful intensity. "How *could* she? Oh, my dear Leila, that's *rather* strong language. But of course—yes, yes, my dear, I *know*—to have your secretary go off at a moment's notice just because her fiancé—oh, Leila, don't! Yes, yes, to be sure, all those lists to be checked. Are you sure you can't put your hand on anyone? No, I'm afraid I don't—that is—no, no, I don't know anyone who would take it on at a minute's notice."

Chloe came into the hall with a rush.

At the other end of the line Mrs. Mostyn Llewellyn was aware of a confused exclamation, after which the line went dead and she said "Damn!" several times with a good deal of emphasis.

Miss Hayman left the receiver dangling, and blinked aghast at Chloe. A young person, a charwoman, rushing out on one, interrupting! What was the world coming to? Bolshevism—sheer Bolshevism! She blinked at it and rubbed her nose.

"I'm so sorry," said Chloe, breathless and ingratiating, "but I couldn't help hearing what you said. But do you, does anyone want a secretary?"—Miss Hayman gasped—"I couldn't help hearing—I couldn't; you, you've got such a splendid telephone voice. And I do want a secretary's job frightfully badly."

A secretary's job—a charwoman! It was really very confusing. Miss Hayman caught Chloe's smile, and really saw her for the first time.

"It's not for myself," she said. "It's my friend, Mrs. Mostyn Llewellyn. She's getting up the big ball for the N.Y.S.Z.K.U.—you must have heard of it—the ball, I mean—the papers full of it—Royalty going and all. And to-day, at the eleventh hour, her secretary—I mean Mrs.

Mostyn Llewellyn's secretary—she's the Honourable Mrs. Mostyn Llewellyn, you know, and—dear me, where had I got to?"

"You'd got to the secretary," said Chloe firmly. "What did she do?"

"Failed her—failed us at the eleventh hour. I'm so interested in the N.Y.S.Z.K.U., you know. Yes, she's failed us. And there are all the lists to check. And, as Leila says, with the ball to-morrow, how can she fill her place?"

"She's quite forgotten who she's speaking to," thought Chloe. "I must have that job—I *must*."

"I think I could do it—I do really," she said aloud. "If you'll call up Mrs. Mostyn Llewellyn and tell her I'm coming, I'll go and see her at once. Just ring up and tell her that I'm here, and that I'm sure I could help her out."

Miss Hayman turned meekly to the telephone. Her impressions of a Bolshevist charwoman had given place to an insistent actuality. Chloe, smiling, sparkling, with the manner and voice of her own world, impressed her as being competent, as being, perhaps, just what Leila wanted.

"I don't—I don't think I know your name," was her only protest.

Chloe picked out her second Christian name and altered one letter of her surname.

"Mary Dene," she said.

Mrs. Mostyn Llewellyn had a much larger and more opulent flat than her friend Miss Hayman. She was also a much larger and more opulent person. She came into the room where Chloe was beguiling a five minutes' wait by gazing at some very up-to-date furniture, a long way after Heppelwhite. The chairs and table combined grey, unpolished walnut with scarlet paint. One might have said, "Heppelwhite in a nightmare."

Mrs. Mostyn Llewellyn was quite as up-to-date as her furniture. She wore a black marocain garment that ended just below the knee and resembled a chemise that was a good deal plainer than chemises are wont to be. Beneath it one divined the sternest control of a figure naturally too generous for the fashion. Her dark-red shingled hair had the appearance of having been kept under a glass case until just the moment before; the most unbridled imagination could not

133 | THE BLACK CABINET

have pictured any disturbance of its perfect wave. Nevertheless, Mrs. Llewellyn was plainly in a state of distraction. She carried a sheaf of papers in one hand, and held a fountain pen in the other.

"Miss Green?" she said.

"Dene," said Chloe.

"What does it matter? Are you from Miss Hayman? Are you the secretary she told me of? *Are* you the secretary she told me about?"

"I am," said Chloe, and nerved herself for a glorious game of bluff.

She might have spared herself the trouble. Mrs. Mostyn Llewellyn thrust the papers and the fountain pen upon her, took her by the arm, and said in a deep contralto voice:

"Thank heaven! Come along and get to work on these lists at once. No, not in here—they'll be laying lunch. My *devil* of a secretary failed me because her fiancé had had a motor smash—and the ball's to-morrow! I'll give you lunch, but you can put in half an hour first."

Talking all the time, she ushered Chloe into a room that contained a littered writing-table. When she had explained very rapidly what Chloe was to do, she departed, stopping at the door to say:

"For goodness sake get the names right, Miss Green."

"Dene," said Chloe politely but firmly.

Chloe got back to Hatchelbury Road at half past ten. She was exhausted but joyful. She met Mrs. Rowse's gloomy disapproval with a flood of light-hearted chatter:

"I've simply written my fingers off—after scrubbing too, you know. And I've mugged up the proper way to address everybody out of Debrett—thrilling! Aren't titles lovely, Mrs. Rowse dear?—written out full on envelopes, you know. The Viscountess Kafoozlum; The Marquis of Carabas; The Lady Capadocia Mount Ararat. It's like a lovely, muddled dream of history, geography, and the best fairy tales. But I wish I'd got a spare hand."

"There's lots that don't hold with titles nowadays," said Mrs. Rowse heavily. "Albert don't for one. And I've kept you a cup of tea—but it's stewed."

"Angel!" said Chloe. "Why doesn't Albert hold with titles?"

"Me and Mr. Rowse don't trouble ourselves—there's only a drain of milk, but you can take two lumps of sugar. Albert's young, and what

I've noticed is, young people always want to set the world to rights—gels are as bad as boys. Now I'll lay you've run away because you think you know better than some that's lived twice as long as you have."

Chloe nodded.

"Lovely hot tea!" she murmured. "May I have three lumps of sugar? I want one to crunch."

"And my advice is, you eat humble pie, and go back to your friends."

"What?—when I've just got a job? Never!" said Chloe. She crunched the lump of sugar with decision. "And look here, I haven't told you half how exciting it is. Prepare for thrills, real thrills"—she made a noble gesture with the empty cup—"I'm going to be Cinderella for the second time in my life. I'm going to the ball."

A gleam of interest sparkled for a moment in Mrs. Rowse's disapproving eyes. It was instantly subdued.

"Lor, how you do run on!—and time we were all in our beds."

"Albert isn't in," said Chloe firmly. "And you know you wouldn't dream of going to bed whilst he's out. I expect his club is having a frightfully exciting time settling just how they'll share everything out when we're all Communists. He's going to teach me to sing 'The Red Flag' so as to be all ready. I shall tell him I've been simply wallowing in titles all day; and to-morrow I'm going to mingle, absolutely *mingle* with an effete aristocracy. He'll be frightfully shocked! Mrs. Mostyn Llewellyn is going to lend me a nice, plain black dress. I do hope it'll cover my knees, because the one she had on didn't cover hers, not really. And I shall see all the people come in—the ball is at The Luxe. And I'm to have a little table in the vestibule and take all the tickets. And every fiftieth person gets a prize—the prizes are lovely. I'm looking forward to it most awfully."

"I don't hold with balls," said Mrs. Rowse in a tone of un-relieved gloom.

Chapter Twenty-Seven

CHLOE LOOKED at herself in the glass in Mrs. Mostyn Llewellyn's spare room, and shook with laughter. The room was emerald green: carpet, floor, walls, ceiling, and furniture. The bedstead had gold knobs and a black eiderdown with gold dragons on it. Chloe was the only other black thing in the room.

She gazed at herself in Mrs. Mostyn Llewellyn's nice, plain black frock, and fell back against the emerald bedstead gurgling:

"It's perfectly, perfectly square; and I expect she paid guineas, and guineas, and guineas for it."

The frock had, in fact, every side equal to every other side. It just touched Chloe's knees coyly. There were no sleeves. Two other Chloes could have squeezed into its ample width. Chloe whisked round, saw her back, and went into fresh convulsions.

"What on earth would Ally have said to this?" She made a face at herself in the glass. "Cinderella up to date! Pouf! I don't like it very much. The shoes at least fit me. But the frock! Oh, I do hope to goodness I shall never weigh thirteen stone—and it would certainly take thirteen stone to fill it. Now have I got *all* the ink off my fingers?" She took a hurried look at them, remembered that she had been given ten minutes to dress, snatched her coat from a fantastic chair, and waved good-bye to her reflection.

A door opened. Mrs. Mostyn Llewellyn was calling her:

"Miss Green! Miss Green!"

"Dene," murmured Chloe automatically, and fled.

The Gold Room at The Luxe was empty when Chloe came into it. Its floor, the best dancing floor in London, shone like water, and like water, took and threw back the reflection of the gold dome and golden walls. Chloe felt like a little black fly in a room that had come straight out of an Arabian Night's Entertainment.

"I'm *really* Cinderella, and I haven't got any business in this fairy story—that's why I feel so queer," she decided, and made haste back to the table where she was to sit and take the tickets.

The lounge of The Luxe, like the Gold Room, has a note of oriental extravagance. In the day-time it is even a little ridiculous, with its ceiling of brilliant blue, its couches upholstered in sapphire velvet, and its great, gilded pillars. But at night, and as a setting for a ball, the brilliant background has its effect.

Chloe's table had been set in the lounge, just where the great double archway lined with mirrors gives access to the Gold Room. She felt very small and insignificant as she sat there waiting for the people to arrive. A momentary wave of depression crept over her. It wasn't nice to feel so small and alone. She would rather be Cinderella in the kitchen at Hatchelbury Road than here at The Luxe in Mrs. Mostyn Llewellyn's horrible dress, with that lovely dancing floor so near—she could see part of it reflected in the mirrors that lined the archway. Presently she would see other people swing by to all those tunes which make you feel as if you could dance to the end of the world and beyond it.

"Idiot!" said Chloe to herself. "Stop it this moment! You're going to have a most exciting evening, and see everybody who is anybody. Only I do wish they'd roll up—I do hate waiting for people."

Twenty minutes later she was breathlessly taking tickets, assisted by a young lady from the booking office, whose golden hair, general efficiency, and remarkable flow of conversation fairly staggered Chloe. Whilst checking off the first fifty tickets, she informed her that she lived at Tooting with a widowed aunt, and found it rather slow, and if it wasn't for her boy—

"After all what I say is this—twenty-five, twenty-six, twenty-seven—if a young lady—no, you've given me two together—what was I saying? Well, after all, it comes to this, if you've got a boy you like, and you go out with him in the evening, it doesn't matter so much where you live—thirty-nine, forty—Aunt's a bit dull; but I'm not there much, and there's something in being able to say that you live with your people. You know what I mean, dear; it gives you a sort of standing. Here, we're just on fifty. Have you got that badge all ready? I wouldn't mind having one of those prizes myself—would you? Fifty!" she announced, and nudged Chloe with her elbow.

Chloe picked up a little gilt badge from a pile on her left, and handed it across the table to the dark, sallow young man who had just given in his ticket.

"What's this?" he said, and stared; he had dull, unhappy eyes.

Chloe explained:

"Every fiftieth guest gets a prize. The prizes will be drawn for after supper. The badge entitles you to draw for one."

"Oh," drawled the dark young man. He looked discontentedly at the badge, stuck it in his button hole, and strolled through the mirrored archway into the room beyond.

"Lord Algernon Du Pré," said the young lady from Tooting—"and I don't think much of him, nor any reason to either, if all they say about him's true. I don't suppose it is though, for there's nothing that people won't say. Only last Sunday my boy told me that a young lady we both know—Florrie Summers her name is, and she's cashier at Watson and Lobbs'—well, she'd told him—my boy, Ernie West, you know—she told him that she'd seen me with her own eyes driving in a motor car with a gentleman that no girl *would* be driving with if she thought anything of herself at all. 'All right, Ernie,' I said, 'you can believe her, or you can believe me. It's not for me to say why she should be set on getting you to believe lies about me. But if you take up with her, you've done with me—and I hope you won't live to regret it.' " The stream of words flowed on without a break, though the voice occasionally dropped to a faint, sibilant whisper. During the arrival of the seven or eight hundred guests Chloe learned that "a girl might just as well be dead as not keep up her proper pride," and that once you let a gentleman friend get the upper hand, he is apt to behave as if his word was law, "which it isn't and never will be—not with me."

Chloe gave out her gilt badges to every fiftieth person who presented a ticket. She had just given one, and Connie Cross at her side was remarking that she wouldn't be seen dead at a pig fair in the dress worn by the recipient, when suddenly she felt her heart stand still.

There was a lull in the arrivals. The lounge had cleared, and she could see the whole length of it. At the far end a man was standing alone, a tall man with his back to Chloe. Her heart jumped, and went on, beating hard. Why had she thought for a moment that the man was—was—? He turned, and her heart stopped again.

It was Martin Fossetter. Two women and another man had joined him. They all came forward together, talking and laughing.

With a whirl of her hand Chloe swept all the gilt badges on to the floor. She knelt behind the table picking them up whilst Connie took the tickets. And, kneeling there, she heard Martin speak:

"My luck's clean out—no prize for me," he said. He laughed, and passed on.

Chloe came up scarlet, her hands full of the little gilt badges.

"My! How easily you do flush!" said Connie Cross.

Chloe stared through the archway, watching the dancers. Presently Martin came into view. He was dancing with six-foot of elegance in a wisp of white ninon, the tallest, slimmest creature Chloe had ever beheld. The couple turned, and by looking into the mirror she could follow them a little farther—Martin's dark eyes with the look of devotion in them; and then, as they turned again, the tall woman's face, small and white above her white dress, with big blue eyes looking out mistily from under a straight-cut fringe of hair as fine and flaxen as a baby's.

"Know who that tall woman is?" said Connie Cross at her ear— "Here, you'll want another badge in a minute; there are a lot of people coming late—They call her a beauty, but what I say is, what's the good of all those extra inches unless you're going to be a mannequin; then, I grant you, it does give you a pull. But in any other line, what's the good of it? And I don't know that gentlemen admire it so much after all—Ernie doesn't, for one. Why I pointed her out to him in the Park one Sunday, and what d'you think he said?" She giggled in anticipation, and patted her hair. "Why, he said she put him in mind of a line to hang clothes on—sarcastic, wasn't it?" She thrust a plump left hand under Chloe's eyes.

"That's his ring—not that we're engaged; but I wear it. You see I was engaged—not to him—; and when you've worn a ring for a year, your finger feels sort of funny without it. Alfred Mendelbaum, the other one's name was—in a jeweller's business, so of course the ring was a better one than Ernie's—but, I couldn't stand him being so jealous."

"Was he?" said Chloe absently. Her eyes were on the mirror.

"*Was* he! Why, I couldn't so much as look the side of the road where Ernie was without having a scene." Her voice went on unceasingly.

Chloe watched the mirror. Martin came into it again, Martin and the tall woman.

"Who is she?" she said, turning suddenly to Connie.

"I said to him, 'Take back your ring!'—who?—her?—didn't I tell you?—I thought I did—about Ernie and the clothes line. That's Lady Alexander St. Maurice. You wouldn't think he'd be so sarcastic to look at him."

The figures danced out of the mirror and were gone. Chloe dug her nails into the palms of her hands. The curtain that had fallen between her and Danesborough had been torn in two. Through the rent she saw Martin and the letters; Mr. Dane's endorsement, "Two letters from Lady Alexander St. Maurice"; that blotted signature, "Your broken-hearted Judy."

Chapter Twenty-Eight

CHLOE FELT very tired before the ball was over. It is a fact that it is a great deal more fatiguing to watch other people dancing than to dance oneself. Chloe could have danced all night, even in Mrs. Mostyn Llewellyn's shoes; but to look on, to watch all these people whom she did not know, and every now and then to see Martin pass—Martin whom she had thought she knew so well—this was altogether another thing.

Connie departed at midnight, yawning frankly:

"All very well for those who can have their sleep out, but I've got to get up at seven as per usual. So long, dear. I'm sorry for you having to stay till the end, but I suppose it's all in the day's work." She turned back to add, "Mind you get paid for your overtime—that's a thing you have to be as sharp as sharp about."

When the last guest had departed, Chloe came down the steps of The Luxe, and began her walk to Hatchelbury Road—it had not occurred to Mrs. Mostyn Llewellyn to ask how her secretary would get home. Chloe knew the way, but she was not prepared for the streets being quite so deserted as they were. She had only seen London all stir and bustle; and now that the roar of the traffic was gone, and the pavements empty, there was something strange and oppressive about the silence and the loneliness. Every now and then a belated car went by. Every now and then she passed a policeman on his beat.

She had been walking for about ten minutes when she first heard the footstep. Some one was walking in the same direction as herself, but a little way behind her and on the other side of the road. She came to a corner, turned, and walked on briskly. It was nice to be out in the open air after all those hours in the overheated lounge. Earlier in the night it had rained; the pavements were dark and wet, the air very soft and still.

Chloe heard the footstep again; it was right behind her now, on the same side of the street, coming up fast in spite of her quickened pace. She began to feel, not frightened, but angry. Instead of hurrying, she fell into a slower walk in order to let the person behind her pass on. Without looking, she was aware that it was a man. Midway between two lamps he came up with her and spoke her name:

"Chloe!"

In the darkness Chloe's cheeks burned with the anger which flared in her at the sound of Martin Fossetter's voice.

"Chloe! Thank God, I've found you! Where have you been?"

Chloe walked as far as the next lamp before she answered. There, under the light, she turned on him, bright-eyed and flushed.

"You've no right to speak to me! You've no right to follow me! I don't ever want to see you again!"

He put out a protesting hand.

"But, Chloe—"

"I don't know how you dare," said Chloe with her head well up.

"Chloe, you don't know what I've been through. I came back to the station and found you gone. I didn't know what to think—I was in an agony about you. In the end I rushed down to Danesborough in case Wroughton—When I found you weren't there I went on to Maxton. And when I saw you to-night—well, you don't know what a relief it was."

One of Mrs. Mostyn Llewellyn's shoes tapped the pavement sharply.

"Look here," said Chloe, "it's no *use*. You told me lies, and I found you out."

"Lies?"

"Yes, lies," said Chloe. She was walking on again, and spoke without looking at him. "Just plain lies. You told me Lady Wenderby was in town—you told me you had seen her two days before. Well, when you had gone to garage the car, I rang up the house because I thought somebody there would be able to tell me of a hostel I could go to. And when I rang up I found that Lady Wenderby had been in Mentone for a fortnight, and wasn't expected back for another two months. I don't know why you lied to me, and I don't want to know. Now will you please go away, because I don't ever want to see you again."

"I suppose," said Martin Fossetter in his quiet, charming voice, "I suppose it didn't occur to you that there might be two Lady Wenderbys?"

Chloe stamped again.

"No, it didn't—and there aren't. As a matter of fact, when I was going through all those tickets with Debrett yesterday, I thought I'd just make sure—and there's only one Lady Wenderby." Her voice broke in an angry sob. "How could you do such a perfectly horrible thing? Please go away, please go away at once! I don't ever want to see you again!"

"Chloe," said Martin, "don't take it like that. I was a fool, but I swear, I *swear*, I never meant you anything but good. I care for you more than I care for anyone else in the world. I want to marry you more than I want anything in the world. I was a fool not to tell you straight out that my aunt was away. The truth is—"

Chloe laughed.

"The truth!"

"Yes, the bed-rock truth. And that is that I was scared to death for you. Wroughton's a horribly dangerous man. You were set on going back to Maxton; and I knew you wouldn't be safe there. I was every sort of fool you like to call me, but it was because I cared so much. I wanted you to come to London—I wanted you to turn to me for help. Chloe, you know, you *know*, that I love you."

Chloe's heart beat furiously. A car came slowly up the road behind them, turned the corner just ahead, and was gone.

"Chloe, you *know*," said Martin Fossetter. His voice was full of a deep tenderness; his hand touched her arm.

"I don't," said Chloe. "How can I? I trusted you, and you let me down—that's what I know."

"I've been an utter, damned fool," said Martin. "But I love you, Chloe, I love you. If you don't believe anything else, you must believe that."

Chloe wheeled round on him with a sort of fierce decision.

"Look here," she said, "it's no good. I don't want you to say these things to me. They *might* have meant something, and they don't mean anything. I don't want to hear them. I want you to go away."

She put out her hands as if she were pushing something from her.

The street was empty from end to end, the houses curtained, dark, indifferent. Martin caught the outstretched hands in his.

"Ah, but you shall believe me. There's something between us— Chloe, you know there is—, something that calls from me to you, and something in you that answers. Chloe, don't you feel it?—don't you feel it now?"

Chloe felt his hands burn on hers. She felt a wave of glamour beat against her resistance; and she saw Martin's face, darkly agitated, very near her own. She wrenched her hands away and fell back against the railing of the house by which they stood.

"No! It's no use," she said. "Wait, Martin, and I'll tell you the truth. I did trust you; I did like you; I did come near to caring for you. But it's all gone, and you can't bring it back again. I couldn't ever care for anyone whom I couldn't trust—and I could *never* trust you again. There—that's the truth. Now will you go away?"

"No!" said Martin. He stood in front of her about half a yard away, and repeated the word more quietly. "Are you so angry with me that you won't let me see you home?"

"I want you to go," said Chloe. She gripped the railing with her left hand for a moment; then she straightened herself and began to walk on without looking round.

Before she had gone a yard Martin was speaking again, close to her, setting his pace to hers:

"Chloe, how can I leave you alone in the streets at this hour? Be reasonable. Let me take you back to wherever you're staying."

"No!"

Martin's voice changed a little; it became tenderly indulgent.

"How are you going to get rid of me?"

Chloe walked on without replying. At the next corner she stood still.

"If you don't go, I shall speak to the next policeman we meet."

"I shouldn't," said Martin. "You'd have to go to Bow Street, or somewhere like that, and give evidence that I was annoying you, after which your address would be public property, and you'd probably have Leonard Wroughton dropping in to tea. Better let me see you home."

Chloe didn't answer for a full minute. Suppose he wouldn't go away. Well, they would just have to go on walking until daylight came and found them, he in evening dress, and she bareheaded, with her old tweed coat over Mrs. Mostyn Llewellyn's expensive dress. She wondered which of them would look the sillier. But go back to Hatchelbury Road with Martin at her heels she would not.

She crossed the road and walked straight on, and as she did so, a car came down the left hand turning, going dead slow. As it came up behind them, Chloe realized that she had no idea at all where she was. If this were a passing taxi, she felt reckless enough to sacrifice a whole day's salary in return for escape from this intolerable situation. As the thought passed through her mind, Martin's arm came round her shoulder.

"Ah, Chloe, be friends," he said. And as he spoke, the car slid up to the kerb ahead of them under a lamp, and stood still. The driver jumped out.

Chloe twisted herself free, and ran forward. In a breathless voice she said:

"Can you take a fare?" And then suddenly she saw the driver's face, and uttered a sharp little cry of, "Michael! Michael Foster!"

Michael put out his arm rather as if he were going to take her in to dinner; it was a curious, instinctive movement. And, as instinctively,

Chloe caught at his rough, damp sleeve with two little shaking hands. Up to this very moment she had been quite steady; but now she began to tremble so violently that her teeth chattered.

Michael put his arm right round her, and said in the nice, ordinary voice which hadn't an atom of glamour in it:

"Can I drive you anywhere?"

It was the nice ordinariness that pulled Chloe together—that and the hard strength of the arm that held her. She said, "Please" only just above her breath, and in a moment the door was open and he was putting her into the car. As the door slammed on her and she leaned back, she heard some rapid interchange of words between the two men. She was so nearly done, so taken off her balance by the sudden release from strain, that it was only an impression, not of words, but of some violent, wordless clash. Then Michael was at the window again.

"Where do you want to go?" he said, his voice so cheerful and unruffled that Chloe lost that impression of having heard it blurred with fury a moment ago. "Where do you want to go?" said Michael.

Chloe braced herself. She felt as if she was slipping down a long, steep hill. She mustn't do that; she mustn't slip. She made a great effort, and said slowly and stiffly:

"Will you go—half a mile—down the Vauxhall Road—and then stop?"

"Right-o," said Michael. He climbed into the driver's seat and started the car.

Chloe began to slip again.

When the brakes went on and the car stopped, she opened her eyes, with the curious feeling that she, too, had come to a standstill. Michael's voice reached her rather vaguely:

"Are you sure I can't take you any farther?"

She roused at that with a start, and looked out into the empty Vauxhall Road. It was so very, very queer to see it all empty and alone like this, with the lamps shining down on the blank pavements.

She said, "No, I can walk from here quite easily," and half expected that he would make some protest. Instead, he opened the door and held out his hand to help her.

She stood in the road, steadying her voice to say "Thank you," and "Good-night"—one must say something, and one mustn't, *mustn't* make a fool of oneself. The words came just above a whisper, and it may be said that they tried Michael's self-control a good deal. Chloe, of course, did not know this. She heard him say pleasantly, "Good-night. And if there's anything I can do for you at any time, you know where to find me; and you know how awfully pleased I should be."

She heard this, and, nodding because she couldn't trust her voice any more, she turned away and began to walk slowly and falteringly in the direction of Hatchelbury Road.

The idea that Michael might follow her never entered her head. She was only conscious of an intense desire to reach the little, cramped room, with its hard, unyielding bed. Every now and then a dreadful doubt as to whether she could reach it pierced the dullness of her mind. At the first crossing, doubt became certainty. She turned the heel of her shoe on the kerb and came down; and being down, she did not know how to get up again.

It was Michael who picked her up. She had really only gone a dozen yards. He picked her up, held her firmly if a little stiffly, and said:

"I say, do let me drive you the whole way."

"I'm all right," said Chloe, in a little, halting voice.

"You're as right as rain; but what's the sense of walking when I can drive you? If you don't want anyone to know where you're staying, I'll forget about it the minute I've dropped you there—I'm an absolute nailer at forgetting things."

Chloe found herself in the car again without quite knowing how she had got there.

"It's 122, Hatchelbury Road," she said, and shut her eyes.

When they stopped again, she had revived a little. Michael at the window was just a shadow, but it was easier to talk. She leaned towards the shadow and spoke, pleased to find that her voice was under control again.

"You will forget—really?"

"If you want me to."

"*Please.*"

"All right, I've forgotten."

She gave him both her hands as she got out. She liked the nice, steady grip he gave them. Suddenly she said:

"Why didn't you come to Danesborough?"

"I did."

"When?"

"On Wednesday week."

They stood facing each other on the narrow pavement hand in hand.

"Oh!" said Chloe. "That was the day I ran away."

"Yes, I know. They told me you had gone away and hadn't left any address. They seemed a good deal peeved."

Chloe gave a faint, faint gurgle of laughter. Michael—Michael was a dear. She became aware that they were still holding hands, and drew hers away.

"I must go in. Good-bye."

She said good-bye, but she stood there for a moment longer, looking at him in a considering sort of way. She could not see his face. He was quite silent and stood like a rock. Chloe said good-bye again, and ran up the steps. But even as she fitted the key into the lock, she was wondering whether she wanted it to be good-bye; she wasn't at all sure that she did. The world, which had been strange and horrid, was beginning to feel friendly again; there was something friendly about Michael Foster.

She half opened the door, and then drew it towards her again. Michael had not said a single word. She turned, still holding the door.

"Aren't you going to say good-bye?"

"I don't want to," said Michael honestly.

"Would good-night be any better?"

"A little."

"Then good-night."

Michael came forward a step.

"Have I—have I still got to forget where you live?" Chloe hesitated.

"You *said* you were so good at forgetting."

"I'm frightfully good at remembering too. I say, don't you think I might remember?—not every day you know, but, say, once or twice a week." He heard her laugh, saw her push the door open and run in.

The door was shutting. It took a long time to shut, because Chloe wasn't sure what she was going to say. Michael waited for the click of the latch, but it did not come. Instead, there was Chloe on the top step.

"You may remember once a week," she said, and was gone.

Chapter Twenty-Nine

CHLOE WOKE at eight next morning, looked at her watch, reflected joyfully that Mrs. Mostyn Llewellyn had told her not to turn up until the afternoon, and plunged into sleep again.

It was whilst she was asleep that a telephone conversation took place which would have interested her very much. One of the parties to it was Mr. Leonard Wroughton, and he addressed the person at the other end of the line as Stran. The conversation was not carried on in English.

"The suit-cases," Stran announced, "are where she left them. They are quite safe and entirely un-get-at-able without the receipt. There must be a great many letters in them. So if the other plan fails—"

"You've made such a damned muddle of it!" growled Wroughton, and was not improved in temper by hearing Stran laugh.

"What a surly beggar you are! Now, I've been up all night, and I'm as fit as a fiddle. What's more, I've got pretty good news."

"What?"

"Her address for one thing. Just take it down:—122, Hatchelbury Road—off the Vauxhall Road. Also I've got a plan."

"Your plans haven't been very successful so far."

Stran laughed again.

"Say something pleasant for a change. We're bound to get something out of this unless our luck's right out. If we don't get anything else, we stand to get the receipt for the suit-cases. But it has much greater possibilities than that. Now, look here…"

Wroughton received a few definite suggestions, and an immediate summons to London, after which he told Emily to expect him when she saw him, and caught the express at Daneham. A little later Jessie, the hard-faced housemaid, came to Mrs. Wroughton with a tale of sudden death in her family: "And if I might go home at once, ma'am, because they'll be wanting me."

Emily became moist-eyed and sympathetic:

"Oh, yes, to be sure—if you think they'll want you."

Jessie gazed at her grimly.

"I'm wanted urgent," she said.

An hour later she, too, was on her way to London.

Chloe found her afternoon's work as dull as such work is wont to be. Mrs. Mostyn Llewellyn was inclined to be cross; she announced herself as sick of the whole thing and wanting to get it all cleared up and off her hands.

"Those creatures at the N.Y.S.Z.K.U. office are unbusinesslike *beyond* what anyone could have imagined. Whenever they've had a chance to make a muddle they've made one. I've always wanted to come across somebody who could tell me why persons engaged in philanthropic work should be entirely devoid of business instincts—they are. Please take down this for the secretary..."

Chloe took it down, while Mrs. Mostyn Llewellyn walked up and down, moving a chair half an inch in one direction, pushing a table a little more into an angle, and fidgeting with nearly every ornament in the room in turn. It was very evidently the afternoon after the night before.

By half-past four Chloe's own temper was a little ruffled, and she began to long for five o'clock and to feel that it would never come. It was just half-past four when the telephone bell rang.

"Tell them to give you a message—say I can't speak to anyone. I can't think why anyone has a telephone—they're an absolute curse when you're busy." Then, when Chloe was half-way to the dining-room, she recalled her sharply:

"Miss Green! One moment, Miss Green! If it's Diana Arabin, I'll speak to her—but *not* Marcia Hayman. Have you got that? And if it's anyone else, I won't, unless they *insist*—and for heaven's sake put them off if you can."

Caught between the bell, which rang continuously, and Mrs. Mostyn Llewellyn's booming contralto, Chloe felt inclined to put both hands over her ears and say "Hush." It was a relief to take up the receiver. A woman spoke:

"Is that Mrs. Mostyn Llewellyn?"

"I'm speaking for her," said Chloe. "Can I take a message?"

"I want to speak to Mrs. Mostyn Llewellyn," said the voice.

Chloe stood for a moment without answering, because she was wondering where she had heard the voice before; then she said:

"I was asked to take a message if possible."

"No, I want to speak to Mrs. Mostyn Llewellyn—I must speak to her."

Chloe could not place the voice, but she was sure that she had heard it before. It was one of those harshly metallic voices.

"I'll tell her. Who shall I say?"

"I'm speaking from the N.Y.S.Z.K.U. office."

Mrs. Mostyn Llewellyn was not pleased. If it is possible to flounce in a dress that barely reaches the knee, she flounced to the telephone; and as she left both the study and the dining-room doors wide open, her side of the conversation reached Chloe with great plainness:

"What did you say? Oh." The tones of annoyance fairly filled the flat. "Yes, I'm *particularly* busy. Oh. What did you say? A diamond what? Spell it please. Good Lord, no one wears necklaces now-a-days—you might just as well tell me they'd picked up a bustle. What *did* you say then? A star? Oh. Well, she hasn't said anything about it; but I'll ask her if you'll hold on."

Chloe rose from her table as Mrs. Mostyn Llewellyn came quickly into the study and shut the door. She looked flushed and angry.

"Miss Green, what's this extraordinary story about some one picking up a diamond star last night and giving it to you? Did you report it to anyone?"

Chloe shook her head.

"It's a mistake—I don't know anything about it."

"Well, there's a shrieking woman at the N.Y.S.Z.K.U. who says that some one picked one up and gave it to you, and now they've got two different women claiming it. And she says will I please send you round to the office with it at once?"

"But I haven't got it," said Chloe. She would have laughed if Mrs. Llewellyn had not looked so much like a thunder storm. "If anyone picked it up, they didn't give it to me."

Mrs. Mostyn Llewellyn returned to the telephone. For such a large woman she was a quick mover. The receiver went to her ear with a jerk.

"Miss Green doesn't know anything at all about a star. It's *not* a star? But you said it *was*. First you said it was a necklace, and then you said it was a star—and now you say it's something else. Will you have the goodness to tell me *what* is supposed to have been picked up and handed to Miss Green!"—this last passage crescendo and with all the stops out. After a moment's pause she snapped over her shoulder at Chloe:

"Miss Green, they say now that it's some sort of ornament—still diamonds I believe, but not a necklace, and not *exactly* a star. Do you know anything at all about it?"

"No—there's some mistake."

Chloe stood in the doorway and heard the rasp of the voice that had seemed familiar; the words she could not distinguish. Every now and then Mrs. Mostyn Llewellyn said, "Nonsense!" or "Preposterous!" or "You're shouting!" In the end she rang off and swung round.

"They want you to go there when you've finished work. I'd kill that woman if I had much to do with her! I can't think why somebody hasn't. They swear that this ornament was picked up and given to you. I said I would send you round to see them about it. You'd better go as soon as you've finished the letter to Mr. Appleby."

"They've probably mixed me up with somebody else," said Chloe cheerfully.

She finished Mr. Appleby's letter. Twice in the course of it she looked up and saw Mrs. Mostyn Llewellyn looking at her. There was something in the look which was new in Chloe's experience. It was not until afterwards that it occurred to her that the something was suspicion.

Chapter Thirty

CHLOE LEFT the flat at five o'clock. It was a relief to get away. Earlier in the day it had been raining, but now no moisture fell, though the air seemed full of it.

Chloe was too preoccupied to notice the weather. Mrs. Mostyn Llewellyn's look played hide and seek in her mind with the voice which had seemed familiar, but which she could not place. If she turned her attention to one, the other came close and was within an ace of being grasped; it was very teasing. She began to try and think, instead, about this puzzling business of the diamond star; and then all at once the meaning of Mrs. Mostyn Llewellyn's look came to her. She gave a little angry laugh and stuck her chin in the air.

"Idiot!" she said with so much energy that an absent-minded passer-by started, stopped, and murmured, "I beg your pardon?"

Chloe dismissed Mrs. Mostyn Llewellyn and her ridiculous suspicions. There remained the voice. Very elusive that voice, and associated in a vague manner with something unpleasant—with Danesborough. Yes, that was the association—Danesborough. A spark of light dazzled, and faded. Why Danesborough? The voice didn't belong to anyone Chloe had known there; she was quite sure of that. Then why?—no, wait a minute, it *was* Danesborough—the study, yes, that was it. She had it now. In a flash she saw herself going to the telephone in the study at Danesborough. The bell had rung, and she had taken off the receiver before Leonard Wroughton could cross the room; and then a voice—*the* voice—had said, "Hullo! I want to speak to Mr. Wroughton."

Chloe nodded to herself. It *was* the same voice; she was sure of it. Her brows drew together in a frown; she walked more slowly. It was ridiculous no doubt, but she began to feel a distinct disinclination to go on and meet the owner of the voice. Of course, she needn't go on: she could simply go back to Hatchelbury Road. But that would mean chucking her job. Impossible to return to Mrs. Mostyn Llewellyn after running away from the voice which had connected her with the mysterious disappearance of a diamond star.

Chloe stood still because this last thought sent a tingling shock right through her. She felt as if she had opened a door into a dark room. She couldn't see anything in the room, but she could hear things moving there. She wanted very much to slam the door and run away.

She walked on a pace or two slowly. She couldn't afford to chuck a perfectly good job; jobs were not to be picked up at every street corner. She mustn't be a fool.

She paused again, and found herself looking fixedly at the letters G.R. on the letter-box of a branch post office. Instantly she had what she described as a brain-wave. Michael—if she could get hold of Michael, the voice and its associations needn't bother her. There was probably nothing in it anyway; but, with Michael in reserve, she felt she could almost have met Wroughton without a qualm.

She ran into the post office, and proceeded to wrestle with the telephone directory. Michael's garage was there. She gave the number, and hoped fervently that Michael would be in the garage. She asked for Mr. Michael Foster, and spoke to three persons in succession, none of whom was Michael. They were all very polite, and said they would try and find him. In the end it was Michael himself who said:

"Hullo! I say, is that you? How topping!"

"Yes," said Chloe, and wondered how she was going to explain.

Michael's voice again:

"Anything I can do?"

"Please. If you're not doing anything else, will you meet me at the N.Y.S.Z.K.U. offices in Victoria Street? I've got to go and see some one, and I don't particularly want to go alone—I mean I thought if you'd just stand by."

"Rather!"

"I'm going there now. I thought perhaps if you wouldn't mind just waiting till I come out—I oughtn't to be long."

"Can't I go with you?"

"No, I don't think so. But I would just like to feel that you were there."

She rang off rather quickly, and had a much more cheerful mood to keep her company for the rest of the way. She was probably a fool, but it would be nice to see Michael—and perhaps they could go and have tea together afterwards.

The N.Y.S.Z.K.U. had their offices on the third or fourth stories of a big block of flats, but in the open hall Chloe was met by a little, dumpy woman with a face like a well floured scone.

"Are you Miss Green? I think you must be, from the description."

"Dene," said Chloe automatically.

The little woman's restless hazel eyes looked her up and down.

"She said Green—I'm sure she said Green," she murmured half to herself.

"She always does," said Chloe; "but it's Dene all the same."

"And you're Mrs. Mostyn Llewellyn's secretary?"

"Yes."

"Then it's all right. We were expecting you earlier, and the secretary's had to go home. But she wants to see you most particularly, so I said I would stay and bring you round to her flat. It's only a step, and she's *particularly* anxious to see you."

She began to move towards the door, but Chloe stood still.

"I don't think I can go on anywhere else. I'm late now, and I really don't know anything at all about the diamond star. If one was picked up at the ball, it certainly wasn't given to me. I don't know whether—Miss Cross was there till twelve."

The little woman's round, expressionless face looked up at Chloe; the hazel eyes shifted.

"Oh, but this was at the very end of the evening," she said in a decorous, soft voice. "It was Mrs. Venables, one of our regular subscribers who picked up the star; and she said particularly that she handed it over to Mrs. Mostyn Llewellyn's secretary, a young person with black hair and a high colour. She gave, in fact, a very accurate description of you."

The girl who would not resent being described as a young person does not really exist. If she did exist, she would, according to Chloe, be a backboneless worm and deserve the further insult of being told that she had a high colour. Just what a worm with a high colour would look like, she made no attempt to explain—imagination jibs at it a little. Chloe was, in fact, sharply annoyed, and the maligned colour became brilliant.

"I don't think—" she began; but the little woman interrupted her.

"I'm sure you must see how necessary it is to lose no time in clearing the matter up. The secretary is expecting us. Shall we come?"

Chloe followed her to the door in a very puzzled, angry state of mind. She now felt more than her former reluctance to go on; and yet she did not see how she could reasonably draw back. The whole thing might be hinged on some perfectly ordinary mistake, or—her thought stopped dead on the threshold of that dark room, refusing to penetrate its shadows.

As they came down the steps into the lighted street with its noisy traffic, Chloe looked quickly to left and right of the pavement, and almost at once she saw Michael Foster standing in front of a shop window a dozen yards away. He saw her too, and made a step forward. The little woman who had met Chloe was talking all the while. Chloe shook her head very slightly. They walked on past Michael and turned to the left. Michael watched them gravely. As soon as they were past, he saw Chloe put her hand behind her back and beckon with it. From this and the head-shake he deduced that he was to follow her, but not to speak. He accordingly followed at a reasonable distance.

The expression "only a step" is, as applied to distance, as misleading as the "bittock" of the Scot. Chloe had time to become dreadfully bored by her companion during their walk. The woman talked incessantly. She asked foolish questions, and then did not wait to have them answered; she made platitudinous remarks about the weather, and evinced a naïve pride in the number of titled persons who subscribed to the N.Y.S.Z.K.U. And the longer she talked, the more certain Chloe was that this was not the voice which had set all those curious fears and suspicions vibrating in her consciousness. This voice induced flat, stale, unprofitable boredom, and nothing more. The "step" seemed to her to have stretched into about three-quarters of a mile, when the woman said:

"Now, here we are. The flat is on the third floor—such a nice position, airy you know, and yet not too high up."

They passed through the hall and ascended to the airy third floor in a small automatic lift. The little woman rang a bell. As they waited for the door to open, Chloe heard a step on the long stone stair.

Chapter Thirty-One

IN THE DINING-ROOM of the flat two people were waiting for the bell to ring. One of them was Mr. Leonard Wroughton, and the other a handsome, black-browed woman of about forty.

Wroughton stood with his back to the fire. The woman had pushed her chair a little away from the table, and was looking at him with a hint of mockery in her fine eyes.

"You're sure?" said Wroughton.

"My good Leonard, how jumpy you are. I am *quite* sure that I can play the secretary to the life—and even sure that I can remember that outlandish jumble of letters. I *am*, in fact, secretary of the N.Y.S.Z.K.U."

"All right, all right."—Wroughton was frowning—"Remember we've got to have the receipt whatever happens. Stran can come in when we've got it, and play the gallant rescuer for all it's worth. It might be worth a good deal, but I'm not counting on it. We don't do too badly if we get the letters."

"Supposing she hasn't got the receipt for the suit-cases on her."

Wroughton moved impatiently.

"She'll have it in her purse—bound to—you said so yourself—you said she'd be bound to have it on her because she wouldn't have anywhere to leave it. What are you getting at, Maudie?"

Maudie twirled a pencil between her first and second fingers; she also tipped her chair a little.

"Oh, run away and play," she said, and then came down to earth with a jerk as the bell rang.

Chloe came into the dining-room from the rather dark hall, and was struck by its neat ordinariness—a red paper on the wall; a fumed oak dining-room suite; an enlarged photograph of the Bridge of Sighs over the mantelpiece; no flowers, no books; a tall woman in navy blue, writing at one end of the table.

Chloe's companion shut the door, and the tall woman looked up, nodded slightly, and said:

"Ah, Miss Green! Good evening." Her voice had a judicial sound, her "Miss Green" a distinct flavour of the prisoner at the bar.

One bit of Chloe felt angry, and another bit of her felt amused. But behind both the amusement and the anger there was just a little quiver of dread, enough to make her hope that the step which she had heard on the stair was Michael's step. She said:

"I am Mrs. Mostyn Llewellyn's secretary. My name is Dene, not Green. You wanted to see me?"

"I asked Miss Smith to bring you round to see me. I wanted to see you particularly. Perhaps you will sit down."

Chloe sat down. (The prisoner was accommodated with a chair.) Miss Smith remained standing by the door.

"You must realize that this is a very serious matter—unless, of course, you have some explanation to give." The secretary's glance was direct, her tone so grave that the words impressed instead of offending.

Chloe ceased to be either angry or amused. She spoke impulsively:

"There's some extraordinary mistake!"

The secretary tapped the table.

"Not on our side. Perhaps it would be better if I gave you the facts. Mrs. Venables, one of our oldest and most valued subscribers, says that she picked up a large diamond ornament in the shape of a star last night at the end of the last dance. It was lying against the wall just by the archway lined with mirrors, which separates the lounge from the ball-room. She says she picked it up, saw you sitting at your table only a yard or two away, and took it over to you. She says you had been pointed out to her as Mrs. Mostyn Llewellyn's secretary earlier in the evening by Mrs. Mostyn Llewellyn herself. She described you to us with great accuracy, and declares that she left the ornament in your charge."

"What *nonsense*!" said Chloe.

The secretary's mouth hardened.

"That, Miss Dene, is not quite the tone to take. You don't seem to realize your position, if I may say so. We have not communicated with the police *yet*—" She paused significantly.

Chloe pushed back her chair and sprang up.

"If Mrs. Venables says these things, she ought to be here!" she cried. "She ought to say them to me! She's making a ridiculous mistake; but I can't prove that it's a mistake unless I see her. Where is she? Ring her up and ask her to come here at once!"

The secretary's eyebrows rose a little.

"Mrs. Venables is out of town," she said. "And I think you should realize your position. This excitement doesn't improve it; it looks, in fact, a good deal like bravado."

"How dare you?" said Chloe in low, furious tones.

The secretary smiled.

"My dear Miss Dene, you're being very foolish. If you are really anxious to prove your innocence, you will not, I suppose, object to the usual search."

Chloe's little, angry laugh rang out:

"If I were to steal a diamond star, do you *suppose* I'd be such a fool as to walk about with it in my pocket?"

"No," said the secretary. "But I think it is quite likely that you would have the pawn-ticket in your purse."

Chloe dived into her pocket, pulled out the shabby purse which had been Rose's Christmas present two years ago, and flung it on the table. It slid a few inches and spun round. The secretary's hand covered it just a shade too quickly; and for a moment her face changed. Chloe saw another woman, eager, avid; the judicial atmosphere was gone—instead, strain, uncertainty, the quick grasp of a hand that had broken from control.

Chloe took a half step back, and remembered that the receipt for the suit-cases was in the inner pocket of the purse. She stared across the table, and saw the secretary's fingers shake a little as they opened it. A ten shilling note in one pocket; six shillings in silver; half a dozen coppers, one of them bad—"Perhaps they'll say I'm a coiner next"—; and in the last compartment, a folded luggage receipt.

"Well?" said Chloe.

The secretary took the receipt, and looked seriously at her.

"This, I think, requires looking into."

"That," said Chloe in a biting voice, "is a left-luggage receipt, not a pawn-ticket."

"Exactly. Luggage left in a cloak-room would make an admirable hiding-place. I think we must ask to see the contents of these two packages." The voice had a hint of triumph and, for the first time, a trace of accent.

The scene in the study at Danesborough came back vividly. This, yes, this, was the voice which had said "Hullo! I want to speak to Mr. Wroughton." Chloe became suddenly very clear and cool. The star and Mrs. Venables were non-existent. This woman who knew Wroughton was trying to bluff her; she wanted the receipt. The whole of this comedy meant nothing less than that. She said:

"Will you please give me back my purse and that receipt." And as she spoke, a bell rang in the hall.

The secretary began to pick up the money and put it back; she picked it up slowly, one coin at a time. The hall door had opened before she spoke.

"You shall have the receipt when we have satisfied ourselves that the missing star isn't hidden in one of those cases."

She pushed the purse across to Chloe, and as she did so the dining-room door opened and a man came in. Miss Smith uttered an exclamation and slipped aside. The secretary rose to her feet. Chloe whirled round, and saw Michael Foster closing the door behind him. She had him by the arm in a moment.

"Michael, make her give me my receipt!"

Michael looked about him. He saw Miss Smith with one hand at her mouth, the other holding on to the back of a chair—a clear case of abject funk. He saw the secretary, composed, enquiring. And he saw Chloe, her face very near him, her eyes wet and brilliant, her lips parted, her breath coming quickly.

"Is anything the matter?" he said.

"Miss Dene—" began the secretary.

Chloe shook Michael's arm.

"Make her give it back to me! Make her give it to me at once!"

"I say, what on earth—"

The secretary's voice broke in on Michael's rather bewildered opening:

"If you are a friend of Miss Dene's—"

Chloe wheeled round, still holding Michael tight.

"He is! And you've no right to keep that receipt—you know you haven't! Please give it back to me!"

The secretary spoke to Michael, ignoring Chloe as one ignores an angry child.

"Miss Dene is in a very serious position, and I cannot get her to treat it seriously."

"Make her give it up! And take me away quick!"—she clutched him tighter—"I don't like this place at all."

Michael looked from one to the other and came forward a step. As soon as he did this, little Miss Smith slipped behind him and ran out of the room. In the hall they could hear whispers and footsteps.

"I don't understand," said Michael; he addressed the woman in the chair. "If you have anything of Miss Dene's and she wants it back, I'm sure"—he smiled pleasantly—"well, I mean of course you'll give it back, won't you?"

"Miss Dene is accused of stealing a diamond star." The secretary's hand was clenched on the paper it held.

Michael said "What rot!" and heard Chloe whisper, "Get the paper and come away. They're thieves." He nodded, and took a stride forward, holding out his hand.

"Miss Dene's receipt, please. You've no right to take it, and you've no right to keep it—you know that as well as I do." The woman faced him, sulky, undecided.

"Who are *you*, anyhow?" she said.

"Come," said Michael, "you're on the wrong side of the law. If you've anything to say about Miss Dene, let's all go round to the nearest police station, and you can say it there. You can't keep that receipt, my dear lady." He smiled at her affably, and saw her blench.

"Oh, you're an accomplice, are you?"

"That's one of the things you can talk to the police about," said Michael. He still held out his hand. "The receipt, please."

She put her hands behind her, scowling.

Michael's pleasant tone changed suddenly.

"Look here, do you want me to smash a window and whistle for the police? I will if you don't hand that thing over. And once the police come in, it isn't Miss Dene that's going to get hurt, I think."

The woman stamped her foot with sudden violence and flung the paper on the floor.

Chapter Thirty-Two

THE HALL was almost dark and quite empty as Chloe and Michael came through it. Chloe did not let go of Michael's arm until they were sinking down, down in the little lift. She let go just before it stopped, laughed shakily, and said:

"I've pinched you black and blue."

"Come and have some tea," said Michael. "I know a place where we can be quiet and talk."

When they were waiting for their tea Chloe laughed again; this time the laughter had a more natural sound.

"That's the second time you've turned up just when I wanted you. How *do* you manage it?"

Michael looked pleased.

"Well, the other night I'd been driving some people to the ball. When I was fetching them, I had to come into the hall with a message; and I saw you. So when I'd dropped them, I came back on the chance of your letting me drive you home."

"Well?"

A tinge of embarrassment crept into his tone.

"Oh, I don't know," he said. "It seemed such awful cheek. I saw you come out, and I didn't like to speak to you. And I didn't think you ought to be walking about by yourself at that sort of hour, so—so I just kept you in sight."

The arrival of the tea here afforded him relief; but as soon as the girl who had brought it had gone, Chloe looked at him teasingly and said:

"So much for last night. What about this afternoon?"

"Well, I was afraid you might think I was butting in. Did you?"

Chloe's smile was suddenly sweet.

"Did you think I did? But I'd like to know what made you come in just then."

Michael stirred his tea with absorbed interest.

"Well, you waggled your hand for me to follow you—at least I thought that was what you meant me to do. I walked up the stairs, and just saw the door of the flat shut upon you. So then I thought I'd find out who lived there, and I rang the bell of the opposite flat. A topping girl opened the door, and she told me the people across the way had gone abroad for a month and let the flat to some people called Smith, and she'd be glad when they came back, because they all thought the Smiths were a bit odd. I thanked her and came away. I thought I'd wait for you down in the hall. I'd just got down when I saw Martin Fossetter come up the steps."

"Oh!" said Chloe. "Are you sure?"

"Well, it was darkish—no, I'm not sure—I *thought* it was. Whoever it was turned sharp round and went back down the steps again. I didn't like it; and I thought I'd come up and see how you were getting along—have one of those sticky buns; they're jolly good." Chloe took a bun, and he added, "I say, don't tell me anything you don't want to. But the whole thing was pretty rocky, wasn't it?"

"I can't think why they let you in."

Michael grinned like a schoolboy.

"They didn't exactly *let* me in. They opened the door, and I put my foot in it and barged in because I heard you call out. No, they didn't exactly let me in! What were they playing at?"

"I don't, mind telling you," said Chloe. "But I hate talking about it. You see, I ran away from Danesborough, and I took a lot of papers which belonged to Mr. Dane. I'm sure, I'm *sure* he meant me to destroy them. But Mr. Wroughton thinks they're worth a lot of money, and he wants to get them back."

"Where are the papers?"

"I packed them into two suit-cases, and they're in the cloak-room at Victoria. That woman wanted the receipt, and I'm quite, *quite* sure that she wanted it for Mr. Wroughton."

"And Fossetter?"

Chloe's cheeks burned.

"No—no—I don't know. Don't talk about him."

"All right."

She blinked once or twice rapidly; then she said:

"I don't know what to do about those papers. They ought to be burned, and I can't burn them at Mrs. Rowse's. If they were burnt, perhaps Mr. Wroughton would leave me alone. You see, it's fearfully complicated. Mr. Dane left everything to me, so I suppose the papers are mine; but I shan't be of age till February, and as soon as I am of age, I'm going to refuse to take anything under his will."

Michael looked up quickly. Chloe nodded.

"I can't take it—I can't take anything from him—I couldn't if I was starving. So I suppose, properly and legally, I ought not to destroy anything."

"No, I don't think you ought."

He saw her colour brighten. She rapped the table vigorously.

"But I'm going to. Even if I was going to be put in prison for it, I'd do it."

"I see," said Michael. He went on looking at Chloe. Then he said, "If it's stocks and shares, I really don't think you'd better burn them."

"It isn't," said Chloe; "it's letters. And they *must* be burnt— they've got to be burnt." She clasped her hands under her chin, set her elbows on the table, and leaned towards Michael. Her eyes were bright and defiant.

"Oh, letters," said Michael in a tone of relief. "If that's all, I'd burn them for you myself. Would you like me to?"

"Would you?—would you really?—not look at them at all, but just burn them?"

"Yes, rather!—if you wanted me to."

Chloe took her hands from under her chin and clapped them.

"Angel!" she said. "If only those beastly things were burnt, I believe I'd get out of this sort of nightmare into something nice and ordinary and every-day again. Will you really do it?"

Michael lost his head a little. He said, "Chloe," and then blushed furiously. "I beg your pardon. I mean I'll do anything you want me to."

"You *are* an angel!" said Chloe. "Why did you beg my pardon? Of course you can call me Chloe. Do you think I'm going to call an angel rescuer Mr. Foster? I'm *not*. But how can I call you Michael if you don't call me Chloe?"

Michael's blush extended to the very tips of his ears.

"It's an absolutely topping name," he said.

"Yes, isn't it?" said Chloe. "If I'd been called Gwendoline, or Gladys, or Emily, or Harriet, I should have gone through life just simply hating my godfathers and godmothers. On the other hand, I should probably have been much worthier. Will you really, truly burn those letters?"

Michael nodded without speaking. Chloe dived into a pocket, produced her purse, and extracted the rescued receipt.

"There are two suit-cases, and they've got Mr. Dane's initials on them—C.M.D. And you'll be frightfully careful, won't you?—because, I'm trusting you *most* tremendously. How will you do it?"

"Take them out on to Finchley Common, sop 'em with petrol, and apply a match."

"You'll be sure they're quite, quite burnt? They're—they're letters, you know,—letters that other people oughtn't to see."

"It's rotten to keep letters," said Michael, frowning. "They're either simply frightfully dull, or else they're like you say—the sort that other people oughtn't to see. Well, I'll undertake that there won't be anything left of this particular lot. I say, if I'm arrested as a dangerous incendiary, and sent to penal servitude for umpteen years, you'll come and see me in prison, won't you?"

"I'll bring you sticky buns," said Chloe. She took one, bit it, and looked at him, sparkling. "They're ripping buns. I'll bring you a dozen in a paper bag every time I come. I could throw them through the bars when the warders weren't looking, and you'd have to be frightfully clever and get a whole one into your mouth every time. I should simply love to see you!"

"All right," said Michael, "that's a bargain. And if I'm not arrested, won't you—I mean, mayn't I—I mean——"

"*What* do you mean?"

"I mean, even if the bars and the buns are a wash-out, I'd like to roll up and report progress—if you'll let me. You'll want to know for certain that I've done the job. I was thinking perhaps I could call for you to-morrow."

"I'm one of the world's workers," said Chloe. "I'm Mrs. Mostyn Llewellyn's secretary, but I don't know that I can go back to her. You see, I want to hide till I'm twenty-one; and that sham secretary woman knows where I'm working; and Mrs. Mostyn Llewellyn knows where I'm living. Oh!" said Chloe. "Oh, Michael!"—the sparkle in her eyes was suddenly drowned in tears—"Oh, Michael dear, I shall have to run away again. And *I am* so tired of running away."

"Must you?"

"Yes, yes, I must. And I've just settled down and got Mrs. Rowse to love me a little. And Albert, who is a frightfully red-hot Communist, was going to teach me how to sing 'The Red Flag,' and save my life nobly whenever the Red Revolution came along—and—and—it's all very well for you to grin like that, but how would you like to have to turn out at a moment's notice and go and look for a room, when you don't know a single person in London and you've only got sixteen and sixpence in the world?"

Michael was considering.

"I don't see why you shouldn't keep on your job. There wouldn't be any need to let your Mrs. Thingummy know that you'd changed your address, would there?"

"N' no. Michael how clever of you!"

"You could carry on for a bit anyhow. And about a room—I'm—well, as a matter of fact, I'm moving out of my own room, and I wondered whether it would suit you."

"You mean," said Chloe with a very direct look—"you mean you're going to give up your room because I'm in a hole. How *frightfully* nice of you!" A wave of warm, honest gratitude seemed to flow from her as she spoke.

"I can find something in five minutes; it's quite easy for a man. I only thought—you don't think it awful cheek, do you?—I mean my landlady, Mrs. Moffat, used to be one of our housemaids, and she's a really topping sort; you could absolutely bank on her."

"She'll hate me at first sight for turning you out."

"Nobody could," said Michael quite simply.

Chapter Thirty-Three

CHLOE WENT BACK to Hatchelbury Road and flung her arms round Mrs. Rowse's neck.

"I've got to run away again. I do wish I hadn't. I'm sure no one will ever be as nice to me as you've been."

Mrs. Rowse looked grim.

"I don't hold with running away. Once, may be, if a gel was really put to it—a step-mother that drinks, or such like—; but to make a habit of it is what I should call unsettling and likely to lead to worse. You go back to your friends, Miss."

"The people who are looking for me are not my friends," said Chloe. "They're horrible, nefarious evil-doers, ever so much worse than a step-mother that drinks. And if any of them come round here and want to know where I've gone, you won't tell them, will you?"

"The biggest blab in the world can't tell what she don't know. But now that we're talking, let me tell you one thing." The voice became very severe, but the bulging eyes rested on Chloe with reluctant indulgence. "I won't say that I'm not sorry you're going, but I won't say that I *am* sorry either. You're a gel that turns young men's heads. And when I see Albert's head getting all ready to turn—well, I won't say I'm sorry you're going."

Chloe flushed.

"Oh, Mrs. Rowse!"

"I don't say that you've any intentions that way."

"I don't ever want to turn anyone's head," said Chloe. "I like people. I can't help it; I do like them; I'm made that way. And when I like them I want to be friends with them. I just hate it if—when they get silly."

"Gels can't be friends with young men," said Mrs. Rowse with extreme dogmatism. "There's too much human nature in the way."

Michael came for Chloe in his car at nine o'clock. She took the seat beside him, and he told her rapidly and cheerfully that he had put in some A.1. staff work, and that everything was satisfactorily arranged. Yes, he'd found a room for himself. No, Mrs. Moffat was not furious, but quite properly delighted to have Chloe instead of himself.

"I've told her she's to bite the nose off anyone who comes there and asks for you. She's a frightfully efficient chaperone. My young sister stayed there with me once, and she said she'd never been so looked after in her life. Then there's Monody—you'll like Monody."

"Who's Monody?"

"Oh, a ripping chap—a bit mad, you know, but one of the best. He does those frightfully good caricatures in 'The Eight-hour Day.' He's a raging Socialist of course."

"I shall learn to sing 'The Red Flag' after all!" said Chloe.

Mrs. Moffat received them with a manner which blended mourning for the departing Michael with suspicion of Chloe as a substitute. She thawed a little on perceiving that Chloe did not make up and had not the golden hair which owes its origin to dye; but the thaw was not sufficient to make the mental atmosphere at all comfortably warm.

"I knew she'd hate me," said Chloe in a little voice as she and Michael followed Mrs. Moffat up the stair. As she said it, Michael felt her bare hand just brush against his; he caught it in a warm, reassuring grasp, and felt it tremble a little. They walked up as far as the landing like that, and Chloe was comforted.

On the landing, Mr. Monody, very long and thin and like a caricature of himself—such an odd, sharp, turned-up nose; and such little, blinking eyes under a thatch of colourless hair.

Michael hailed him with a shout, whereupon he at once dropped the portfolio he was carrying and stood by, rumpling his hair, whilst

Mrs. Moffat, Chloe, and Michael retrieved his scattered drawings. Michael, on his hands and knees, effected an introduction.

"This is Monody. He's always doing this sort of thing. Monody, this is Miss Dane. You know—I told you." Then in a stage whisper to Chloe, "I say, I forgot to ask you if you wanted to be Miss Dane here—Dene or Green will do just as well if you'd rather."

Chloe gurgled with laughter. She heard Mr. Monody remark with perfect gravity, "Too many names spoil an alias. I should stick to Dane if I were you." And, before she could recover, he was gone, running down the stair at top speed, whistling the "Hymn to the Sun" from the *Coq d'Or*.

Mrs. Mostyn Llewellyn received Chloe next day with a marked absence of enthusiasm.

"I think," Chloe told Michael in the evening, "in fact, I'm sure, that she's suddenly realized that she doesn't know anything about me, and that she never even asked me for a reference. I know that she went and rang up the real secretary of the N.Y.S. thing. She was perfectly priceless about it. She looked at me in the most suspicious way, and said the whole thing was very strange, and how did I account for it."

"What did you say?"

"I put it to her quite firmly that I couldn't possibly be responsible for what people said to her on the telephone. I said I'd told her all along that there was some idiotic mistake. And that was that. She was peeved. Michael, I'm afraid my job is fading before my eyes. You'll have to find me another."

"All right," said Michael, "I will. I burnt those letters this morning."

"You did?"

"Yes, it took about a gallon of petrol; but it's done."

"Ouf!" said Chloe. She drew a long breath and slipped her hand for a moment into Michael's arm. "You don't know, you really don't know, what a frightful relief it is. How did you get time off?"

"Ah!" said Michael, "that's what I was going to tell you about. I don't drive cabs any more: I only collect dividends. From to-day I'm a full-blown partner. And we're going to dine and do a show to celebrate the event."

It was next day that Chloe lost her job. Mrs. Mostyn Llewellyn paid her, thanked her coldly for her assistance, and intimated that she had now made other arrangements. Chloe was both angry and dejected when she came out into a deluge of rain and found Michael waiting for her. He did his best to console, but found her in a thorny mood.

"I *hate* looking for jobs. I *hate* people who snork and say, 'What experience have you had?' And I simply *loathe* people who ask me for references."

Michael blundered badly.

"I suppose it's natural they should want them," he began.

Chloe stamped her foot in a puddle; the muddy water flew up and drenched her ankles.

"What's the use of their asking me for references when I can't give them any? What's the good of references anyhow? If I was an unscrupulous adventuress, I should have lots of perfectly lovely ones, *beautifully* forged so that no one could *ever* find out. So that's how much good references are. I tried to explain that to one woman, and she turned pale magenta and opened her mouth like a fish. Hateful people!"

"I thought you liked people."

Chloe's April smile flashed out suddenly.

"I do—when I'm not in a raging temper."

Mrs. Moffat really thawed that evening when Chloe came home "sopped"—the expression was Mrs. Moffat's own. And when she discovered that she had nothing to change into, sympathy and conversation became the order of the day.

"You're fair *sopped*. Now whatever could Mr. Michael have been thinking of to let you get that wet?"

"It was raining," said Chloe, "and I stamped in a puddle. It felt frightfully nice at the time because I was just blazing with fury; but afterwards I was sorry, because there's something discouraging about having one's ankles wet. Oh, Mrs. Moffat, how frightfully kind! Will you really lend me a dressing-gown and dry my things for me? I haven't got any clothes because I ran away. I expect Michael told you."

Mrs. Moffat ran out of the room and returned at top speed with a crimson flannel dressing-gown and a pair of solid black felt slippers.

Chloe snuggled into the warm flannel, while Mrs. Moffat went down on her knees and held the slippers one at a time for the little cold feet.

"You won't hate having me here any more, will you?" said Chloe— "not after being so frightfully nice to me. I told Michael you'd hate me for turning him out. He said you wouldn't; but I knew you would. But you won't go on doing it now, will you?"

Mrs. Moffat, still kneeling, looked up and saw Chloe's mouth tremble, and the tears come into her eyes. She laid her hands on Chloe's knees.

"He loves you true."

If Chloe was taken aback, she didn't show it. She pushed aside a wet curl, looked wide-eyed into Eliza Moffat's plain, sharp face, and asked as a child might have done:

"Does he?"

Mrs. Moffat nodded, swallowed, and repeated with emphasis:

"He loves you *true*."

"How do you know?"

"It doesn't need knowing—not for anyone that's got eyes and ears, and their seven senses. And it doesn't need telling neither, though he told me sure enough with his own lips in this very room. 'Lizzie, you'll be nice to her?' he says. But I says to him, 'What 'ud your pore ma say, the way she brought you up and all?—you to be bringing goodness knows who into a respectable house like mine, and asking me to mix and meddle in goodness knows what! No, Mr. Michael, I says I'm not the woman, and this isn't the house, for goings on.' But he turns round and says to me solemn-like, 'Lizzie, I love her true,' he says."

Chloe twisted round in her chair, dropped her head on her hands, and burst into a passion of weeping.

Chapter Thirty-Four

THE BUSINESS OF looking for a job began again; also the business of wearing out shoe-leather. Chloe was on her way home, and had just become aware of a hole in her right shoe, when she was overtaken by Mr. Monody with a portfolio under each arm. He looked vaguely at her without salutation; but as he continued to walk by her side, she imagined that he had recognized her. It was in the middle of a rather difficult crossing that he suddenly addressed her in a voice which was well calculated to penetrate the roar of the traffic:

"What attracts me to you so strongly—"

At this intriguing juncture Chloe had to flee before a motor bus. She reached an island and looked back, panting. Mr. Monody and his portfolios were intact. Next moment they were beside her, and the road being clear, Chloe ran across to the pavement and trusted him to follow. He did so, and instantly resumed speech:

"What attracts me to you so strongly is the fact that you have run away."

Chloe looked up with dancing eyes.

"How frightfully nice of you!" she began.

But Monody was not looking at her. He strode along, presenting a jutting profile and talking with rapid intensity; if he had not been carrying two portfolios he would certainly have waved his arms.

"I've spent my whole life running away," he said.

"I'm a little tired of it," said Chloe, and received a momentary glance of reproach.

"There is only one damnation," said Mr. Monody; "and that is accepting the accepted. The minute you do that, whether it's in religion, or art, or life, you're dead and damned—buried, you know, under a neat grassy heap of conventions, with something symbolic in stone at your head and feet. You've got to run away if you want to keep alive. You've got to be revolutionary if you're not a born cauliflower." For a moment the sharp profile was replaced by the misty gaze which seemed to see, not Chloe, but something a good many aeons away. Chloe certainly felt herself to be a mere speck, just one little speck floating with millions of others in a vague and speculative mist. It was not at all comfortable.

"What is history?" said Mr. Monody.

Chloe ceased to be a speck, and became Chloe again.

"It's generally dull: and it ought to be so exciting," she said.

Monody frowned. It was quite obvious that he expected to do all the talking himself.

"History is the statement and re-statement of one tragedy. Dynasties, and wars, and politics, and politicians are just so much clutter. The real thing is the continual appearing of ideas—lots of them, streams of them, vigorous, vital, dynamic. What happens all through history? The same old crime, the same *damned* crime. Nobody wants 'em, nobody can do with 'em; they're alive, they're uncomfortable, they're disturbing. Take them away, and smother them up and bury them deep—everybody's ready to lend a hand. If you want to save an idea alive, you've got to run away with it—the wilderness, you know; every one's hand against you, and yours against every one; fighting like blazes all the time till your idea is strong enough to fend for itself. Then a few things get smashed."

They reached Mrs. Moffat's doorstep as Mr. Monody paused for breath. Chloe felt rather dazed and, for once in her life, at a loss for words; Mr. Monody seemed to have used them all up, for the time being at any rate. He now began to walk up the stairs in front of her. Half way up he dropped one of his portfolios, and they both descended to the bottom to pick up the scattered drawings. As they knelt in the dark hall on either side of the open portfolio, Monody began to talk again.

"I began," he said, "by running away from my name. My parents cursed me with the deplorable name of Adolphus. They meant well of course—parents always mean well. To them it had a rich, fruity sound; it suggested something in the City—something rich and fat and Adolphian. I ran away from it."

He picked up the portfolio, and this time remembered to stand aside and let Chloe pass him. When she had nearly reached the top, she heard him coming up behind her three steps at a time. She turned to meet the misty gaze.

"I say, you *are* Michael's girl, aren't you?"

Chloe burst out laughing.

"What would you do if I said 'No'?" she said.

"I don't know," said Mr. Monody. "I want to make a sketch of you. Shall we say to-morrow at ten?"

"I don't think—"

"To-morrow at ten," said Mr. Monody firmly. He went into his room and shut the door.

Chloe ran downstairs again, still laughing, and penetrated into Mrs. Moffat's kitchen. Mrs. Moffat was making apple dumplings, but she allowed Chloe to stay; she even let her make a dumpling for herself and mark it with a large, irregular C.

"It's frightfully difficult to get a good initial in dough, isn't it?"

"It all comes with practice," said Eliza Moffat. "Not that I've ever tried," she added.

" 'M," said Chloe, sucking the dough off her fingers. "Is Mr. Monody mad, Mrs. Moffat?"

Eliza Moffat looked up sharply.

"Mad?" she said. "I don't call the likes of him mad, nor I don't hold with shutting them up neither. Who's been telling you such things?"

"Oh, I don't know. He seems odd."

"Odd's one word and mad's another," said Mrs. Moffat, opening the oven door and putting in a tray of dumplings. "Now, say a gentleman was to take the kitchen chopper and bash his wife with it—I'd give in to his being mad. Or a young lady what tries to throw herself off of a crowded bus in the middle of Hammersmith Broadway—well, I'd say likely enough as she was mad, pore thing; for who's it going to help a-throwing of yourself from buses when all's said and done? That's what I calls mad. But if a gentleman likes to write poetry, who's he a-harming of?"

"Does he write poetry?"

"Strews it all about the floor. And what I say is, it's a crool shame to shut the pore things up so long as they're harmless and don't go throwing of themselves down off buses and such like." She banged the oven door with decision.

Chloe gazed at her, fascinated.

"Do tell me some more," she said. "Did a girl really throw herself off a bus in Hammersmith Broadway? Was she hurt?"

"Not her,"—Eliza Moffat sounded a little disappointed—"fell on a perliceman she did."

"How perfectly thrilling!"

"Fell on a perliceman what was holding up the traffic, and knocked him flat. There he was, one minute throwing a chest, and holding his hand up, and looking as if he'd bought London; and the next minute down she come and knocked him flat."

"Good gracious!" said Chloe.

"Mr. Moffat's sister seen it," said Mrs. Moffat. After a pause she added: "Their banns was called on Sunday."

It was that afternoon that Chloe saw Emily Wroughton. Emily was coming down the street towards her, holding up an umbrella against the incessant rain; she held it much too high, and a steady cascade descended upon a limp black ostrich feather, and from thence to a sagging shoulder.

As soon as Mrs. Wroughton saw Chloe, the umbrella came down like an extinguisher, and she scuttled into a side street. Chloe caught her up easily enough, and took her by the drier arm in friendly fashion.

"Why on earth do you run away from me? I'm the one to run—I'm going to too, in a minute. But I *did* want to say,"—here she squeezed the bony arm impulsively—"I did just want to say 'Thank you.'" Emily, having failed to keep the umbrella between her and Chloe, let her mouth fall open, and said, "Oh!" She sniffed also, and her nose began to get pink. "It was ripping of you to give me the chance of getting away. I don't believe I ever thanked you. I—I was horribly frightened really, you know. But afterwards I thought how absolutely topping it was of you."

Emily said "Oh," again; her mouth stayed open; the tears began to run down her nose. "I shall have to tell Leonard," she said in a miserable whisper. "I shall have to tell Leonard that I've seen you."

"All right," said Chloe quite cheerfully. "Tell him I've got a nice post in a detective's family, and that we shall all be frightfully pleased to see him any time he likes to drop in."

Emily produced a handkerchief and took three little dabs at her face—left eye, nose, right eye. Then she gave a rending sniff, and said:

"Oh, Miss Dane, have you really? Oh, I'm so glad! But please, please, *please* don't tell me any more, because I shall have to tell Leonard what you've said."

"But I want you to. You go home and tell him that the detective is most frightfully anxious to meet him. I *do* hope he'll come and see us."

"Don't tell me the address," said Emily quickly.

Chloe laughed and shook her arm lightly.

"Why don't you stamp your foot at him and tell him to go to Jericho? Just try some day, and see what happens. I believe he'd go off pop like a burst tyre. Anyhow, if he wants to know where I am—"

"No, don't tell me!" Emily put up a protesting hand.

Chloe gave her another little shake.

"Tell him to ask at Scotland Yard," she said, and ran back along the way that she had come.

If she had looked behind her when she came to the corner, she would have seen that Emily was no longer alone. Wroughton had come out of a house near by and joined her. When he had listened to half-a-dozen tearful sentences, he, too, ran to the corner round which Chloe had disappeared and, turning it, proceeded to follow her at a safe distance.

Chapter Thirty-Five

CHLOE SAT to Mr. Monody next morning in Mrs. Moffat's sitting-room. Mrs. Moffat herself did not use it for sitting in, but it contained all the things she valued most on earth. It had, therefore, the atmosphere peculiar to such shrines, and the first thing that Mr. Monody did was to fling the windows wide and let in the north-east wind.

Chloe perched on the arm of a large chair upholstered in crimson plush, and swung her feet.

"Are you one of the people who put an eye in one corner of the picture and another somewhere in the middle of next week?" she asked anxiously. "I saw a painting like that once, and it gave me the cold grues."

"I'm neither a cubist, nor a vorticist, nor a vertiginist. Tilt your chin and think about running away. Think about running for your life from all the conventions that ever were. And just run your hand through your hair, will you—it's much too tidy. Don't look at me—I want your profile. Look at the wall above the fireplace."

Chloe looked, and found her attention riveted by a print which hung there, an obvious heirloom. Beneath it in flourishing letters its title, "The Broad and Narrow Ways."

Chloe forgot Mr. Monody and everything modern, and stared, fascinated, at the picture. Right at the top was a single, enormous eye, coloured blue. Beneath it The Broad Way ran steeply downhill. The Broad Way was exactly like Maxton High Street; there were shops on either side of it, and swarms of little black people laughing, talking, and shopping; at intervals there were roundabouts, and people dancing; at the bottom of the street, instead of the bridge, there was an awful chasm which revealed a most authentic Hell, with lots of smoke, and flames and devils. The Narrow Way, which occupied the left-hand side of the picture, was like the course of an obstacle race, a terribly difficult obstacle race. First there was a stream with little jags of rock in it and holes to fall into; a pilgrim could be seen in one up to his neck and looking most uncomfortable. Next came a ladder fixed to the face of what Chloe called a more than perpendicular cliff; a pilgrim, who had almost reached the top appeared to be hanging by a single finger. At the top of the cliff there was a chasm with the flames of Hell coming out of it, very pointed and terrifying. After that there were piles of black stones. And right at the top of the picture there were three fat angels with Georgian smiles and stout calico nightgowns.

Mr. Monody did not talk whilst he was working, and he worked at lightning speed. By the time Chloe had assimilated Eliza Moffat's great grandfather's print he was saying, "Thanks," and shutting up his sketch-book. Chloe uttered an incredulous "Oh!" and jumped down.

"How quick you've been—how frightfully quick! But I must see it!"

"I never—" began Mr. Monody, and at that point found that he was no longer holding his sketch-book.

Chloe ran to the window with it, turned the leaves, and exclaimed. She saw herself running down a steep hill with a tearing wind behind her; her hands were stretched out; her hair was blown about her face; the one brief garment with which Mr. Monody's pencil had endowed her also blew in the wind. It was a very clever piece of work. She looked at it and said:

"How do you draw the wind? I can see it blowing."

He came and looked over her shoulder.

"Most people can't see it. If they could see it, they'd be able to draw it." He spoke in the abstracted tones of one who informs an infant that C.A.T. spells "Cat." Then he took his sketch-book out of Chloe's hands, twisted a piece of worn-out elastic round it twice, and began to drift away. At the door he seemed to wake up; he actually looked at Chloe as if he could see her, and not some fantasy in his own mind.

"You did say you were Michael's girl, didn't you?"

Chloe's colour brightened; her eyes danced.

"No, I didn't say anything of the sort."

Mr. Monody rumpled his hair.

"Ah!" he said. "Some one said it—but perhaps it was Michael. I think you'd better shut those windows, because she likes this room kept nice and stuffy. Michael's a very good chap."

He was half way out of the room, when Chloe's voice arrested him; it sounded severe, but her eyes still danced.

"Mr. Monody." She emphasized the name with a tap of the foot.

"Yes?" said Mr. Monody vaguely.

"Where were you brought up?"

He brightened.

"Everybody asks me that sooner or later. In future I've decided to say that seven maiden aunts took me in infancy to a South Pacific island. Don't you think that covers the whole ground?"

That afternoon Chloe had an adventure. She hunted jobs from half-past two till past-half five, when she had promised to meet Michael and have tea with him. Once or twice during the afternoon an extraordinary feeling of discomfort came over her. It was rather difficult to describe and very disturbing. When it came upon her she found herself turning round to see if she was being followed; she had to struggle against a desire to run as fast as she had been running in Mr. Monody's sketch. It was in a fit of extravagance induced by this curious, recurrent sense of dread that she expended twopence on a tube fare.

It was too early for the evening rush, but the train was full enough, and the lift in which she found herself at her journey's end was closely packed. Some one had an elbow in the middle of her back, whilst a massive lady with a feathered hat made it impossible for her to move even half an inch forward. "Pass along, please," said the lift man. "Pass along there, pass along." The elbow became a gimlet. Chloe surged forward into the ostrich feathers, which smelt horribly of dye; and at the same moment she felt a hand in the pocket of her coat. Two thoughts bobbed up in her mind simultaneously—"A pickpocket," and, "My purse isn't there, thank goodness." That was what she thought. What she did bore no relation to it, and must have been quite instinctive. With a lightning dive her hand went into the pocket and found, not another hand, but another purse. Like a flash she had it out and was holding it up high above all those crowding heads.

"Whose purse is this?" she called at the top of her clear young voice; and every soul in the lift heard her, stopped talking, and twisted their necks to look. The lift stopped with a jerk. "Somebody put this into my pocket. Whose is it?" said Chloe to the silence. What she had done had been without thought; but just at this moment thought came into play again. The gate of the lift opened, and the lift man came across to her.

"What's all this, miss? Had your pocket picked?"

She had begun to shake and feel cold.

"Some one put this into my pocket. It's not mine."

Nobody claimed the purse, which proved to contain nearly a pound in silver. Chloe had to accompany the lift man to an inspector to whom she repeated her story, and with whom she left the purse.

"Some one sneaked it of course, got a fright, and tried to get rid of it. But if you ask me why nobody claimed it, well you ask me something that I haven't got an answer to. Just give me your name and address, miss, will you."

Chloe met Michael and had tea with him. When they were walking back together she told him what had happened. Half way through the story she took his arm because she felt that it would be nice to have something to hold on to. The hand shook, and Michael felt it shaking. Chloe's voice shook too.

"If I hadn't pulled it out and held it up like lightning, I should probably be in prison at this very minute," she said. "Michael, it's the second time in a week—and next time perhaps it'll come off."

"What do you mean?" said Michael blankly.

"Some one in that lift was all ready to say I had stolen that purse. If I hadn't felt their wicked, prowling hand, and got in in front of them, that's what they'd have done; and I should have been in prison instead of having tea with you, because there was that wretched purse actually in my pocket—nobody could say it wasn't."

"But who on earth—"

"The same people," said Chloe with a gasp. "The woman on my right—I didn't see her face properly until just as she went out of the lift—she'd white hair and sort of old lady clothes, but I'm sure it was that sham secretary dressed up."

Michael didn't say anything; he did not, in fact, speak at all until they were standing in Mrs. Moffat's hall, which seemed to be quite full of the smell of cabbage. Then he opened the sitting-room door and said rather shortly:

"Will you come in here? I want to speak to you."

He lit the gas, and a mantle with a large hole in one side shed a fluttering light upon the red plush suite, the crimson Axminster, and the striped green wall-paper up which there climbed endless rows of pale magenta sweet peas. Over the mantelpiece the great blue eye in the ancestral print gazed severely upon Chloe's shivering attempt at composure and Michael's set pallor.

Michael shut the door and turned.

"Look here, all this has got to stop," he said.

Chloe nodded.

"I wish it would."

"It's got to! Something's got to be done. Will you let me go to the police about these people?"

"No!" said Chloe. "No—no—no!"

"Why not?"

Chloe saw herself climbing over the garden wall in the dark and running away with Martin Fossetter. She saw Emily Wroughton sniffing and dabbing her pink eyelids. She saw headlines in evening papers: "Heiress Elopes." She stamped her foot and said through chattering teeth:

"No, no, you're not to!"

"Will you let me consult a solicitor then?"

"No, no, I won't—not till I'm of age—not till I can sign something and get rid of Mr. Dane's horrible money. I won't do anything except hide till I'm of age. A solicitor would say I oughtn't to have taken the letters; and he'd try and make me take the money, and ask all sorts of questions. No, I won't go near one till I can say what I mean to do, and *do* it."

"Who gets it if you don't?"

"Mr. Hudson told me I ought to make a will as soon as I was of age, because otherwise the money all went to the Crown."

"It seems a pity," said Michael slowly.

Chloe flared.

"It doesn't—it isn't—you say that because you don't know—no decent person could touch a penny of it—I'd rather go to prison for the rest of my life!"

Michael looked at her, frowning.

"You want some one to look after you."

"N' no—I don't."

"You do. My people have gone to Madeira for two months, or I'd have got my mother to take a hand—she'd have done it like a shot. I can't think what people want to go to Madeira for. But they've gone, so that only leaves me."

Chloe darted a look at him. He was very pale.

"Chloe," he said, "I'd look after you if you'd let me." And in her own mind Chloe heard Eliza Moffat say, "He loves you true"; and then again, "He loves you true." She said,

"Would you?"

"Yes, I would," said Michael. "I've wanted to ever since the second time I saw you; and you don't know how frightfully I've wanted to since you came here. When I see you going about looking for some beastly job, it makes me feel like running amok and smashing things. And when it comes to these damn blackguards,—" he took a big stride forward and caught Chloe's hands in his—"I can't stick it. You've got to let me take care of you."

"Oh," said Chloe; it wasn't a very audible sound. She pulled her hands away and tried again: "M-Michael, d-don't glare at me like that."

Michael put his arms around her.

"I love you frightfully," he said. "I love you *frightfully*."

"Why?" said Chloe with a little sob.

"Because I do. It's—it's just me. I mean there isn't any me that doesn't love you—I'm all in. I—Chloe, can't you—won't you—couldn't you like me a little?—enough to let me look after you?"

His arms were very strong. Chloe had stopped shaking, and she had stopped feeling cold. She looked straight up into Michael's face, and the tears began to run down her cheeks. Michael kissed her.

"M-Michael," said Chloe.

Michael hugged her.

"M-Michael, will you always be frightfully nice to me?"

"What'll you do if I'm not?"

"Run away of course."

Michael laughed rather unsteadily and laid his cheek against hers.

"I've got a beast of a temper," he said.

"Have you? What do you do when you lose it?"

"I don't do anything—I just want to smash things up."

"I stamp my foot," said Chloe.

"Yes, I've seen you. Chloe, let's get married at once."

"What do you call at once?"

"Well I asked a parson, and he said it took three days."

Chloe put both hands in the middle of his chest and pushed him away.

"Don't talk nonsense! D'you know, pushing you is exactly like pushing a stone wall."

Michael looked pleased.

"I am pretty hard. Look here, it isn't nonsense; it's the only thing to be done."

Chloe whirled to the other side of the room, blew him a kiss, and said, "Pouf!"

"No—really. You see, I can't look after you properly until we're married. And—and I do so hate these beastly jobs you keep looking for."

"Perhaps," suggested Chloe brightly. "Perhaps there's a most fearfully nice and lucrative job waiting for me round the next corner—and perhaps I should like it ever so much better than being married to you."

"Perhaps you would. On the other hand—" his tone was rather grim—"you might walk into another of those infernal traps."

The sparkle died out of Chloe's look. She put out her hands with an involuntary gesture, and found them taken and held very tightly indeed.

"Chloe! Sweetheart! Darling! Don't look like that. What a brute I was to say it!"

"I'm a perfect fool," said Chloe in a little, sobbing voice. "It's no good your saying I'm not, because I am. I'm a rabbit, and an idiot, and a fool. But oh, Michael, I *am* frightened. That business this afternoon was a sort of last straw; it scared me stiff."

"I'm going to take you right away from it all. I told you I'd gone into partnership. Well, I can get a week or ten days off, and we'll go away and have an absolutely ripping time. Look here, this is Friday; and if I go and wrestle round, we can get married on Tuesday, and just go off anywhere you'd like to. What about Paris?"

"Lovely!" said Chloe. "But won't it cost a lot?"

Michael became very business-like.

"We shan't be rich, but we ought to be able to rub along. I've got about five hundred a year of my own, and I expect to do quite well out of the business. We'll go to Paris and have no end of a time."

Chapter Thirty-Six

CHLOE'S WEDDING DAY dawned wet and windy. The clouds instead of lifting darkened to a day of settled gloom.

"It's just as well," said Chloe to Mrs. Moffat, "isn't it, Moffy dear?"

"'Happy's the bride that the sun shines on,' is how the proverb goes. But where there's real true love like Mr. Michael's got for you, there's always sunshine in a manner of speaking—not but what a lift in the weather wouldn't be a treat too."

Chloe shook her head.

"It's not going to lift; and it's much better it shouldn't, for of all the dowdy, disreputable frumps of brides, I'm sure I'm the dowdiest, and disreputablest, and frumpiest."

"Oh, miss!" Eliza Moffat was obviously shocked.

"Moffy dear, I *am*. Just look at me! Wouldn't I make a perfectly sweet paragraph in one of the Society papers?—'Miss Dane absolutely riveted the eyes of all beholders by her daringly original choice of a wedding dress. Exquisitely gowned in brown tweed, her raven locks crowned with priceless felt, she had only to be seen to be admired. Her stockings were the latest thing in darned needle-work, and her feet displayed the new open-work shoe which, a little bird tells me, is to be *all* the rage.' Oh, Moffy dear, if you love me, *does* the hole show very much?"

"It shows," said Mrs. Moffat—"no one can't say that it don't show. But they're shined up lovely."

"I *would* have liked a proper wedding dress," said Chloe. "I've thought so often what I'd be married in; and I never, never, *never* dreamt of its being brown tweed."

"Didn't Mr. Michael—"

Chloe's cheeks flamed.

"He knows I wouldn't let him! He'll just have to make the best of the shabbiest bride in London."

"My dear," said Eliza Moffat, "do you think he'll see your clothes? When a man loves a girl true like Mr. Michael loves you, he don't see anything except just her, and the way he loves her. You take it from me, my dear, you'll be all in shining white for him, because that's the way he thinks of you."

Chloe flung her arms round Mrs. Moffat's neck and kissed her.

"Moffy you *dear*!" she said.

Chloe and Michael were married in a little dark church with Mr. Monody, Mrs. Moffat and Mrs. Rowse for witnesses. The responses echoed in the empty space. A red angel with yellow hair looked down at them from a little stained glass window; he held in his hand a pair of scales.

The parson murmured, and Michael murmured.

Chloe said, "I, Chloe Mary, take thee, Michael—" Her voice dropped to inaudibility on his second name because the young parson had boggled at it. Stannard or Standen—she must ask him afterwards what it really was. Ridiculous not to know one's husband's second name.

"I pronounce you man and wife," said the young parson; and a voice deep inside Chloe spoke to her so loudly, clearly, and insistently that she stopped hearing anything else. "You're married," said the voice, "you're married—you're married—you're married." The words went over and over, and on and on. Suddenly the parson's voice broke in upon them; it had a tone of finality about it: "As long as ye do well, and are not afraid with any amazement," he announced, quoting the Apostle Peter.

Michael and Chloe walked into the little vestry, followed by an abstracted Mr. Monody, a composed Mrs. Rowse, and a highly tearful Mrs. Moffat.

"I knew Lizzie would kiss me," said Michael in Chloe's ear.

"Ssh," said Chloe. She herself kissed Mrs. Rowse and Mrs. Moffat, and, to her extreme surprise, received an absent-minded salute from Mr. Monody. Then Michael's hand on her arm.

"Come and sign this register thing. I've done it. Why do you suppose they want to know what one's father's Christian names are?"

Chloe laughed.

"It does seem odd."

She came forward, still laughing, took the pen which somebody put into her hand, and bent over the register.

"Just here," said the young parson. "Your full names, please."

Chloe wrote Chloe Mary Dane, and then looked at Michael's signature above her own. The names stood out black in a clear, boyish writing. Chloe stared as she might have stared at death. The names stood clear and black:—Michael Stranways Fossetter.

The laughter and the warmth were struck out of her, leaving her colder than she had ever been in all her life before. She was not faint, or ill; she was able to say, "Lawrence John" quite clearly and steadily in response to a request for her father's Christian names. She said "Thank you," and smiled when the parson shook hands with her and offered her his good wishes—he only thought that her hand was very cold.

Next moment the little cold hand was on Michael's arm, and they were walking down the aisle together. Chloe walked to the steady beat of one insistent refrain, "Stran—Stran is short for Stranways." It just went on and on in her head like a chance-heard tune that one can't get rid of—her own question, "Who is Stran?" and Leonard Wroughton's answer, "Stran is short for Stranways."

They came out into the damp, draughty porch, and down the wet steps to the horrible rhythm. She got into Michael's car, and heard the engine beating out the same measure, "Stran is short for Stranways—Stran is short for Stranways."

Michael spoke to her, and she answered him.

"Is anything the matter? Are you cold, darling?"

Chloe said, "Yes, I'm cold." And behind the question and answer the maddening beat went on, "Who is Stran?—Stran is short for Stranways."

They stopped at Mrs. Moffat's door and got out. In the hall a letter lay face downwards on the floor. Michael picked it up and handed it to Chloe.

"Come along in to the fire," he said, and put his arm about her. "I haven't kissed you yet, Chloe, I haven't kissed you yet."

Chloe detached herself with a queer, jerky movement. The letter was from Emily Wroughton. She said, "Wait—please wait," and began to open it.

Michael watched her. What had happened? Why on earth was she looking like this? He had seen her look cold, tired, angry, and frightened; but he had never seen her look like this. There was no expression in her face; a smooth, even pallor seemed to have blotted all feeling from it. He looked at her, and felt afraid.

Chloe let the envelope fall on to the floor. Her face never changed as she unfolded the letter and read it. There was no formal beginning:

"I *must* tell you, because he has found out where you live. I didn't tell you the truth at Danesborough—I told you what Leonard had told me to tell you. The real plot was to frighten you into marrying Stran. He was to make you keep the money. That was the real plot—to marry you to Stran. The rest was only lies. I couldn't bear it when you thanked me."

The words were smudged and blotted. There was no signature.

Chloe put out her hand and let the letter fall into the fire. Well, the plot had succeeded. Emily's letter was too late. She had married Stran.

"Chloe, my darling!" said Michael, and put his arm about her.

With all her strength she thrust him away, and turned to face him with her head up.

"If it was because of the money you married me—I shall never take it—you will never get me to take it!" The bleak voice and slow utterance were of all things in the world most unlike the Chloe Michael knew.

He could only stammer her name.

"Nobody can make me take the money!"

"I don't know what you mean," said Michael. "Are you ill?"

She shook her head slightly.

"No, I'm not ill."

"What is it then? What was in that letter? Chloe, what is it?"

Mrs. Moffat opened the door, looked in, and withdrew hurriedly.

"You know!" said Chloe. "You know! I didn't know until I saw your name written down. But I know now."

"My name! But you knew my name—you knew it was Fossetter."

"No. You called it Foster—every one did."

"Every one does who knows us. On my honour, Chloe, I thought you knew. Meeting you at Miss Tankerville's and all, I didn't know that you had never seen it written—how could I? I thought you knew Martin was a cousin. We talked about him, and I told you I barred him—I always have. Chloe—Chloe darling, don't be angry!"

Chloe backed away from him.

"Don't touch me!—don't touch me!"

Michael stopped dead. His outstretched arms fell to his side.

"I won't touch any woman who doesn't want me to touch her—you needn't be afraid. Have you gone mad, Chloe?"

"Yes," said Chloe. "I was mad when I trusted you. And I was mad when I married you. But that's the end. I'm not going to go on being mad any longer."

Michael was as pale as she was.

"Will you tell me what you're accusing me of?"

"Yes, I will," said this new, icy Chloe. "I'm accusing you of having lied to me and deceived me. I'm accusing you of being a blackmailer. I'm accusing you of marrying me in order to get hold of Mr. Dane's money." She paused, dropped her voice to its lowest tone, and said, "But you won't get it—you'll never get it, Michael!"

All the time that she was speaking she watched him with a hard stare. When a sudden flush ran up to the roots of his hair and he made a half step toward her with clenched hands, she felt a little stab of exultation. She was hurting him. He looked at her with a blaze of fury in his blue eyes, and she laughed. Then she turned her back on him and went out of the room, and so up the stairs and into the room which had been Michael's before it had been hers. Everything in her was bent to the one purpose—she must get away. Her mind was cool and clear. She must get away before this coldness melted and turned to burning pain. She must get away from Michael, who wasn't Michael any more, but Stran.

On the bed was her grey coat and the travelling case which Michael had given her. The things she had brought away from Danesborough were already packed in it. She took them out and made a parcel with the brown paper and string which Eliza Moffat had taken off the new travelling case only an hour or two before—her admiring comments sounded faintly in Chloe's memory, coming back as though across long, intervening years. Chloe laid the parcel on the bed beside the empty suit-case and put on her coat. Then she took out her purse and opened it. There were two shillings, a threepenny bit, four pennies, and a very battered halfpenny. She picked up the parcel, crossed the landing, and knocked at Mr. Monody's door.

Mr. Monody opened it in his shirt sleeves. When he saw Chloe he rumpled his hair and said:

"I can't come down and eat cake at this hour—and what's more, I won't. If you could get Mrs. Moffat to believe that I won't, I shall never stop being grateful to you. She's a most pertinacious woman."

"Yes," said Chloe. "Will you lend me some money, please?" She spoke without a tremor, and held out her hand just as a child might have done.

With equal simplicity Mr. Monody replied:

"How much?"

"A pound." She dropped her voice because a sound came up from below.

Mr. Monody extracted a pound note from his waistcoat pocket and gave it to her.

"Thank you," said Chloe. "I'll pay it back. Good bye."

Without another word she went to the top of the stairs and stood there listening. Then she went down four steps and looked over the banisters. She held her parcel in her left hand.

Without any warning Michael burst out of Mrs. Moffat's sitting-room. She had no time to move or go back. She saw him cross the hall at a stumbling run. He wrenched the front door open and plunged out. The door banged with a violence that set the gas pendant swaying and rattling; the tiny flakes from the broken mantle fluttered down from it like snow. Chloe watched them fall.

The hall was empty. She came down into it noiselessly, and reached the front door. It opened, and she slipped out and stood for a moment on the step. Michael's car still stood by the kerb. But there was no sign of Michael. The door closed gently, gently. She let go of the handle, and went down into the street.

Chapter Thirty-Seven

CHLOE WENT down the street, crossed over, and took the first turning that she came to. She kept on walking and taking turnings without thinking where she was going. She had not, indeed, begun to think at all. She only wanted to get away, to hide, to bury herself where Michael couldn't find her.

She did not remember what she had said to him, or what he had said to her; but the unspoken clash between them had been so violent that the instinct of each was the same—blind headlong flight. She thought of Michael's rush through the hall, the momentary glimpse that she had had of his face convulsed with rage, and fierce little stabs of anger began to break through the icy cold which had come upon her when she bent over the register and read Michael's names. In Eliza Moffat's sitting-room he had looked at her as if he would like to take her up and break her; she had at least stung him to that. And, for the rest, he should never find her—*never*.

She found herself all at once on a crowded bus route. She could get away quicker by bus. She got into the first one that stopped, and sat rigidly upright, her parcel on her lap, staring out at the shops, the other buses, the streams of people flowing like water along the pavement.

"Where to?" said the conductor.

Chloe had no idea. She said, "A pennyworth;" and took her ticket. She crumpled the thin cardboard in her hand and tried to think. She couldn't go to Maxton because Michael would look for her there. She couldn't go to Mrs. Rowse. She couldn't go to Danesborough. She couldn't go any distance by train because Mr. Monody's pound and her own two and sevenpence halfpenny were all the money she had, and you can't go very far or live for very long on twenty-two and sevenpence halfpenny.

She went on looking out of the window, and presently saw the great block of The Luxe slide into view. The bus stopped with a jerk, and as it stopped, Chloe got up and followed the stream of descending passengers. She crossed over and walked up the steps of The Luxe, a composed, shabby figure carrying a brown paper parcel. The ice in her was fast melting into flame, and between icy pride and flaming anger there was no place at all for self-consciousness or shyness. She walked into the hall and approached the porter.

"I am Mrs. Mostyn Llewellyn's secretary. I have a message for Miss Cross, one of the clerks employed here." Neither voice nor manner failed her, and the porter actually ceased to be conscious of the brown paper parcel. He said, "Certainly," waved to an underling, and a minute later Chloe was resting her parcel on a counter of polished mahogany and looking over it at Connie Cross.

"Hullo!" said Connie, looking up; and then added in a different tone, "My! You do look bad! Anything wrong, dear?"

Chloe shook her head. She didn't quite know why she had come to Connie. She had just seen The Luxe and walked in without having any definite idea of what she was going to do next. In the daylight Connie's hair looked several shades more improbable than it had by night. But Connie's voice was friendly.

"You do look bad all the same," she repeated.

"I'm all right," said Chloe. She stood at the counter, leaning on it a little and looking down at its polished surface.

Connie put a warm hand on her wrist.

"Look here, what is it? For the Lord's sake, don't go fainting in here!"

Chloe pulled herself together just in time.

"I want a place to go to—a room. I thought—can you help me?"

"Well, dear—" Connie began, and then broke off, considering; the new wedding ring had caught her eye.

"Just for you?" she asked.

Chloe followed the direction of her eyes. The gold band stood out on her ungloved left hand. She turned so white that she frightened Connie, and said:

"I'm alone—I'm quite alone."

"My!" said Connie. "Has he let you down already? Don't you take it too much to heart—that's my advice. Men aren't worth it—that's the truth. Ernie now, that I told you about, he's treated me something shameful—took up with that girl that was trying to get him away from me. Well, she's got him, and I hope she likes her bargain." She tossed the impossibly golden head. "I'm not going to break my heart for him, not if I know it. I shan't lose my beauty sleep worrying over Ernie. And my advice to you is, keep smiling and don't let any man think you care enough to worry. There, that's good advice, dear,—you can take it from me it is. Leave 'em and they come running after you; but you start running after them, and, Lord help you, they'll keep you running."

"Don't!" said Chloe. Then she looked Connie straight in the face. "I've nowhere to go," she said in a piteous whisper.

The easy tears sprang into Miss Cross's large blue eyes. She gave them a perfunctory dab with a highly scented handkerchief.

"Oh, Lord, dear, don't talk like that, or I shall cry. Look here, you can share with me till you get something else. Aunt's the difficulty of course; but you take care she sees your wedding ring, and she'll be all right. I wish I could come along with you myself. But I'll write you a line—and don't you take any notice if she's disagreeable or inclined to talk pious, because that's just her way. She's not such a bad old sort; only she thinks a girl's going straight to the devil if she powders her face and has a gentleman friend. And what I say is, where's the harm?—and, anyhow, what'ud life be like if you didn't?"

She scribbled rapidly on a piece of paper as she spoke, scrawled her name at the bottom, and resumed:

"There, you give her this. And tell her I'll be home at my usual. Here's what I've said:

'DEAR AUNT,

'This is my friend Mrs. Dene,'—"Will that do?"—'Her husband has had to go off and leave her most unexpected, and I've told her she can share with me while she looks round for something.'"

She wrote the address,

Mrs. Cross,
    7, Blanesbury Terrace,
        Tooting.

and added some practical advice as to the shortest way of getting there.

"And mind you keep smiling, dear," she concluded. "See you this evening."

Chloe said "Thank you." She tried to say more, but the words wouldn't come. Contact with human kindness had thawed the last of the ice. Pride was gone; she felt defenceless against pain. She went out of The Luxe, and followed Connie's directions carefully. With all her heart she hoped that she would reach 7, Blanesbury Terrace before the last of her strength gave way. She found she was talking to herself, as she used to talk to herself when she was a child: "You can't cry in a bus. You mustn't cry in a bus. You mustn't cry or faint in front of all these people." An old man opposite her was reading *The Poultry Keeper's Journal.* She wondered what he would think if she were to break down suddenly. "You mustn't do it. You can't do it—not in a bus."

She came to Blanesbury Terrace at the end of her tether, and put Connie's note without a word into the hand of the tall, grim woman who opened the door of No. 7. She did not speak, but she searched Mrs. Cross's face for comfort; it did not promise very much. A conviction of the sinfulness of most other people had drawn hard lines about the eyes and mouth. The iron-grey hair was tightly plaited after an obsolete fashion. The black alpaca dress reached almost to the floor.

Mrs. Cross looked up from her niece's note with sharp grey eyes.

"I'm sorry," she said in the stiffest of stiff voices. "I'm sorry; but Connie's taken too much on herself. She rents a room in my house, but I'm not prepared for her to share it with her friends. Good morning, Mrs. Dene."

She began to shut the door. Chloe took a step forward, caught at the door-post, and clung there.

"Mayn't I come in?" Mrs. Cross could hardly catch the words.

"Connie takes too much on herself," said Mrs. Cross. "I don't let apartments."

Chloe had ceased to mind what she said or did. She looked at Mrs. Cross with the eyes of a hurt animal and said:

"I've nowhere to go."

Mrs. Cross became a little more erect than before, her voice carefully refined.

"I'm *reelly* very sorry."

Chloe's eyes shut. She said "Oh!" quite softly, and sank down fainting at Mrs. Cross's feet. When she recovered, it was to the feel of horsehair under her cheek. She was, in fact, lying full length on the old-fashioned horsehair sofa in Mrs. Cross's parlour; there was a very hard bolster under her head, with a horsehair button at either end.

There was an antimacassar on every chair, and spangled shavings in the fireplace. The room was very cold, and her hair was wet.

Chloe sat up, and as she did so, Mrs. Cross came into the room with a cup of hot soup in her hand. When Chloe had drunk the soup, Mrs. Cross looked at her searchingly.

"You're a married woman?"

Chloe remembered that she was married; she remembered that she had married "Stran." She looked as if she was going to faint again as she caught her breath and said:

"Yes."

Mrs. Cross took the empty cup, put it down, and planted herself grimly on a chair. Chloe, shivering on the edge of the sofa, saw purpose in the very way in which the bony hands were folded.

"Where is your husband?" said Mrs. Cross.

"I don't know." The words shook and tumbled over one another.

"Has he deserted you?"

"N-no," said Chloe out of her breaking heart.

A gleam of pleasurable triumph altered for a moment Mrs. Cross's harsh contours.

"I knew it," she announced. "And what, may I ask, do you make of your duty and of the Bible? 'Wives, obey your husbands', Mrs. Dene,— what do you make of that, may I ask?"

Chloe put out her hand and laid it on Mrs. Cross's knee.

"Did you ever trust anyone very much, and have them fail you?" she asked.

The older woman frowned.

"Put not your trust in princes, nor in any child of man, for there is no help in them," she said.

"No, there isn't, is there?" said Chloe with the tears running down her face. "I thought he was good; and he isn't."

"What's he done?" said Mrs. Cross sharply.

"I can't tell you—I can't tell anyone. I came away because if I'd stayed, he would have tried to make me do a wicked thing."

"Lord, have mercy!" said Mrs. Cross. "Was it as bad as that?"

"It was money," said Chloe. "I couldn't take it because it had been come by wickedly. But if I'd stayed, he would have tried to make me take it. I *had* to come away." She spoke to something in this forbidding woman which she could trust. Mrs. Cross looked at her very hard. Chloe rose to her feet.

"I'm sorry I troubled you. I'll go now. It was kind of you to give me the soup."

"I'm a woman that does her duty," said Mrs. Cross. "No one can ever say I'm not. I took Connie without a penny; and I'd have brought her up pious if she'd have let me. If you can give me your word that you're a fit companion for her, you may stay. No one can say I'm the woman to turn any respectable young woman from my door if she's got nowhere to go to. Look me in the face, Mrs. Dene, and tell me the gospel truth. Are you a good-living young woman, and fit to be with Connie? For mind you Connie's worldly, and takes no heed of religion; but she's a good-living girl, and some day, I'm in hopes, she'll turn her mind to serious things."

Chloe's eyes met the hard, grey stare with perfect simplicity.

"I won't hurt Connie," she said; and quite suddenly a most dreadful desire to laugh came over her. She buried her face in her hands, and Mrs. Cross saw her shoulders heave.

"I'm dishing dinner," she said. "You come along in and sit down."

Chapter Thirty-Eight

MRS. CROSS proved to be a woman of some efficiency. Within an hour or two of Chloe's arrival she had actually obtained work for her with a little dressmaker who attended the same chapel.

"She can't afford much in the way of wages, but she's a God-fearing woman, and you won't hear any loose talk in her house."

Chloe took the work thankfully, and submitted to a thorough examination by Mrs. Cross, at the close of which her contribution to the household expenditure was assessed.

"You won't do better than that anywhere else—and seeing that you're here, it may be that it's laid on me to look after you. There's plenty of roaring lions going about seeking whom they may devour, and a young married woman that isn't living with her husband can't be too careful."

Chloe settled down to a life of outwardly placid routine. All day she worked for Miss Morrison, who made terrible clothes for the elder members of the congregation. In the evening she sat and mended her own things, whilst Connie went out to meet a "gentleman friend." It was only by the most constant mending that Chloe's things held together at all. Mrs. Cross approved her industry, and, herself occupied in like manner, discoursed at length on such exhilarating subjects as:

The Worldly Tendencies of The Young;
The Iniquity of Face Powder;
The Prevalence of Divorce; *and*
The Danger of Gentlemen Friends.

Chloe grew thin and lost her colour. The nights were the worst. Towards two or three in the morning she would have welcomed the gloomiest and most acid of Mrs. Cross's discourses. She lay cold and rigid in the narrow iron bed next to Connie's, listening to her hearty breathing, and struggling to repress the low, heart-broken sobs which threatened to overwhelm her during the long, dark hours. If she could have gone on feeling proud and angry it would have helped; but it wasn't in Chloe's heart to go on being angry with anyone. Her anger against Michael was all gone. The trouble was that the Michael she had known was gone too. He was quite gone. It was like the old stories where a person changed before your eyes into something horrible— wild beast or dragon. She had trusted him and loved him with all her heart. But the Michael whom she had loved and trusted had never really existed. She was lonely and cold and heart-broken for Michael. But there wasn't any Michael; there never had been any Michael. There was only Stran.

As she lay awake through the long hours, she went over and over all the things about Stran. Mr. Dane's warning, "Don't trust him a yard." The endorsements on those terrible letters: "From Stran"— "Two letters from Stran." The first thought of the letters brought her bolt upright in bed, her hands clutching the sides of it. She had given the letters to Michael to destroy. No—no—no—there wasn't any Michael: she had given the letters to Stran. That was the very bitterest moment of all. She had gone through so much to save the letters, and then in the end she had let herself be tricked into handing them over to Stran.

Even as the thought stabbed her she saw Michael's face looking at her as he had looked when she gave him the letters, and again when he told her how he had destroyed them. How could he look like that if he was Stran? There was no answer.

Chloe had been at Blanesbury Terrace for about ten days. She had saved five shillings towards repaying her debt to Mr. Monody, and she had written to Eliza Moffat. Connie posted the letter on the other side of London; it was very short:

"DEAR MOFFY,

"You were heavenly good to me, and I shall never forget it. Don't think me an ungrateful beast.

CHLOE."

"She will, of course," Chloe thought. "They all will, unless they think I'm mad. Oh, why can't one just wake up and find it's all a horrible dream?"

Sometimes she just let herself think that it was nothing but a dream after all, and that at any minute she might wake from it and find Michael. She didn't dare to do this very often because it hurt so much, and she mustn't cry in the day time, she mustn't think of anything but her mending and what Mrs. Cross was saying.

"Aunt loves you because you're such a good listener," Connie said, laughing. "I'm fond enough of her, but I can't be bothered listening to all the old stuff she talks. It stands to reason a girl's bound to be fed up with being told she's going to hell. I told her so straight only the other day. 'If I was going to be hanged, Aunt,' I said, 'I wouldn't want some one telling me about it all the time first.'"

Chloe sat and sewed. Mrs. Cross, on the other side of the table, mended Connie's silk stockings with a disapproving air. Every now and then she looked searchingly at Chloe. The ticking of the clock on the mantelpiece seemed to grow louder and louder.

Mrs. Cross rolled up Connie's stocking, put it on one side, and said:

"It's laid on me that maybe it's your duty to go back to your husband."

Chloe looked up, startled; her face was white in the gas-light; there were dark circles under her eyes.

"It's laid on me," said Mrs. Cross, "to tell you faithful that a wife's got her duty, and that, bad or good, marriage is marriage."

"I can't," said Chloe just above a whisper.

"The Lord don't take 'can't' for an answer," said Mrs. Cross. "And we're not in this world to do what's pleasant, like all you young folk think. We're here to do the Lord's will; and it's not His will for a wife to leave her husband and live separate. And you needn't think I'm talking about what I don't know. I married a man that was a heavy drinker, and I thought I was going to reform him. Well, I didn't. But I saw my duty, and I didn't leave him. I'd fifteen years of it; and a woman that's lived fifteen years with a drunkard has got the right to tell you what I tell you now. A wife's duty is with her husband."

"I can't," said Chloe again.

Mrs. Cross's sharp eyes dwelt for a moment on the quivering face.

"Did you quarrel?" she asked quite suddenly.

"Yes," said Chloe, "we did."

"I thought as much. You've a hasty temper, Mrs. Dene, and you'd do well to make it a subject for prayer. What did you quarrel about?"

"I can't tell you."

Mrs. Cross nodded.

"That generally means there isn't much to tell. I've kept quiet and watched you. You're hasty. It's my belief you spoke hasty and acted hasty. Did you wait to hear what he'd got to say for himself?"

Chloe flushed; the shaft was a pointed one.

"No."

"I thought as much." She took a needle with a larger eye, threaded it, and picked up a black woollen stocking of her own. "Everyone's got a right to a hearing. The Lord knows that man is full of vain excuses. But it's your duty to hear what they are, whether you like it or no."

The colour sprang to Chloe's cheeks in two scarlet spots. She jerked her chair back and got up, letting her work fall on the floor.

"Duty! Duty! Duty!" she said. "I'm sick of the word. I never heard it so often in all my life!" She stamped her foot and ran out of the room, slamming the door behind her.

Mrs. Cross watched her go, and nodded again.

"Hasty—very hasty," she said, and went on darning.

Half an hour later Chloe came back and begged her pardon. Her eyes were red with crying.

"It's not for us poor human beings to say we forgive or don't forgive," said Mrs. Cross. "You remember that when you think about your husband, Mrs. Dene. There, don't look like that. I forgive you fast enough. There's worse things than a hasty temper—not but what you oughtn't to strive against it all the same."

"It just goes off bang," said Chloe—"and then I'm frightfully sorry afterwards." She took one of Mrs. Cross's hands and squeezed it in both her own. "You've been an angel to me, and I'm a bad-tempered beast."

Mrs. Cross shut her mouth with a snap. Then she pulled her hand away and said:

"Don't talk so light about angels—no, nor beasts neither. We're both poor sinners that need the Lord's mercy."

Chapter Thirty-Nine

CHLOE LAY AWAKE that night. She did not cry any more; she just lay quite still with her hands clasped behind her head, thinking. If you cried, you did not think clearly; and she had got to the place where she must be quiet and think. It was Mrs. Cross who had brought her to this place. That dreadfully pointed, "Did you wait to hear what he had to say for himself?" would not away from her mind; the point of it went deeper and deeper.

Chloe set out her facts and tried to look at them impartially.

Michael's name was Fossetter, not Foster. That had naturally been a shock to her, but she could not say that he had deceived her about it. She had never seen it written until she saw it in the register; the mistake might have come about without any deception on his part. Then the other name—Stranways—it was the shock of that that had taken her right off her balance. "Stran is short for Stranways." You couldn't get away from that. And then Emily Wroughton's letter: "the real plot is to frighten you into marrying Stran."

Chloe tried to consider it all quite calmly, as if it had happened to somebody else.

She had married Stran. *Had she?* She looked into the darkness and saw Michael's face, Michael's eyes. Suppose she believed what his eyes said, and what something very deep down in her own heart said. Suppose, oh, suppose that she could really wake up out of this nightmare and find that Michael wasn't Stran at all. Chloe sat up and pushed her hair back from her face. What then? She said Michael's name in a quick, frightened whisper, and began to tremble violently. If Michael wasn't Stran; if he was Michael, her lover and her friend; why, then he would never, never forgive her.

"You didn't wait to hear what he'd got to say for himself." No, she hadn't waited—not an instant—before she flung dreadful words at him and fled. Nobody could ever forgive a thing like that—at least a girl might, but a man wouldn't. She didn't see how Michael could forgive— if he were really Michael and not Stran. Chloe went on thinking. Whether he forgave her or not, she'd got to be sure. She couldn't go on here, sewing black bead trimmings on to black cashmere dresses, and not be sure. How was she going to be sure? She could go and ask Emily Wroughton; but that wouldn't make her sure, because Emily, by her own confession, told lies when she was frightened; and she was nearly always frightened. No, there was just one way in which she could be sure. The envelope with "Stran's receipts" was still in the safe at Danesborough. When she took the last of the letters out she had thrown it back on the account books; and if Leonard Wroughton had not succeeded in opening the safe since, then it would still be there, and inside it the name and the handwriting of the man who was Stran.

A curious rush of mingled feelings carried her to the point of decision. She *had* to know who Stran was; and if she had to go to

Danesborough to find out, why then she would go to Danesborough. After all, everything that could happen had already happened. If Michael were Stran, why then the plot had succeeded in so far as it could succeed; they had the letters, and she was married to Stran. And if Michael wasn't Stran, the letters were burnt, and the plot had failed, because she was married to Michael. No, there was nothing that could happen.

Chloe sewed for Miss Morrison next day as usual. Whilst she sewed she made her plans. At six o'clock she went back to Blanesbury Terrace and told Mrs. Cross that she was going to be away all night on business. Mrs. Cross proved so hard to satisfy as to the necessity of any business that kept a young woman out all night that Chloe in the end told her the plain truth:

"I'm going down to my old home to get some papers which will tell me whether the things I've been believing are true or not."

"About your husband?"

"Yes. I *must* go—I really must."

"Well, the Lord go with you," said Mrs. Cross.

Chloe passed Connie at the station, and stopped for a moment to speak to her. Connie was in a state of giggling excitement.

"What do you think? I've been followed all the way from The Luxe—a handsome young chap too! Never offered to speak or anything like that, and quite the gentleman by his looks. First he asked one of the other girls if that wasn't Miss Cross—there's two or three of us come off together—and when she said 'Yes,' he followed me. I thought he was going to speak once, but he didn't." She tossed her head. "They think all the more of you if you're not too free. Wait a minute and I'll point him out to you. No—that's odd now, I can't see him."

Chloe took her ticket, only half listening. Connie had some such adventure as this nearly every day in the week. She got into her train, and was glad to sit still and shut her eyes; she did not, therefore, see Martin Fossetter cross the platform and get into the next carriage.

She caught the last train to Daneham. It was half-past ten when she left Daneham station behind her and started on her seven mile walk to Danesborough. It was black dark, wet under foot, but not raining; it was not cold either. A great, buffeting south-west wind moved the trees far overhead, but left the heavy air unstirred between the hedgerows.

Chloe walked quickly. She was not afraid of the darkness or of the lonely lanes. After London with its hurrying crowds it was good to be alone, to feel oneself covered and sheltered by the dark. When she had gone about half a mile, a taxi passed her, going fast. She flattened herself against the hedge to let it go by. Someone who had come by the same train as herself driving to one of the houses in the neighbourhood. She gave it no further thought until, nearly two miles further on, it passed her again on its return journey. Except for this double encounter she neither met anyone nor did anyone pass her on the road.

She came to the gates of Danesborough just before half-past twelve, and there for the first time it came to her that she might find them locked. The thought terrified her. Why had it not occurred to her before? She had been thinking of the safe and of the paper in the safe; she had never thought that the gates might be locked against her. She came to them, put out her hand quickly, grasped the handle, and pushed. With a creak one half of the gates swung inwards. Chloe went through, closed it behind her, and began to walk up the drive.

In her two hours' walk her eyes had become accustomed to the dark; she could see the shrubbery dead black, and the trees like a blurred pattern smudged in Indian ink on a background of soft gloom. Overhead the wind came and went, setting the bare, wet branches creaking, shaking the rain from the evergreens in sudden make-believe showers.

It was between two gusts, when she had stopped to take breath for a moment, that Chloe heard the footstep behind her, a quiet step, rather slow, a man's step following her own. She walked on quickly, listening; and before the wind drowned every sound but its own she heard the footstep quicken too. The wind came battering, driving, shaking everything. The air was full of noise and wetness.

Chloe ran as fast as she could to the turn of the drive, and there cut off on to the grass. She felt no fear, but a great sense of exhilaration. Ever since she had run away from Michael, days and nights had been full of a dull, flat weariness. That, at least, was broken. She ran along under the terrace, and then stood still, listening intently. She could hear nothing but the wind and the swish of the trees. She slipped up the steps on to the terrace, turned the corner of the house, and stood close to the end window of the drawing-room, the big one that looked east, and listened again. If anyone were to cross the gravel, she would hear them, however lightly they stepped.

As she stood there flattened against the wall, the words of the old fairy tale slid into her mind:

"Sister Anne, Sister Anne, what do you see? What do you see?"

"I can see the grass growing and the wind blowing."

The wind was blowing; but the following footstep was gone. She gave a sigh of relief, turned to the window, and broke it with her shoe. It was really extraordinarily easy to burgle a house. The little tinkling sound which the glass made would never have been heard in the servants' wing even if the night had been dead still. She wrapped a fold of her thick tweed coat about her right hand, and pulled away the broken glass until the hole was large enough to let her in. Then she crawled through the gap, parted the curtains, and began to grope her way to the fireplace.

The darkness in the drawing-room was quite different to the dark outside. It was a flat, even gloom out of which things jabbed you—the hummocky back of a chair, or the sharp corner of a polished table on which your fingers slid. Chloe moved with the greatest care.

The settee on the right of the fireplace was her landmark. When she reached that the rest was easy; she had only to pass along the back of the settee and feel for the shaded lamp on the table against the wall. She put the light on, and looked back to make sure that the curtains were quite closed. She must have a light; but she did not want to advertise her whereabouts to the owner of the footstep in case he should still be following at a distance. The pale folds hung straight and close from valance to floor.

She took the key of the cabinet from her purse and opened the doors. The golden river caught the light for a moment; the little men stood unmoved amongst the water reeds. They had never changed or moved since Chloe was a child. There was something assuaging about the unchangingness of Henry Planty and Timmy Jimmy.

Chloe let herself have these thoughts because deep down in her there was a dreadful eagerness and a dreadful fear. Just on the other side of that thin sheet of steel there was something that was going to change her whole life for good or bad. Once she had opened the long envelope and read Stran's signature, there would be no going back: there would be certainty.

Chloe stood with the door of the cabinet in her hand, and was afraid.

Chapter Forty

IT WAS REALLY only for a moment that she hesitated. "You've got to be quick," she said to herself with a little stamp of the foot. "Do you hear? You've got to be as quick as lightning. Suppose the person who was following you was a real burglar; and suppose he came in before you had time to open the envelope."

It wasn't so easy to open the safe without an electric torch. When she had lifted out the middle section of the cabinet, she had to get the reading lamp into the gap. The cord was only just long enough, and she had to tilt the lamp sideways and prop it with a book. This did not leave a great deal of room for herself; but she managed to crawl in, and, crouching there, she set the combination and opened the scarlet door of the safe. It creaked a little as it swung back, showing an empty upper shelf, and below, a little pile of ledgers and the long yellow envelope.

Chloe took it in her hand and backed out. She did not wait to move the lamp, but, holding the envelope close to the tilted light, she broke the big black seal and pulled out a little sheaf of papers.

Just for an instant she shut her eyes. She couldn't look. Sometimes certainty stabs too deep. She shrank as from the edge of a knife. It was only for an instant. Then she opened her eyes and looked.

The little sheaf of papers caught the light full. The first one told Chloe everything that she had come there to learn. Right across it in a sloping, flowing hand, ran the signature that she had come to see:

"Martin Stranways Fossetter."

Chloe leaned her forehead against the smooth lacquered face of the cabinet. For the space of three full breaths everything stood still with her.

There was a little sound. It came to her, but she did not know what it was—she was so far away, in a silence where she looked at Michael and Michael looked at her, and she knew that he was Michael and not Stran.

The sound brought her back again. She turned round and opened her eyes. The room behind her stood clean and cold in the light of all three chandeliers; the old cut-glass lustres made a dazzle of little rainbows.

Martin Fossetter stood by the door smiling at her.

"Well, Chloe?" he said.

Chloe leaned against the cabinet. Her eyes went from his face to the signature under her hand. She read the short, damning receipt from end to end:

"Received, for two letters of Lady Alexander Fitzmaurice, the sum of £50 (Fifty pounds).

"MARTIN STRANWAYS FOSSETTER."

Martin crossed the room.

"Well, Chloe," he said again, "what have you got there? It must be something very interesting, or you would at least say you were surprised to see me."

Without a word Chloe put the papers into his hand. She looked away because it did not seem to her that one could watch a man whilst he read such shameful words. She felt no anger, none of the feeling which had made her fling insulting words at Michael and watch, exulting, to see how the shafts went home. She had wanted to hurt Michael, more than anything on earth she had wanted to hurt him. She did not want to hurt Martin; and she couldn't look at him.

The silence really only lasted a moment. Martin's voice broke it. It was a wonder to Chloe that his voice should be so like itself.

"Well?" he said for the third time; and then, "Are you making me a present of these?"

Chloe nodded. Her lips were stiff; she tried twice before she managed to say, "Burn them." Martin put them in the pocket of his long, light overcoat.

"The old man kept them pretty carefully—and I don't mind betting he told you to keep them too. Why don't you? They'd be a splendid guarantee of good behaviour." He laughed quite lightly and easily.

Chloe shook her head.

"I can't do things like that. Besides"—she made a little movement with one hand—"it's all over."

Martin bent down, looked into the safe, and whistled softly.

"Letters all gone! I told Wroughton you'd made a clearance, but he clung to hope—he's an optimistic creature. Personally, I hadn't much hope once you ran away from me at Victoria—damned bad luck that was, and it's never any use to fight your luck. The letters, I take it, are gone west."

"Burnt—Michael burnt them."

"I thought so. Well, now that all the cards are on the table, can't we be friends?"

"No."

"All or nothing? Is that it? It was very nearly all, Chloe."

Chloe's hands held each very tightly. The part of her that had come near to loving Martin was sick and ashamed; she couldn't look at him. Martin came nearer.

"It was you, not just the money. You know that, don't you? And I'd have run straight if you had married me."

Chloe did look at him then, very mournfully.

"For how long, Martin?"

His mouth hardened, but almost at once he smiled at her with his eyes.

"Oh, well, there would have been a pleasant absence of temptation."

"I see. You were to marry me and get me to keep the money. Did you really think I would keep it? Did you really think you could make me keep it?"

He laughed at that, an amused, confident laugh.

"You wouldn't," said Chloe, and shut her lips tightly.

He laughed again.

"Oh, Chloe, you child! Well, it's a pity; we'd have had some good times together."

"No, you would have broken my heart." She spoke quite dispassionately.

"Perhaps—even probably. But we'd have had our good time first, and hearts mend—I think I could have mended yours." He came quite near and laid his hands lightly on her shoulders. "Chloe, I've been a bad lot; but you could make me different. I love you. Let the money go. I love you enough to let everything go."

Chloe stepped back. Her heart felt cold and sad. She shook her head without speaking. And then, as she put out her hands to keep him off, he saw her wedding ring.

"What's that?" he said sharply, and touched it with one finger.

"Didn't you know? I thought you would know."

His face had changed.

"No. Who is it? Michael?"

"Yes, Michael."

Martin burst out laughing and stuck his hands in his pockets.

"That's damned funny!" he said.

There was a pause.

Chloe took the reading lamp out of the cabinet and put it back on the table. Then she shut the safe door and locked the cabinet. She was aware all the time of the frowning intensity of Martin's gaze. He said at last:

"And why aren't you with him?"

"I ran away."

"Quarrelled with him?"

"I thought he was Stran when I saw the name in the register, so I ran away."

"That's funnier still," said Martin. "Michael, the Virtuous Apprentice! Did you tell him?—too bad if you didn't." His bitter, jesting voice hurt Chloe sharply.

"Yes, I told him. He'll never forgive me."

Martin looked at her with a little twisted smile.

"I shouldn't wonder if you're right. Michael's a very stiff-necked sort of chap—always was. Once he got an idea into his head, you couldn't shift it. Now I could forgive you anything, my dear." There was an exquisite inflection of tenderness on the last words.

"Don't!" said Chloe. "It's all gone, Martin. Don't you know enough to know that?" There was a weary finality in voice and look.

Martin caught her hands in his, held them so tight for a moment that she nearly cried out, and then quite suddenly dropped them.

"All right," he said with a complete change of manner, "that's a wash-out. Now, as one human being to another, tell me one thing. Aren't you hungry?—because I am. And as I followed you all the way from your abominable suburb, I'm in a position to know that it's about seven hours since either of us had anything to eat. I'm going to forage. You needn't run away this time."

Chloe sat down on the settee. She felt the softness of the cushions at her back, and she felt the draught that blew in through the broken window. Anything beyond this she was incapable of feeling. She sat up with a start when Martin came in. As he opened the door the clock in the hall sent out a single, heavy stroke.

Martin had a tray in his hand. He balanced it, shut the door, and came forward.

"Full marks for efficiency this time," he said. "Soup; cold ham; bananas; cheese. I got the soup hot on the spirit lamp Emily plays with at tea."

It was like a sort of dream picnic. Martin talking gay nonsense; and Chloe not speaking at all—not because she had any resentment in her mind, but because her mind felt quite, quite empty.

"Now," said Martin, "the best thing you can do is to go up to your own room and go to bed. Your things are still there."

Chloe spoke then:

"Who's in the house?"

"Not the Wroughtons,"—he was quick to read her fear—"only old Blayne and his wife, and the under housemaid, the bun-faced girl from the village. Jessie's up in town with Len and Emily. You get off to bed, and I'll knock up Blayne in the morning and tell him you got here late. Then you can give your own orders about breakfast and catching a train."

207 | THE BLACK CABINET

Chloe got up. She came quite close to him, lifted her heavy eyes with a great effort, and said:

"I'm so tired—I can't think. Is—it—all—right?"

Martin Fossetter experienced emotions. He answered her very gently.

"Yes, it's all right. You get off to bed and go to sleep. It's quite all right."

"Thank you," said Chloe.

He put on a light in the hall, and took her to the door of her room.

"I'll send the bun-faced girl to you in the morning. Good-night, Chloe's ghost," he said, and was gone.

Chloe went into her room and locked the door. It was strange to be there again, to see her things scattered on the dressing-table. She took off her tweed coat and her shoes. She did not mean to sleep, but she thought she would lie down. She pushed the bed across the door, crept under the warm eiderdown, and was instantly very deeply asleep.

Chapter Forty-One

CHLOE WOKE to the sound of knocking close to her head. It seemed at first to be inside her head; but by the time her eyes had opened she realized that the sound came from the other side of the door. She pulled the bed away and let the housemaid in.

"And if you please, miss, I was to ask you when you'd like breakfast, and whether there was any orders for the car."

Chloe ordered an egg on a tray, and said she would like to catch the nine-forty-five. After a moment's hesitation, she asked:

"What is Mr. Fossetter doing?"

The girl's eyes stared at her blankly.

"Mr. Fossetter caught the eight-fifteen, miss," she said. "And please, miss, there's a note on the tray."

Chloe read the note when the girl had gone. It had the merit of brevity and contained only a single line:

"I hate an anti-climax. So good-bye."

It was just after twelve when Chloe came back to the house she had been married from. She had left her box at the station, and came back as she had gone, on foot.

"Oh!" said Mrs. Moffat. She stood with her hand on the door and looked accusingly at Chloe.

"Oh, Moffy dear, *don't!*" said Chloe.

"If you went, why did you come back?" said Mrs. Moffat.

Chloe came in, shut the door, and put her back against it.

"I won't cry in the street," she said—"you shan't make me. Oh, Moffy dear, be nice to me, because I'm very unhappy. Is he here?"

"Ah," said Eliza Moffat, "you should ha' thought of that before."

Chloe took her by both arms and shook her a little.

"Is he here? *Is* he?"

"If you'd stayed where your place and your duty was, you wouldn't have had to ask me that, miss."

"Oh, Moffy, *don't!*—not now. You can scold me afterwards, and I won't say a word. But tell me first, is he here?"

"He's come back here to lodge, if that's your meaning," said Mrs. Moffat very stiffly.

"Is he in?"

"No, he isn't, and won't be for a good half hour. And what I ask is, what ha' you done to him?—you that he brought in from nowhere and married honourable. You to go and leave him on his wedding day!—Mr. Michael that any young lady might ha' been glad to have for a husband." Her thin nose twitched with emotion as she spoke; she was stiff with angry resentment.

"I can't explain," said Chloe. "I thought things that weren't true, and I've come back to say I'm sorry."

Mrs. Moffat pulled herself away, marched down the passage, and flung open the sitting-room door.

"It's not me you've to say it to," she said sharply. "You can wait in here, and when Mr. Michael comes home I'll tell him you've called."

Chloe sat down in the cold, crowded room, and waited with what heart she might. Mrs. Moffat's greeting had frightened her. It was dreadful to have to wait for Michael to come in, straining one's ears, and getting colder and more frightened all the time. The eye in the picture of The Broad and Narrow Way stared at her relentlessly. She moved her chair to get away from it; but it was no use, it looked straight at her still. She shut her eyes, and through the closed lids still felt the accusing stare.

It was a long, long time before the front door banged and Michael's step sounded in the hall. Then a sickening pause. Eliza's step; Eliza's voice. And at last, Chloe on her feet with clenched hands, and Michael coming in slowly, shutting the door behind him, and standing close to it, looking at her.

Chloe looked at him. He was very white, and his jaw was set square and hard. But it was his eyes that frightened her. She had not known that blue eyes could look like that; there was a sort of sparkle in them like the sparkle on ice, and the blue of them was the blue of ice, so hard and so cold.

"Well," he said, "it's you."

"Yes," said Chloe. Her heart was beating so violently that she thought Michael must hear it. She wanted so much to be calm, to explain, to say the things that would make Michael forgive her; and she felt frozen and powerless. She had said to herself, and she had said to Martin, that Michael would never forgive her. But she hadn't really believed it until now; she hadn't believed it because, deep in her heart of hearts, she knew something about herself and Michael which it was difficult to put into words. The nearest she could get to it was with the one word *home*. Where Chloe was would always be home to Michael; and where Michael was would always be home to Chloe. But Chloe had come to her home and found it cold and barred against her.

"Why have you come back?" said Michael roughly.

Chloe dug her nails into her palms.

"I've come back," she said.

"So I see. Why?"

Chloe began to seek desperately for words. She had always had words at her command. Why had they all gone, and failed her at her need?

"You didn't try—and find me." She didn't know why she said it; but if he had looked for her it would give her a little hope.

"Didn't I?" said Michael. "Well, you're wrong there as it happens. I remembered that girl at The Luxe, and I found out where you were next day."

"Oh!" said Chloe. It was an involuntary gasp of pain, because if Michael had known where she was and had not come to her, it really did mean that there wasn't any hope.

The courage that comes when hope is gone came to her. She lifted her head, and found words:

"I see. I didn't know, or I wouldn't have come here. But I only came to say that I knew you weren't Stran."

"Stran?" said Michael quickly.

"Yes. I thought you were. Mr. Dane warned me. He kept on talking about Stran; he said, 'Don't trust him a yard.' He told me he'd got a hold over him—receipts that he'd made him sign. Afterwards I opened the safe, and I found out about Mr. Dane. He was a blackmailer—that's how he'd got his money. They were all blackmailers, he and Mr. Wroughton and Stran. Only I didn't know who Stran was. I asked Emily Wroughton, and Mr. Wroughton said, 'Stran is short for Stranways,' and wouldn't let her answer me. When—when I saw your name in the register I thought—Michael, I thought—"

"You thought I was a blackmailer. I remember you told me so."

It was no good, but she went on:

"I didn't think at all—I couldn't—it was such a dreadful shock. I didn't even know that your name was spelt Fossetter, or that you and Martin were cousins. After I got away I tried not to think, because it hurt so. And then, when I couldn't stop thinking, I remembered that the envelope which Mr. Dane had kept was in the safe at Danesborough—I threw it back when I took the letters out, the letters I gave you to burn. It was marked 'Stran's Receipts.' So I went down to Danesborough, and I opened the safe and the envelope. And it was Martin. It wasn't you at all; it was Martin."

"Yes," said Michael, "I could have told you that. I've never been called Stran in my life. It was his school nickname."

There was a long silence. Then Chloe came a step nearer.

"You can't forgive." It was a statement, not a question.

"No," said Michael.

There was another long silence. Then Chloe said:

"Why?"

"I don't know—I can't—you've smashed something."

Chloe's heart broke then. She knew why people used just that word, because she felt something crack and give way, and it hurt terribly. She had not thought that anything could hurt as much as that. She wanted to go away and hide herself. It wasn't right for Michael to look at her whilst her heart broke.

She moved towards the door. Michael was standing there with his back to it, just as he had stood ever since he came in. She looked up at him and spoke gently, as if to a stranger.

"Please—will you let me pass?"

Then Michael stood aside; but he didn't open the door. She was groping for the handle, when he caught her suddenly in his arms and lifted her right off the floor.

"You're not to go," he stammered.

She had a glimpse of his face, and saw the icy hardness gone, everything broken up, agonized. Her own tears blinded her; but she knew that she must comfort Michael, that Michael needed comfort more than she.

Presently she was in one of the chairs, with Michael kneeling beside her, his head against her shoulder, his hard, difficult sobs shaking her from head to foot. Chloe held him tight.

"You've broken my heart," she said. "Oh, Michael, you've broken it."

"No!" said Michael. "No!"

He felt a flutter of soft kisses on his cheek, his ear. Chloe's kisses were very soft.

"You have— I felt it break. Oh, Michael, it hurt!" Her arms were round his neck. She rubbed her cheek against his, and felt it wet with his tears. "I thought you'd stopped loving me—I did."

"I couldn't!" His voice broke.

Chloe kissed him.

"I thought— Michael, Michael, you're breaking me! Oh, you are!"

Michael's grasp relaxed a shade. He lifted his head from Chloe's shoulder.

"I've got you back—I've got you back—I thought I'd lost you."

"You couldn't—we belong—it's just us."

A good deal later Chloe said:

"That *horrible* money—you'll help me to get rid of it as soon as possible, won't you?"

"Rather!" said Michael. "We'll go and see my step-father's solicitor at once. He's a most frightfully respectable old boy—the family heirloom sort. He always treats me as if I were still at school. He'll know just what to do; and he can get everything ready for you to sign as soon as you're of age. I had it all planned, and then—Chloe, let's play we were married this morning!"

"Yes," said Chloe—"yes." Her soft, brilliant colour had come back, and her eyes shone.

"Moffy'll feed us. Then we'll see the solicitor. And then we'll go off into the blue together with the car. Will you come, Chloe—*darling*?"

Chloe's eyes sparkled behind the wet, black lashes.

"Will you promise not to break my heart again? Oh, Michael, it *did* hurt!"

"I'm a brute," said Michael. "But you mustn't run away. It's when you run away that I feel like breaking everything in sight."

He took her by the shoulders and held her. Chloe put up her face to be kissed, like a child.

"This time I've run home," she said.

THE END

Made in the USA
Columbia, SC
13 January 2020